SLAVE GIRL
of
NENUPHAR

(THE ATKOI WAR TRILOGY, BOOK 3)

HENRY SPARROWHAWK

This is a work of fiction. Any resemblance to actual people, living or dead, events or locales, is entirely coincidental.

ISBN – 13: 978 - 1500916800
ISBN – 10: 1500916803

DEDICATION

To my wife.

CONTENTS

PROLOGUE

Some excerpts from *Slave Girl of Nenuphar*, Volume 3 of *The Atkoi War Trilogy*

(i)

"Get me the dumb slut," said Jak bluntly.

Roxana understood what he wanted. Jak had heard that the Maidens had acquired a mute girl. The new pleasure house known as Seen But Not Heard was proving quite popular, and Akkadis Leisure did not want to be left behind. One of the new girls from the Maidens of Nenuphar had been sent to have the same treatment.

The operation to cut out a slave girl's vocal chords was safe and inexpensive. The girl could be back at work in ten days.

Roxana went to the reception and fetched the mute.

The girl was beautiful. She had a lovely figure, tall and slender, and a pretty face with dark blonde hair which she wore in kittentails which hung down prettily each side of her head. Like all the Maidens that evening, she wore a short, flared wraparound skirt and skimpy top. She glanced nervously at Jak and blushed prettily, feeling his eyes upon her. She smiled shyly, curtsied and pressed her palms together as if in supplication. She stood perfectly straight. Gentlemen did not like girls who slouched, she had been warned.

It was very important to make the gentleman like her, she knew. She could not speak any more, and it was more important than ever to show by her body language that she would be both pleased and honoured to entertain the man and do everything he wanted.

Jak reached out and lifted her chin. He saw the scar, a vertical line on her throat. It was red and raw, but it was healing cleanly.

“She’s charming, isn’t she, Mr Zadkine?” smiled Roxana.

Jak nodded. “All right. I’ll have her,” he said, and stood.

The girl smiled as if genuinely delighted. She held Jak’s hand and led him towards the till.

(ii)

Radmilla was going to have to kill her husband.

It would have to be tonight. There was no other way. Timing was everything. She had deferred the dreadful moment for as long as possible in the hope that it would prove unnecessary. But now she knew that if she hesitated a moment longer, she and her sons would lose everything.

There must be no clue linking her to the Kzam’s death. She would need an instrument, an unwitting puppet who she could manipulate and who would later take the blame. A slave girl would be ideal. The girl would be impaled afterwards and the truth would never come out. For the plan to work, the girl would have to be very beautiful.

The choice was obvious. She would use Kyra.

(iii)

Emma was dancing on the stage. The pretty brunette was blushing and completely bare, thrusting and gyrating to the powerful rhythmic beat, repeating the steps she had been taught. As always when she danced, she tried not to meet the eyes of the men watching. It was too humiliating. That was why she had been dancing for several minutes before she saw the young man sitting at a table with Trixi, halfway across the room.

The young man was staring at Emma, transfixed. Emma did not know how long he had been watching her.

The young man was Lance.

For the briefest instant Emma gasped and covered her breasts and pudenda, ashamed to be seen by Lance like this, dancing naked in a brothel in front of a hundred men or more. Then she remembered her training. She continued dancing as if nothing had happened. She looked around for Roxana, hoping that her blunder had not been noticed. Girls at the Maidens of Nenuphar had been stretched over the flogging stool for lesser offences than this. It was mortifying, but she had to dance as normal.

(iv)

Amanda saw Lavendro's face in the intense light of the radiation blast from his neutrino pistol. She remembered his features clearly. It was the man who had murdered her husband.

Can I kill Lavendro? Can one powerless woman defy the authorities of a whole planet?

But I am not powerless, she thought. *I have the pistol.*

This would be her one chance to kill Lavendro, she knew. If she missed, Lavendro would see her and fire back. Lavendro would not miss. He was wearing night vision goggles. He was highly trained. In a few seconds Mrs Carno would be dead and Lavendro would turn his attention to hunting Amanda.

She took a deep breath, held it, and chose a moment when he was not moving. She held the pistol firmly in both hands, praying that it would actually work. She aimed it at Lavendro's chest, where his body was widest, and pulled the trigger slowly, as Michael had taught her.

(v)

Damn the bastards. *Damn the bastards!* Voragine had worked his whole life to serve Ziandakush, and this was his reward. The Kzama Radmilla and her fellow conspirators had cost him everything he had. They had stolen his career, his security, his worldly goods and his pension. And what could be he take from the Kzamate? Nothing. Absolutely nothing.

No. There was one thing, one thing of theirs he could take. He could go to the police station and fetch Kyra. He had the authority to remove her from the headquarters. Why should the slave girl be skewered if he could save her with no additional risk to himself? She was a beauty, a virgin and trained to serve a Kzam. He was fleeing the Kzamate anyway. If he could reach Imperial territory he could sell her for a tidy sum in the slave markets of Nenuphar or Petwen. He could begin a new life with the proceeds.

(vi)

Abi and Trixi knew they were lucky to be aboard the Erebus, crowded though it was. Millions of refugees were still trapped on the planet below. They would not escape now. The Atkoi would arrive within hours.

They had been standing in the queue for the toilets for almost an hour before Abi reached the front and was allowed in. A minute later her sister Trixi was also admitted.

Trixi looked around but saw no sign of her sister. The pretty brunette was confused. Suddenly two crewmen appeared from behind her.

“Good evening, miss,” said one of them. “This toilet is not yet operational. Please come with me.” He seemed a little brusque, not as polite as Trixi might have expected. He gestured her towards another door. Despite the hum of the extractor fan, Trixi could faintly smell something burnt. She hesitated, sensing something was wrong.

“What do…?” she began. “Ouch!” The other man had suddenly twisted her arm behind her back and forcibly marched her out of the small room.

The girl was pretty, he thought. She would be worth keeping. His colleague closed the door. They were in a hurry. The next shuttle was due in soon. Trixi was thrust stumbling along a corridor and into another room, unhurt but terrified.

Their mother, Michaela entered the room next. She sensed the two men behind her. She may even have glimpsed one of their neutrino pistols as the man raised it and pulled the trigger.

It is said that a victim neither sees nor hears nor feels the bolt of neutrino plasma which kills him. It kills more quickly than the human senses or brain can function. There was a brief hiss as the narrow beam of brilliant light cut into Michaela's head and boiled the soft tissue of her brain. Her body flopped limply and vertically to the floor. The two men dragged it away, to pile it with the other corpses. It was only worth saving the young women, the prettiest ones.

It was time to leave Chimaera, Pitogo decided. He would not send the shuttle back down to the surface. They had kept forty-eight of the refugees, all of them young women. Altogether they had made an excellent haul. The refugees had paid with cash, gold and cinerium. All the girls worth keeping were locked safely in the hold now. The bodies of the other passengers would be ejected later. They would never be found. Even if they were, there would be nothing to link them to the Erebus.

The Erebus was not truly going to Bodnant, of course. It was going into Atkoi territory. The Atkoi were glad to pay for any cinerium they could buy. They were paying more than the Empire, because they were building more ships. Atkoi, building ships! That would have been laughable not so very long ago. And the Atkoi would not raise any objections if a few dozen slave girls were landed and sold without deeds of ownership, especially not if they were Imperial citizens.

It would take a few weeks to get there. The Erebus was not a warship. It was a freighter, and relatively slow. But Pitogo and his crew need not be bored. They had entertainment readily available. There were two brunette sisters he especially liked the look of. Their names were Trixi and Abi. They seemed well educated, too. That always made it more fun.

(vii)

Chief Eunuch was dead!

Nenuphar had been blasted from above and its defenders had fled. Six divisions of Atkoi berserkers had landed and some of them were even now looting the burning Imperial Palace.

Jemima ran lightly towards the huge doors at the far end of the dark deserted hall, her blonde hair flowing behind her. She was grateful for the regular physical training sessions now. She could hear Dawn screaming, and knew with sickening certainty that one of the terrible soldiers, the ones they called 'berserkers,' must have caught her friend. They had also caught Lydia, and probably Strawberry too. Jemima wondered how long it would be before she too was caught.

If only the Emperor had remained on Nenuphar, the whole Empire would have stood together and fought. Everyone said that. Now, everyone could see they were losing the war. There were even rumours that some ships' crews had mutinied and deserted because they did not want to fight.

For weeks the girls of the Imperial seraglio had heard the rumours of the advancing enemy, but they had known that of all places in the Empire, the Radiant Palace was the safest. Then the Emperor had fled. No one had dared use the word 'fled.' The girls had been told that their master was on a 'diplomatic mission'. But with Aethelstan gone, everyone knew that Nenuphar could not be defended.

The girls had listened fearfully to news broadcasts and exchanged horrified gossip about what the Atkoi did to young women when they captured a planet. But Chief Eunuch said they would all be safe. They were the personal property of the Emperor himself and no one could touch them. No one.

But now the Atkoi had arrived on Nenuphar, and Chief Eunuch was dead.

Jemima ran desperately through the dark, deserted corridors and into a large dining hall. She heard a sound from the corridor she had just left and she knew that the berserker was still following her. He must be close behind her now. She reached the doors at the far end of the huge hall and pushed the handles.

Nothing happened. Panicking, she wasted precious seconds pressing down the handles with all her weight, but they were locked and solid. She heard another sound. The man must know which way Jemima had gone. He would be here in seconds, and there was no exit. She looked around desperately for somewhere to hide. There was no furniture in the hall. It had not been used for years, not since Aethelstan had ascended the throne.

But there were places to hide. Along the entire length of the hall, on both sides, were high windows. There were perhaps a dozen windows on each side of the hall. Each window stretched from the floor up to above head height. Thick, beautifully embroidered curtains hung over each window and they were all pulled shut. Without further thought Jemima dashed to a nearby window and slipped behind the curtains, making sure they were pulled tightly closed. She had chosen a window halfway along the hall, about the fifth or sixth in the row.

She found herself in a tiny recess. The walls were two feet thick, giving her sufficient space to stand between the curtains and the duraglass window.

It was still dark outside. Jemima could see the dim outline of ornamental trees in a quadrangle surrounded by more buildings. Above the roofs she could see the flickering glow of the burning buildings in another part of the palace. It was the seraglio proper, from which she had just fled.

She realised that Dawn had stopped screaming. She was silent now.

Jemima could still hear the occasional shouts and laughter of men and screams of girls, but they were further away. The thick duraglass windows kept out most of the sound. They were built to resist anything except a direct prolonged blast of a neutrino rifle. They could not be opened. There was no escape that way.

Then she heard the door rattle as the man entered the hall. He activated the chandeliers, bathing the room in light. She heard the man's footsteps as he hurried to the other doors and tried the handles. She heard his laugh as he discovered that the doors were locked. He could easily open the doors. He had a rifle. But there was no point. He knew that Jemima was locked in the room with him.

"Come here, little birdy," he said in a mocking, singsong voice in heavily accented Inglic. There was only one man, Jemima thought, but he was armed and strong. All the berserkers were strong. They were strong, and pumped full of drugs that made them aggressive. "Come here, my lovely birdy. I won't hurt you." Jemima was trapped and the man knew it. He knew she was hiding in one of the window recesses but he did not know which one. He was enjoying the hunt.

"Come to me, little birdy," Jemima heard. She stood perfectly still and tried to keep the sound of her breathing under control. She listened to each unhurried, heavy footstep as he walked slowly to the first window on her side of the hall.

She heard him tug each curtain open. She heard the sound of the curtain rings as they slid along the pole and snapped sharply together.

He walked to the second window and opened those curtains too. "Come out, little birdy," he said in the same mocking tone. Jemima heard the rings snap together. "I won't hurt you if you come to me now… but if I have to come and find you, I'll be angry… don't make me angry, little birdy."

He went to the third window, and then the fourth. At the fifth window he tugged the curtains so sharply that they were torn from the pole.

Jemima realised that the next window was hers. Within seconds she would be discovered.

"Come to me, my little birdy," he said. She heard his footsteps, slow and deliberate. He must be very close now. Should she run for it and at least have the advantage of surprise? Perhaps if she bolted for the door he would blast her and kill her instantly. Jemima would prefer a quick death. That would be better, far better, than what they had done to Lydia and Dawn.

Then it was too late. He had stopped. He must be just inches away from her now. She dared not breathe. She felt her heart thumping, and wondered whether it was possible for him to hear her heartbeat. Why did he not simply pull the curtains?

He did. He grinned. He looked at Jemima, and grinned. She was a beauty, with long blonde hair and a slim flat waist and nicely curved hips. Her breasts were small but firm. He saw how they pressed against the thin cloth of her pyjama top. The top was cropped short and it left her waist bare. Her pyjamas were a pale blue-green colour. The trousers were thin and low cut. Her feet were also bare. She was wide eyed, standing pressed against the window behind her, as far away from the berserker as she could. She stood very straight, with her feet together and her hands crossed across her breasts as if to protect herself from what he was going to do. She was everything he had hoped for, when he first caught sight of her fleeing across the courtyard in the pale light. The Emperor had good taste, and the money to indulge it.

The berserker's name was Katto. Katto knew that the war could not last much longer. The Imperials were retreating as quickly as the Atkoi could advance. When it was over, the Kzam would reward him with land. Katto had already chosen the world where he would settle. It was called Tungstall.

Tungstall was an Earth type world, with rolling green hills and valleys and rivers. To Katto, who came from the semi desert world of Envermeil, Tungstall seemed so green it scarcely seemed natural. When Katto had first seen Tungstall, he knew what the Valleys of the Righteous must be like; and he could live there, in this life.

Katto had been part of the invasion force which had conquered Tungstall. There had been very little resistance. The inhabitants had heard of what had happened on New Wessex, and they had decided it was better to surrender immediately. After the war, Katto would claim his land, send for his family and settle on Tungstall. Many of the lads who had been with Katto said they would settle there too, if they survived the war.

Katto thought he would survive, now. He had survived this far, and soon it would be finished. With the loot he found on Nenuphar, he would return to Tungstall a wealthy man.

But the others would be here, soon. They would all want their turn with this girl. Katto would satisfy himself with the little birdy first, and then go looking for more valuables.

He grinned, drinking in Jemima's beauty. Then he said, "Take your clothes off."

Jemima stared at him, too frightened to run, or speak, or obey him, or move at all. Like all berserkers he had a red stripe across his face and tunic. He looked horrible, terrible. He had already been looting. Two heavy gold candlesticks hung from his belt, leaving his hands free to hold the rifle.

Katto raised the rifle and pointed it directly at Jemima. "You do like I say, else I blast you. Top first, then trousers." He grinned in anticipation. It was an ugly grin, Jemima thought, a frightening grin.

Jemima belonged to the Emperor. No other man was allowed to see her naked. For that matter no other man was allowed to see her clothed. She tried to say, "Please," but no sound came from her mouth.

Jemima did not at first understand what happened next. There was a flash of light so bright that for several seconds Jemima could not see properly, and she heard a girl screaming hysterically, very loud and very close by.

Then she realised that the girl was herself. It was her own screams that she could hear.

1: INSPECTOR TOZEUR INVESTIGATES

A good memory is needed, after one has lied.
Corneille: Le Menteur, IV: 5

Amanda did not yet know what terrible weapons of interrogation Inspector Tozeur had at his disposal. Soon, Tozeur would teach her what fear was: true, utter fear unlike anything she had yet felt despite what she had already been through.

Fear was useful. Fear would be used later, in the second stage of interrogation. But first, Tozeur wanted to make his prisoner feel more comfortable; relaxed even, so that she would be off her guard. It was not necessary, at this stage, for her to feel afraid.

"Mrs Alba. Amanda," smiled Tozeur. It was an ugly, insincere smile, Amanda thought. "Is your tea satisfactory?" he asked.

Amanda nodded, not daring to speak in case she unwittingly betrayed a closely guarded secret.

Tozeur and Amanda sat on opposite sides of a large desk. She had been given clothes to wear, garments gleaned from a former prisoner of Diskobolus who no longer required them.

"Amanda, I would like you to run over the facts again. I will ask you a number of questions. You will answer them immediately, without thinking or planning what you are going to say. Your best course of action is to tell me the truth, fully. If you lie, or embellish the truth, or omit anything, I will know. Whatever you may imagine about the Commission for Public Safety I assure you that we are civilised. We prefer to arrive at the truth without any… unpleasantries. I would also prefer not to have to bring in… Thomas and Honeysuckle." (He glanced at a sheet paper to remind himself of their names.) "However, I hate lies. No one likes a liar. I can detect lies straight away. It's a skill you develop in this job. Do we understand one another?"

Amanda nodded. Tozeur smiled. "Good. Then let's begin. The method you used to kill Henderson, or Scamander, to use his real name… it is very difficult to kill a man by biting off his penis. At least I imagine it is; I do not propose to try. But you say you were acting under duress, under orders from Mrs Knott and Mrs Carno. Why did Mrs Knott not simply supply you with say, a knife?"

It was an obvious question. Amanda had planned her answer.

"Inspector, we were not allowed knives. The house is run very strictly. If a knife were used, it would prove that I had an accomplice, someone in authority."

The woman was clever, Tozeur thought. Cunning. She had tricked Lieutenant Lavendro when she was first proscribed, and almost escaped. But she was not going to trick Norizs Tozeur.

Tozeur was intelligent, suspicious and persistent, as became a Chief Inspector in the Commission for Public Safety. The question on his mind was not *who* had killed the envoy, but *why*. What had motivated her? If the pleasure slave was merely the instrument, or agent, then who was the principal? Was it Mrs Knott, Mrs Carno, Senator Thrux or one of the oligarchs? Or did the plot extend higher still? Was it the Imperial authorities, or the Kzamate?

Mrs Carno insisted it was a straightforward murder of a client by a deranged slave woman. Scamander was known to be cruel and vicious and the slave may have had a real or imagined grievance against him. He may even have been responsible for having the woman's family proscribed in the first place. That would certainly be a motive.

On the other hand, Scamander had been involved with some very powerful people. Dangerous people. He had apparently been accepting bribes as well as paying them, deceiving both the Imperials and the Kzamate, perhaps playing them off against each other.

Carno and Knott certainly had something to hide. They had waited twelve hours before reporting the crime, and they had tried to conceal the body. No innocent person would have needed to conceal a body.

Amanda claimed that they had forced her to kill Scamander, using threats against her and her offspring. She claimed that there was some illegal business arrangement between Scamander and Mrs Carno. She said she thought Scamander was blackmailing Carno.

At first it had sounded to Tozeur like a rather desperate attempt to shift at least some of the blame away from herself. Nevertheless he had ordered that the properties of Akkadis Leisure be searched thoroughly. The pleasure slave's offspring, Honeysuckle and Thomas, had also been questioned but claimed to know nothing. Tozeur was inclined to believe them. They could be brought back to Diskobolus at any time though, if need be. They might be very useful. He could use them to encourage Amanda to be more forthcoming with the truth.

But the search of Mrs Carno's properties had unearthed something else of interest. Various clients, including Scamander, had been recorded while availing themselves of the services of the Maidens of Nenuphar. Tozeur, Lavendro and their colleagues had watched the recordings with considerable interest. It always amused Tozeur that quite ordinary seeming, respectable citizens sometimes had such unusual personal tastes. The evidence was being evaluated and catalogued at the moment, and some of the recordings would certainly prove useful. The Commission was not averse to using blackmail itself on occasion, not for any greedy or selfish reasons but simply to influence certain individuals for the public good.

The existence of the recordings strongly suggested that blackmail was a motive, but that Scamander himself was being blackmailed.

Under interrogation, Mrs Knott admitted making the recordings, but she said that Mrs Carno had forced her to make them. She had also said Mrs Carno had forced Amanda to kill the Archpriest.

The Carno woman had been detained and questioned, but she denied all knowledge of the recordings. If she had indeed ordered Scamander to be blackmailed or murdered, Tozeur needed to know who, if anyone, had persuaded her to do it.

It was known that Scamander had spent several hundred million solidi, under various different names, paying bribes to different public officials on Akkadis, causing people to be proscribed, influencing the elections, and paying huge sums to several senators and oligarchs. This would certainly have incurred the wrath of powerful and ambitious men with no compunctions about having someone killed. Scamander may not have realised quite how dangerous certain Akkadisi oligarchs could be.

There was also reason to believe that Scamander himself had received several very large payments from the Kzamate, made through intermediaries. If he had been selling the Kzam sensitive information, and Imperial authorities had discovered his treachery, might they have eliminated him? Or might he have double crossed the Kzam and been murdered in revenge?

The Commission had been watching Scamander. Tozeur also knew that Mrs Carno had visited the Imperial Embassy more than once. Perhaps she had gone to see Scamander. But would a blackmailer be that brazen?

The problem was that the people who wanted Scamander dead, tended to work through intermediaries. Carno and Knott, if they were guilty, might not even know who they were really working for, much less the slave woman Amanda.

But Tozeur would find out. He always found out.

A thousand light years away, the mind of the Emperor Aethelstan IV was troubled by no such doubts. “That bastard did it,” he announced. “It’s obvious.”

It was sometimes difficult to follow the thread of Aethelstan’s conversation. The subject might suddenly leap from one topic to another as if those he were addressing were expected to follow his unspoken thoughts telepathically.

In this case though, the Lord Chancellor Thomas Arbuthnot-Samar did not require supernatural powers. He knew what the Emperor meant. The Great Kzam must have ordered Scamander assassinated. The Akkadisi authorities had been blackmailing Scamander. That much was obvious. The evidence had been found. Scamander must have refused to do what they wanted. But the Oligarchs would never have dared kill Scamander without the order coming from the Kzam.

Arbuthnot-Samar nodded. It was a reasonable assumption. But why? And why now? Had Rurik wanted to silence Scamander? Had the cleric discovered something? Why such a provocative move, from a man usually so cunning? What did the Kzam know that the Empire did not? Was war so imminent that the Atkoi had nothing to lose by provoking the Empire? Was it connected to the absurd Atkoi accusation that Princess Athanasia had tried to poison Rurik?

"I don't believe in coincidences, Thomas," the Emperor continued. "Not when the man concerned is dealing with matters that affect the future of worlds. *Was* dealing. And he was known to have enemies. Dangerous enemies. His methods were sometimes… unconventional. You said so yourself."

Arbuthnot-Samar nodded again. He was a well-intentioned man who wished to avoid war, and if war was inevitable, wished to win it speedily with a minimum of suffering. The Emperor's interpretation of the facts was probably correct, but it was Aethelstan's response to the events which the Chancellor feared.

"We can't allow them to do this with impunity," the Emperor continued. "They can't be allowed to benefit from what they've done. We know what they want. They want a naval base on Akkadis. They can't have it. I've already spoken to Seguier. He agrees with my analysis of the situation."

The Chancellor nodded. Admiral Geoffrey Seguier was what the Emperor called 'a good man' and 'a strong leader,' which meant that he agreed with what the Emperor said. This was what Arbuthnot-Samar had feared most.

"Geoff knows what to do," continued Aethelstan. "The Tolon fleet are on manoeuvres at present. They will continue those manoeuvres, but much closer to Akkadis. I want them in the immediate vicinity of Akkadis, ready to take the planet and deal with the Kzam's fleet if they make any hostile move. I've also spoken to Aanrud. He's in full agreement."

This was worse than the Chancellor had imagined. If Minister of Defence Frederik Aanrud also supported such a move, it would have the backing of the Senate.

"Majesty, are you certain this is wise? It is provocative. We could hold off from any immediate action and recall Admiral Bazan. With his experience, he ought to be commanding the Tolon fleet, not stuck on the Nizami Marches. The Nizamis have been peaceful for three hundred years. You may remember that Bazan strongly recommended that if we ever came into conflict with the Kzamate, we should gather a combined fleet, a much longer force, to crush the Atkoi once and for all. It would take a little longer, but it would assure us of victory. With a little...."

"Hold off?" interrupted Aethelstan. "They've killed an archpriest! An anointed archpriest of the Holy Orthodox Church! In my grandfather's day no one would have dared to even imagine that. No, no, if we delay, we lose the initiative. Tolon would be in immediate danger. Immediate!" He hardly needed to add that if Tolon fell, the whole Empire would be in jeopardy. "I want Bazan just where he is. With a crisis with the Atkoi, you simply don't know what the Nizamis might try. We have to defend our back door, too."

The Emperor fears Bazan, the Chancellor realised. *He knows Bazan is the most competent admiral in the fleet. Bazan is also popular with his men. Aethelstan senses that such a man might harbour great ambitions. In the Empire's long history, more than one Emperor has been dethroned by an admiral.*

"If we play this right, Thomas, we won't have to fight a war. We can face them down. If we get cold feet now, the Atkoi will sense weakness.

I don't want a war with them. They've got Athanasia. But if they think we're scared, the Atkoi will be at our throats."

Arbuthnot-Samar swallowed the insult. Aethelstan was not a man to be impressed by intelligent argument. He did not realise his own intellectual limitations. He needed to be managed, guided towards the right decision. To his dismay the Chancellor realised that Aethelstan, like the situation in general, was beginning to slip out of control.

2: THE SHADOW OF DISKOBOLUS

False face must hide what the false heart doth know.
Shakespeare: Macbeth 1:7

On Akkadis, at the Commission for Public Safety headquarters at Diskobolus, Chief Inspector Tozeur looked serious.

"Amanda, I think it is time we dispensed with the silly stories. This is the stage at which I sometimes warn a prisoner, especially a female prisoner, that if she does not cooperate fully she will soon become much better acquainted with a number of my junior officers. Some of the lads would find the experience very entertaining. You are, after all, an attractive woman. So is your daughter, if I may say so. However, I can assure you that the experience would not be enjoyable to you or to Honeysuckle. And as for your son, well, he could watch."

Tozeur paused for his words to sink in. "However, I realise that given your… occupation, this threat may not hold quite the horror it usually does. The alternative though, is possibly even worse." Amanda wondered whether anything could be worse than what she had already suffered at the Maidens of Nenuphar.

"I am talking about truth drugs," said Tozeur. "We have developed a very powerful cocktail of drugs, a mixture of several powerful mind altering chemicals. At first, you will want to tell us everything you know. But they have a strange effect on the human mind. With repeated use – and you will be receiving repeated doses – they destroy the personality. They leave you with just enough brain to eat and drink and fight and fornicate, and that's all. You become, in effect, an animal. You will not be able to dress yourself. You will have no desire to keep clean. You will evacuate your bowels and bladder whenever you feel like it, with no sense of shame. You will still respond to pain. You will become quite promiscuous, if given the opportunity. We used to keep a number of such prisoners, male and female, together in a cage, and they were at it all day. Even with their own children. That, and fighting, was about all they ever did. One of them lived for twenty years, if you can call it life. You won't retain the power of speech. You will not recognise your own children if you meet them. You will not be physically dead. Your body will still be alive, but your memories, your experiences, your character and personality, everything that made you who you are, in fact your soul, will be gone forever. Do you believe in God, Amanda?"

Amanda nodded.

"So do I," continued Tozeur. "At least I think I do. But I wonder sometimes. Where does the soul go, if the body is virtually brain dead but still technically alive?"

Tozeur apparently did not expect a reply, because he continued his explanation. "You will be like a vegetable, or perhaps more like a lower animal. And all for no useful purpose whatsoever. If you don't tell me the truth, Mrs Knott and Mrs Carno will. We call the process a 'complete chemical lobotomy.' Have you ever heard of it?"

Amanda had heard of such mind-dead creatures. It was said that some men kept them as sexual playthings, but it was not a popular entertainment. They were animals in human form, as Tozeur had said, lacking all human responses. Akkadis Leisure did not keep any such creatures, as far as Amanda knew.

Than Tozeur added, "I think I'll do one of your children first, and then give you one final chance. Do you have any preference? Which one would you like us to do first? The buck, or the filly?"

"No," said Amanda. "No. I'll cooperate fully."

Mrs Joan Carno seethed with helpless rage. Because of that stupid, lunatic whore, she had been subjected to the indignity of arrest. Of course they had found no evidence. She had not been blackmailing Henderson, or whatever his real name was. She had not known anything about any blackmail. If Mrs Knott was blackmailing anyone, Mrs Carno hoped the Commission would strangle her. Clients needed to know they could visit her houses in the strictest privacy and confidence. If it became public knowledge that anyone had been recorded at the Maidens, or in any of her houses, Akkadis Leisure would be ruined overnight.

Eventually Mrs Carno had convinced the fool Tozeur that she was innocent of any blackmail. At least she thought she had convinced him. The problem was that the situation was rather more complicated. The Commission had searched her house. They suspected her of something. They might be looking for the package.

Senator Thrux had brought her the package the day before. It was exceptionally heavy this time, but she had hidden it very carefully. She was quite proud of her foresight in that respect. It was not hidden in her own house at all, nor even in the grounds.

She had hidden the package in the grounds of the neighbouring property, which she had bought from that ingratiating little toad Nargal, who had been awarded it when the Alba family was proscribed. She had wanted the property for years. The grounds were lovely. Alba had refused to sell it.

Fortunately, thought Mrs Carno, the fool Tozeur had not yet realised that she had bought the Alba property. Now Tozeur's stupidity and lack of imagination had probably saved her life. She had the opportunity to move the package, to hide it better. She would bury it properly, somewhere very obscure in the woods behind the Albas' old house.

Tozeur had eventually ordered Mrs Carno, Alicia and Gumbo to be released. He had been quite apologetic towards Mrs Carno. He had questioned Amanda only briefly. There would be time to interrogate her properly later on. First, he intended to follow Mrs Carno.

Tozeur sat in his aircar, looking at a screen. Dots representing Mrs Carno, her daughter Alicia, and the repulsive thing Gumbo, were moving together across the screen. None of them realised that they had each ingested several microscopic homing devices or direction finders in their food. Tozeur saw Alicia's dot separate from her mother's. But Gumbo's dot remained with Mrs Carno. That was interesting. Mrs Carno never took Gumbo anywhere. Gumbo was virtually brain dead, but physically very strong. He would make a good bodyguard. Did Mrs Carno need protection? Who was she going to meet? Was she reporting to her superior?

Tozeur knew that Mrs Carno was frightened. There was something Mrs Carno was not telling him, he sensed. But he was close to discovering it. He hoped she would lead him straight to her accomplices.

There was more to Mrs Carno than met the eye. She had been a slave once, he had discovered. Mrs Knott was also a freedwoman. Perhaps they had been friends as slaves and were still working together. Amanda would be skewered, of course, after he had finished interrogating her. You couldn't have a slave woman murdering people, not even vermin like Scamander. And the Knott woman would be strangled. It was Carno who was important. She could lead him to her accomplices, to whoever was controlling this whole affair.

Mrs Carno was taking a circuitous route, even changing landcabs twice. *She thinks she can avoid being followed,* thought Tozeur. *That's good. It's very good. It means she's leading us somewhere.*

Then she began to head towards her own home. *Does that mean her accomplice is meeting her there?* Tozeur wondered. He felt a thrill of excitement. *If I catch whoever planned Scamander's death, it'll mean promotion. I could be Head of Ops in a few years. Spong can't go on forever.*

He nodded to Lieutenant Lavendro sitting next to him. "Follow them," he said. "The mother, not the girl. Keep your distance, though."

"Should we get back up, sir?"

"No," said Tozeur. "Do you want Top Floor to think we can't sort this out without help? No, two of us, both armed, we'll be all right. She can't get away. Not with the markers she's swallowed."

3: ROBBING PETER

Everything in Rome has its price.
Juvenal

Amanda lay on her hard bunk with no thought of sleep. They would kill her soon, she thought. She wondered whether Tozeur would keep his promise to spare her children. Amanda had tried to tell him the truth. She had admitted that Mrs Knott and Mrs Carno had not been blackmailing anyone and had not ordered her to kill Scamander. No one had forced her to do what she did. Strangely, Tozeur did not seem to believe her. He was only interested in what he thought was Mrs Carno's part in the plot. Amanda would even have told him about Aimee helping her, but Tozeur ended the interview suddenly. He said they would continue the next day.

It was a dark night. Phlegethon, the huge moon of Akkadis, had not yet risen. Tiny Caedmon had risen, but its light was dim and Diskobolus was far enough from the metropolis for the city lights to be a mere glow on the horizon.

When the first blast came, the light reached Amanda's tiny cell. It had no window, only a grating in the door. Amanda knew she was below ground level, but light wells from the surface penetrated down to the lower levels of the complex filling the corridors with natural light during the day. But now it was night, and the light from the surface was anything but natural.

The sudden light gradually faded again. Seconds later she heard a dull but prolonged and thunderous boom. *Lightning?* she wondered. *No. The light persisted for too long.*

Then there was another blast, then another, then another. Soon the thunderous booms merged together into a continuous low roar. She heard shouting, not in panic but in excitement. Prisoners were shouting to one another, asking what was going on. Strangely, no one ordered them to be silent.

Then the first of the blasts hit Diskobolus itself. The blast knocked her from her pallet onto the floor. For a few moments Amanda was blinded, deafened, and confused. Desperately uttering prayers, at one point she thought, *if I die now in this earthquake, or explosion, or whatever it is, I have won. They can't kill me again. I have already killed Scamander. They can never take that away from me.*

Possibly she was unconscious for a few moments. Then she was aware of more shouting, and the sound of neutrino pistol fire. She was coughing uncontrollably in clouds of dust. She could hear cries of pain.

Part of the complex must be on fire, she thought. In the dim flickering light from the grating she could see that the walls to her cell were still standing solidly. Whatever had happened to the rest of the complex, Amanda was still held securely. *The cells were built to be blast proof,* she thought. *Escape proof.* After a few minutes the sound of firing stopped, although she could still hear distant voices.

Then she heard a voice from the corridor outside. "Hello! Is anyone in here?" It did not sound like a guard. It sounded too polite. Amanda made herself known.

"Stand back from the door," came the reply. "Stand well back." Amanda scarcely had time to obey before several blasts of neutrino fire melted the door locks. Her rescuer must be in a hurry. The room was uncomfortably hot.

She had never seen the man before, but he had broken down her cell door to set her free. *In Diskobolus, all men are brothers*, she thought.

"Sorry," said her rescuer. "There are no keys. It's all palm operated. You'd better take this," he added, handing her a neutrino pistol. "Do you know how to use it?"

Amanda nodded. Michael had showed her. "Kill any guards you see," the man added. "Then get out of here fast. There could be another blast any moment."

"Who is… blasting us?" Amanda asked.

"I don't know," he said. "It's not just Diskobolus. It's the city too. It could be Imperials. Their ambassador's just been killed. The Oligarchs probably had him done in, to suck up to the Kzam."

Is this my doing? Amanda wondered, shocked. *Have I brought this down upon us?*

Much later, she realised that she had never thanked her rescuer, and she was ashamed of her thoughtlessness.

She saw bodies in the corridor, some of prisoners, but mostly of guards killed either in the original blasts or by escaping prisoners. *Is Tozeur dead?* she wondered. She hoped so. *Is Lavendro dead?* Lavendro had killed Michael. Amanda would have liked to kill her husband's murderer, but the complex was too large to search.

Emerging from the ruined complex, Amanda found a row of empty landcabs and inserted a credit stick stolen from a dead guard. If she was to survive in hiding for any length of time, she would require money. She and Michael had hidden a supply of cash in the grounds of their house. It was unlikely to have been discovered. She would collect it now. In this confusion maybe no one would be looking for her. Then she could think about where to hide, and how to rescue Tom and Honey.

At first, Amanda had hoped to head in a straight line towards her old home. Diskobolus and her old house were both about twenty miles from the city centre, but in opposite directions. She soon found she could make no headway against the flood of refugees already fleeing the city. Nor did she see a single vacant landcab after leaving Diskobolus. There would be no opportunity to change landcabs. Eventually she was obliged to take a more circuitous route, which took about five hours.

Amanda used the opportunity to scrutinise the neutrino pistol. It was different to the one Michael had obtained. She dared not test it inside the cab. She could not find the charge indicator, but perhaps that did not matter. She found the safety switch and enabled the pistol. A tiny light came on. Should she keep it switched on? *Yes*. Anyone who challenged her tonight would be experienced and trained with weapons. She could not afford any delay. She would need every advantage she could get. Regular blasts were still illuminating the sky and there was a pale glow on the horizon in the direction of the city centre. Amanda knew that a ruthless enemy could eliminate a large city with a single blast. These repeated, smaller blasts must be from neutrino cannon aimed at particular targets. She prayed that Honey and Tom would be safe. Thankfully Tom was on a farm. There would be few targets outside the city, she thought.

The blasts seemed smaller, with longer intervals between them, as she arrived in the neighbourhood of her former home. She dared not enter the property from the front, but scrambled over a wall and across a neighbour's land much as she had left it with Tom and Honey all those months ago.

Reaching the stream, she took a long drink. The cold water refreshed her. She crept closer to the house. It must be past three o'clock in the morning, she thought. There would be no one about, surely, but she paused frequently to listen. She found the large tree whose roots made a small dam across the stream. Then she turned away from the stream, counting the paces towards another, smaller tree. This was the spot, she thought. She carefully put down the pistol and scraped away the leaves. She used a stick to begin scraping away the soil, pausing every few seconds to listen for danger.

Then she tensed. She had heard a noise. Hardly daring to breathe, with her heart thumping in fear, Amanda crept forward. There were some bushes ahead, and beyond the bushes was a small clearing. She crouched in the undergrowth with the pistol at her side.

Phlegethon had risen now, and in its pale light Amanda could faintly see two figures approaching, one slight, and the other bigger, carrying something. The slight figure gave instructions to the bigger one, and he began digging. It must have been a spade that he was carrying. Amanda could not distinguish the words spoken, but she could not mistake the tone and pitch of the voices. The two figures were Mrs Carno, and Gumbo.

Despite Amanda's hopes, Lavendro was not dead, nor was Tozeur. They had been in Tozeur's aircar, flying towards Mrs Carno's house when they saw the horizon light up with the first blasts. At that point they had no more idea than Amanda that these were the first shots of a war which would rage across the inhabited galaxy and change it forever. A blast of air rocked the aircar, causing it to spin and lose altitude, but it righted itself. One did not require very great skill to pilot an aircar. It was only necessary to type the direction or the coordinates of the destination into the keypad. The vehicle itself planned the journey and navigated a course along authorised routes.

Tozeur had tried without success to contact Diskobolus. The blasts must be causing interference, he thought. He decided to proceed with his plan. If the city was being attacked, it was a military matter. He could not help in any way. His task was to catch those who had brought about the murder of an Imperial envoy. *Has the murder provoked this attack?* He wondered. *If so, it's all the more important to find out what the Carno woman is up to.*

The aircar hovered half a mile from Mrs Carno's house. The two officers watched their screen. Mrs Carno and Gumbo were no longer moving. For a while, Tozeur and Lavendro waited in silence. *Are we wasting time,* Tozeur wondered, *or is Mrs Carno still waiting for her accomplice to arrive?*

It was almost three o'clock before the two dots began to move again. Mrs Carno and Gumbo were making their way towards the neighbouring house. No, not the house itself, thought Tozeur. The grounds. They're going to meet someone, in the woods.

Tozeur and Lavendro landed their vehicle softly and entered the woodland on foot, each wearing night vision goggles. They caught occasional glimpses of the two ghostly figures of Gumbo and Mrs Carno which disappeared and reappeared as they passed behind trees. Unaware they were being watched, they did not try to hide. They stopped walking. Lavendro and Tozeur crept closer, until they could actually hear Mrs Carno quietly talking.

Then Lavendro saw a third image, small, unmoving, perhaps twenty yards beyond Gumbo and Mrs Carno. The figure appeared only as a pale outline on the screen of their goggles.

Lavendro did not know it, but the third figure was Amanda.

Tozeur had also seen the third figure. "Yes," he whispered. "There he is. That's our man. He's here to meet the Carno woman."

Lavendro nodded. It seemed logical. "I'll approach from this side," said Tozeur. "You go round the back. Keep your distance. Go quietly. They may try to escape through the woods. Don't blast them unless they try to escape. We'll need to question him. I want to see who this guy is. Atkoi or Imperial."

4: IN A HOLE

Three may keep a secret, if two of them are dead.
Benjamin Franklin

Mrs Carno appeared alert, watching carefully in all directions and yet unaware that she herself was being watched. Amanda looked on, fascinated, as Gumbo dug ever deeper. Was it possible that Mrs Carno had come here for the same purpose as Amanda, to dig up something? Valuables? A body? Or did she intend to kill and bury Gumbo? But why?

In fact Mrs Carno had no intention of killing Gumbo, but Amanda had been correct when she guessed that the owner of Akkadis Leisure had been hiding a secret concerning the deformed creature.

Joan Carno had not been born to a wealthy family. She had not been born free at all. She was bred and raised as a slave on Seven Fountains Farm. Its owner, Nathan Carno, had fallen in love with her, freed her and married her. They had one child: their daughter, Alicia.

Joan was an ambitious woman. She considered her marriage to be the greatest achievement of her life. It was rare for a slave girl to be freed while she was still of any use to her master, and rarer still for him to marry her. She was determined to allow nothing and no one to take away what she had achieved. She knew that above all her husband wanted a son and heir. If Joan had been able to give him a son, his happiness would have been complete and Joan's future would have been guaranteed forever.

But then her husband had taken the slave girl Rosemary as a concubine. Mrs Carno recognised something of herself in Rosemary: they were both beautiful, charming, confident and very ambitious. Mrs Carno saw all of this in Rosemary, and she knew that the slave girl was a threat. She tried her best to persuade her husband to dispose of the girl, but to no avail.

Then the terrible Abaddon Virus struck. Half the girls at Seven Fountains caught it. Many of them died and most of the unborn babies were aborted. Rosemary was infected, but recovered. Her baby was born terribly deformed. Rosemary must have passed the infection on to her master, Nathan Carno. Within a week he too was dead.

Mrs Carno was a widow. She was consoled by the fact that she would at least be an extremely wealthy widow. She found her husband's will in his desk. It was hand written; Nathan Carno had not believed in wasting money on lawyers.

But when Mrs Carno read her late husband's will, she was consumed by rage and disappointment.

Any child whom Nathan Carno had fathered by any of his slave girls was to be freed. This alone was fairly harmless and not an uncommon provision in wills. But if Mr Carno died leaving no son by his lawful wife, then his eldest son by a slave woman would inherit his properties and businesses.

Carno had fathered only one son by a slave girl: George, Rosemary's son. *The bulk of my husband's wealth, my daughter's rightful inheritance, is to go to that diseased freak, that slave girl's whelp,* she thought bitterly. Alicia would receive a modest dowry when she married: a hundred thousand solidi. *A hundred thousand, out of an estate worth ten million or more.* Mrs Carno herself was to have the use of the marital home for the remainder of her life, and an income from the business. The rest would go to George. *And to add insult to injury, I am expected to raise the whelp as my stepson,* she thought.

If only her husband had not insisted on a son to inherit the business, and if only he had not died so young, this disaster need not have happened. Now her life and Alicia's life and their futures were ruined because of the slut Rosemary.

Then she had an idea. She would consult Raphael Thrux. He was discreet, and a useful friend of the family. He was powerful, he knew the law and he was good at dealing with difficult legal problems. He had helped her husband before, she knew. Perhaps the will could be overturned.

Senator Thrux had examined the will. It was entirely valid, he said. Then he delicately mentioned another possibility: since the will was not registered, if Joan destroyed it, her late husband would be considered intestate. Then Alicia, as her father's only legitimate child, would inherit the estate. Joan, as Alicia's mother and guardian, would control it and have a right to an income from it.

Naturally she must on no account kill George. He was legally free, and Joan, as a freedwoman herself, could be impaled if she was ever convicted of murder.

Nor was it even necessary to kill George. No one need know that he was Nathan Carno's son. The farm manager was dead. George himself need not be told about his origins. His medical condition was well documented and they already knew that his mental capacity would never develop beyond that of a two year old child. Rosemary was a slave: she could be silenced quite legally. There was no law preventing an owner from destroying her own property. George himself could simply be sent to somewhere else to live. Then if the truth ever did emerge, Mrs Carno could produce him, alive and well, and say that she was looking after him as best she could.

Rosemary knew, just before she died, that she was going to be destroyed.

She had been sent to the farm manager's apartment, which was unoccupied now. The new manager had not yet arrived. She heard a noise and turned round to see Mrs Carno. Rosemary curtsied, but she noticed a strange look on Mrs Carno's face, a severe, determined look. Rosemary's blood ran cold.

Mrs Carno said simply, "Bowser," and someone else entered the room. He was young, no more than eighteen, and physically strong and tough looking. Rosemary had never seen him before, but from his clothes she guessed he was a slave labourer. He had the same hard expression as Mrs Carno. He was carrying a sack and some cord. Bowser and Mrs Carno exchanged a look, and Mrs Carno nodded. Bowser stepped towards Rosemary.

That was when Rosemary knew that they were going to kill her. She begged and pleaded and screamed hysterically. She struggled frantically, but she was no match for Bowser. She was tied, gagged and thrust into the bag. Bowser carried her to the bath, still squirming and whimpering. It was already full, and he held her beneath the water. She struggled and twisted for a long time. She died believing that her son George would also be destroyed.

But Mrs Carno did not destroy George. When he was learning to speak, he began to call himself Gumbo. It was a garbled form of 'George'. Mrs Carno sent him to live in one of her pleasure houses, where no one knew him. Years later he was moved to the Maidens of Nenuphar. Bowser was freed and offered a job. He was a good worker.

Years later Mrs Carno was glad she had not killed Gumbo. That was when Thrux began asking her to do small favours for him. It emerged that he had kept a copy of the will. Thrux could still ruin her life, but at least she was not guilty of murder. He could not hold that over her.

It was because of one of those favours that Mrs Carno was now retrieving a package buried in a shallow hole in her woodland.

Mrs Carno thought she heard a faint noise, and told Gumbo to stand still. She listened for a few moments, looking around intently. No, it was nothing, she decided. She shivered in the cool night air. She told Gumbo to continue his work. The sooner they were finished and out of these woods, the better. She knew that Tozeur suspected something. Thanks to his stupidity, she now had an opportunity, a brief opportunity, to move the package.

She already knew what was in the package. She had looked. It contained money: bars of cinerium, several hundred, she estimated, and each one probably worth a hundred thousand solidi in today's prices. Someone must have been bribing Henderson, or Scamander, or else he was blackmailing someone, or selling something that was not his to sell. Information, perhaps, or influence. If Tozeur found this, no one would believe that she was innocent. She could be accused of murder, blackmail, bribery, treason or anything.

Fortunately she had Gumbo to dig holes for her. He was a perfect accomplice. He was physically strong, but he could not tell tales, even if he wanted to, or even if the Commission tried to make him. He could neither remember what he had done, nor explain it. She would have him dig a hole six feet deep, deeper into the woods.

The blasts and flashes of light did not help Mrs Carno's nerves. It was obviously the Marines, training, she thought. Some of the flashes seemed to come from the direction of Agrinova, where their base was. Then she tensed. For the second time, she thought she heard a noise close by. Again she told Gumbo to stop digging until she was certain it was nothing. She was getting jumpy, she knew.

"Mrs Carno, I presume," said Tozeur, switching on his torch. "Doing a spot of late night gardening, I see." It was moments like this that made Norizs Tozeur's job worth doing. This was why he had joined first the police, and later transferred to the Commission for Public Safety. "You are under arrest for trespassing." He paused. "And murder. And treason," he added.

In the dim light, Tozeur had not seen the pistol in Mrs Carno's hand. He realised, just before he died, that his joke was not especially funny.

5: THE LADY VANISHES

The condition of man…is a condition of war of everyone against everyone.
Thomas Hobbes: Leviathan, 1:4

Without speaking a word, Mrs Carno pulled the trigger. A bolt of flame shot from the muzzle of the pistol and hit a tree several feet from Tozeur, engulfing it in flames. She had never fired a weapon before. Tozeur leapt aside, at the same time raising his own pistol. Mrs Carno kept her finger on the trigger, swinging the weapon around so that its blade of fire cut through the air and incinerated Tozeur's upper right arm and chest.

He managed to scream briefly before he died. Mrs Carno overcompensated, swinging her weapon too far and succeeded in incinerating another tree and nearly hitting Gumbo. He was not seriously injured, but his face and arms were seared. He screamed in terror and ran, unable to comprehend the pain, the fearsome beam of fire, Tozeur's screams or the burning trees.

Mrs Carno ran to hide in the nearest thicket. She knew Tozeur would not be alone. Then she heard running footsteps. Lavendro was pursuing her. A blast of light and heat missed her by inches. She ducked and dodged sideways behind the thick trunk of a larger tree just as a second blast almost hit her. In the darkness, she could not even see her pursuer, but she knew that he must be well trained, experienced and well equipped.

Amanda was still crouching in the undergrowth some yards away. She had seen Lavendro's face in the intense light of the blast from his pistol, and she was shocked. Earlier, she had wondered whether she would recognise Lavendro if she ever met him again. Seeing her husband's killer now brought back her memory of his face. She remembered his features clearly.

Can I kill Lavendro? Can one powerless woman defy the authorities of a whole planet?

But I am not powerless, she thought. *I have the pistol I took from Diskobolus.*

This would be her one chance to kill Lavendro, she knew. If she missed, Lavendro would see her and fire back. Lavendro would not miss. He was wearing night vision goggles and he was highly trained. In a few seconds Mrs Carno would be dead and Lavendro would be hunting Amanda.

She took a deep breath, held it, and chose a moment when Lavendro was not moving. She held the pistol firmly in both hands, praying that it would actually work. She aimed it at Lavendro's chest, where his body was widest, and pulled the trigger slowly, as Michael had taught her.

The pistol did work. A shaft of fire shot out, but Amanda was inexperienced and her hands were shaking. The radiation blasted into Lavendro's legs. He screamed, collapsed and twisted and arched his body, trying to roll away from the white beam. Amanda adjusted her aim and incinerated his upper body and head, keeping her finger on the trigger far longer than was necessary. Long after he was dead, she kept the beam of radiation trained on his body, staring transfixed at the crisp charred remains as the beam blazed sun hot for perhaps a minute before suddenly fading. Amanda had exhausted the charge of the pistol.

When Lavendro was killed, Mrs Carno was unable to move for a few moments. When she regained at least some of her self-control she raised her own pistol and said to Amanda, "Stand still. Drop it."

Amanda dropped the useless pistol, backed away and dived over a fallen tree trunk as Mrs Carno fired. Desperately Amanda rolled, dodged and ran as Mrs Carno fired twice more, setting light to some fallen leaves and blasting a deep hole in the tree trunk. Amanda rolled again and headed for the cover of some more trees.

Mrs Carno had to kill Amanda. Amanda was a witness. She had seen the murder of Tozeur, and the buried money. True, she had saved Mrs Carno's life, but it was Amanda's fault they were in this terrible mess in the first place.

Mrs Carno thought she heard a noise, and blasted again ineffectually at some undergrowth. She paused to listen, then continued pacing through the trees. Amanda paused too, desperately trying to control her breathing in case Mrs Carno could hear it. The trees were thicker here, and neither woman could see the other, but Amanda knew that Mrs Carno, with her pistol, would inevitably find her soon. In the pale light of Phlegethon, Mrs Carno would see her and blast her as soon as she tried to flee the shelter of the little thicket. If she remained still she would survive a little longer, but eventually Mrs Carno would see her anyway.

Despair almost overwhelmed Amanda. *I was so close,* she thought. *I nearly escaped. Perhaps I could have rescued Honey and Tom.*

But Mrs Carno was becoming impatient. Lavendro and Tozeur would surely not have been alone. Others would arrive at any moment. If she could kill Amanda now, she could blame her for killing both officers.

Perhaps a more conciliatory approach might be productive. "Come here, Amanda," she said. "I'm sorry I got a bit panicky just then. I only want to thank you. You saved my life. I only want to talk to you. You can go free, and so can your children. We can split the money, half-half. We can all be winners."

Mrs Carno sounded quite reasonable, although Amanda did not understand the remark about the money. She remained silent.

Suddenly Mrs Carno's patience snapped. "Come here now, you mad slut, or I'll roast you in the trees," she barked.

"No! Not!" Amanda heard Gumbo's screams. "You not roas' Manda in trees. Manda nice!" As Mrs Carno fired a blast into the small copse,

Amanda saw Gumbo running towards Mrs Carno, still carrying his spade.

Mrs Carno hesitated. She still needed Gumbo to help her. "Gumbo, Gumbo, listen to me," she said, urgently. "Listen to me. Your name is not really Gumbo, it's George. George, you are my stepson. You are my little boy and I love you. I am your mummy, George. I will always look after you, always. I promise."

But Gumbo was not listening. Driven mad by the pain of his seared skin, the bright bolts of flame, the fire and the screams, he still understood that Amanda was in danger. Gumbo ran at his stepmother, swinging his spade wildly with all his strength. Too late, Mrs Carno raised her pistol and pointed it at him, but the flat side of the spade struck her cheek with all the force which Gumbo had to command just as Mrs Carno pulled the trigger. A blast of neutrino fire caught Gumbo low in the stomach before the pistol fell harmlessly from her grasp. Mrs Carno's head cracked sharply to one side and her body flopped limply to the ground.

Amanda heard a high, keening wail. It was a sound like no other she had heard before. It was Gumbo, crying. He was kneeling beside Mrs Carno's body, rocking back and forth and clutching his stomach.

Amanda crawled out of the bushes. "Gumbo, it's me, it's Manda. Thank you, Gumbo. You saved Manda's life."

"Manda, it hurts. Make it stop, Manda," he said.

"It will stop hurting soon, Gumbo, I promise. Try to rest. Keep still."

Gumbo lay on his side, still clutching his stomach. "Manda nice," he said. "Gumbo loves Manda."

"I love you too, Gumbo." She squeezed his hand. "Good boy, Gumbo."

Perhaps Gumbo was about to say something else, but Amanda felt his hand go limp.

George Carno, the rightful heir to the Akkadis Leisure empire, was dead.

Amanda listened. She heard neither aircars, nor landcabs, nor voices nor communicators. Then she realised that the blasts of neutrino cannon fire over the city and from the Marines base had stopped.

She went to the hole that Gumbo had dug. It appeared empty. She prodded the soft soil with a stick until she felt it hit something hard. She pulled a heavy carbonite bag from the hole. It contained bars of cinerium: a king's ransom, or more precisely an Imperial envoy's bribe.

This was what Mrs Carno must have meant when she spoke of sharing the money, Amanda realised. She wondered whether Mrs Carno had told anyone where it was. Probably not, but she would not take that chance. If the Commission even suspected it was there, they would have the equipment needed to detect it. She filled in the empty hole and covered it with leaves.

She swopped the spent cartridge from the pistol from Diskobolus with the one from Tozeur's pistol; they were of identical design. She left Mrs Carno's and Lavendro's and Tozeur's pistols beside their bodies. She made no attempt either to hide the bodies or the pistols, nor did she attempt to take the aircar. The Commission would find two dead officers and two dead suspects. Let them draw their own conclusions. No one would expect that Amanda would return to her old house. She kept the pistol from Diskobolus and the spade.

Amanda took a long drink from the stream and washed the blood from her clothes and skin. She adjusted her hair to cover her ear tag. Perhaps later she would be able to get it removed altogether. She felt light headed. Murder was easy, the second time.

Hefting the heavy bag as well as the much smaller bag of money which she and Michael had buried, and the pistol and the spade, she made her way back to the landcab.

The early light of dawn revealed pillars of smoke on the horizon, from fires that were still burning. A thick pall of smoke shrouded the city centre. Columns of hapless refugees limped confused and exhausted from the city, carrying bundles of their possessions. Amanda blended in with the other refugees. No one saw her drop the spade into a stream. Later, she abandoned the landcab too. When she looked back, someone had already hired it. She joined the columns of exhausted refugees heading towards the hills. All the traffic was in one direction, away from the city. Streams of landcars overtook the pedestrians, but as the hours passed, they grew fewer and fewer.

6: SPOILS OF WAR

The Corps of Berserkers were the shock troops of the Kzamate, trained, indoctrinated and drugged to be violently aggressive counterparts to the borbods recruited by the Empire. They inspired terror in those they faced....

Itchenor, E: The Causes and Consequences of the Atkoi War, Vol. 3. (Cornubium University Press: Nenuphar, 3020)

The Imperial Fleet patrolling off Akkadis had been attacked. The result was worse than a defeat. It was a rout, complete and utter.

The Emperor coped poorly with any setback. He preferred certainty and permanence. "How long will it be before our forces can regroup at Tolon? Is there any word from Seguier yet?" Aethelstan seemed to be forcing himself to accept that what had happened was real.

"Aanrud said it would take them ten days to reach Tolon," replied the Chancellor. "Sir, we have to bear in mind that only ten ships have so far reported their positions. As yet there is no word from Admiral Seguier himself. We would normally - "

"Ten?" Aethelstan did not attempt to disguise his shock, but it was mixed with something else. A reluctance to believe the unwelcome truth, Arbuthnot-Samar thought. "But we had thirty-five ships at Akkadis. Six of them were cruisers."

"And the Kzam had close to sixty ships, we believe. He's been building them faster than us. It appears they never had any intention of honouring their arms limitations commitments."

Aethelstan appeared unable to reply. The Empire had also built more warships than it admitted to, but apparently the Kzam had been arming his navy on an altogether more massive scale.

"Seguier was meant to scare them off, not start a war," said the Emperor. "Who actually fired the first shot?"

"We did. There was an Atkoi fleet on manoeuvres just outside Akkadisi space. One of the Atkoi cruisers tried to drop into close orbit around Akkadis. Seguier fired a warning shot. That's all it was meant to be."

The Emperor nodded. To allow an enemy cruiser into orbit around Akkadis would have meant conceding control of the planet to the Kzam. A cruiser could destroy any target on the planet at will.

The Chancellor continued. "They ignored the warning shot. Seguier tried to land a peacekeeping force on the planet. Intelligence believe a powerful faction there favour the Kzam. The authorities certainly tried to keep Scamander's death a secret, for several days. They may have been trying to take over the government. But the Atkoi said that the peacekeeping force violated Akkadisi neutrality. They said it was an act of war. They attacked the fleet first and gave the reason afterwards."

The Emperor nodded. "Then by now the Atkoi must control Akkadis. What about our peacekeeping force?"

"We have not been able to contact them, sir. We destroyed as many anti Imperial targets on the planet as possible. We blasted their seat of government, the homes of all their oligarchs and senators known to favour the Kzam, their secret police headquarters, regular police, and all the military and marine bases. The naval base will be out of commission for a while yet. But that doesn't stop the Kzam's fleet."

"But… Scamander never told us there was any risk of a coup on Akkadis. He always said the anti-Imperial faction were weak. Disorganised. He said they could be won over with bribes."

"Sir, there seems to be a lot that Scamander never told us. Intelligence are reassessing everything he gave us."

The Emperor remained silent, digesting this remark. "We will regroup at Tolon. The future of the Empire will be decided there. I want every available ship gathered there. That was Aanrud's plan, if ever the situation became this bad. Well, now it has. Admiral Hric will bring his entire fleet there, from Terminor. Every planetary garrison will be put on full alert. Every planet will resist the enemy advance with all the means at their disposal. That will slow them down. At Tolon, we will stop them. We will destroy them. This is a terrible loss, Thomas, but not a fatal one. We can still beat the Kzam."

A light flashed above the Emperor's door. "That will be Aanrud now," he said. Then he added. "I'm afraid Seguier would have contacted us by now, if he could."

"Sir, there is one more thing," said Arbuthnot-Samar, as the Minister of War entered the room. "The Kzam's fleet. It's led by Prince Ozim."

"Ozim? He's a nasty piece of work, I hear, but he's not experienced. Why would the Kzam let him lead anything?

Ozim was cruel. On a scale of cruelty he went above and beyond the pragmatic cruelty of most Atkoi rulers. He enjoyed cruelty for its own sake. This was the reason his father had given him command of the Central Fleet. But the Kzam was not a fool. Ozim's military decisions would be guided by an experienced, trusted senior naval officer.

The Great Kzam of All the Atkoi knew about his eldest son's cruelty and he would not choose Ozim as his successor, whatever the boy or his mother might imagine. Nevertheless he would employ him gainfully. Those Imperial planets which surrendered swiftly would be shown mercy. But those who resisted would be punished with a severity which would be remembered for generations. Their people would not die in vain. Their example would bring conquest and peace to other worlds.

This war was to be no smash and grab, no mere raiding party. The conquered worlds would belong to the Kzamate forever. They would be settled by loyal Atkoi, men who had served in the Kzam's forces and who would be rewarded with land and property. They would become the ruling class on all the conquered worlds. In time they would be joined by those oiku, those Imperials who converted to the Arian faith. Those converts would share rights of citizenship in the Kzamate. They would be spared the burden of the blastung, the poll tax.

Many would consider the Great Kzam Rurik III a barbarian, he knew. Perhaps he was, if the word was defined so as to include all those who believed in swift punishment for heretics and libertines. The Empire was effete, corrupt and immoral. It needed cleansing. In its place Rurik would create a better Empire, a purer, more honest society, a more civilised polity. A barbarian merely destroyed. Rurik intended to create.

But to create, the Kzam needed resources. The Empire was decadent, but it was also enormous and wealthy. Rurik knew that he could win battle after battle, but still be worn down by the cost of the enterprise and the sheer size of the Empire.

Therefore the war would have to pay for itself. Those planets which were conquered, especially if they had resisted, would pay for their own subjugation. Land and fixed property would be confiscated, not only to reward loyal soldiers but to be sold to Atkoi settlers. Anything movable and of value would be repatriated to the Atkoi worlds to help defray the cost of war. Money, metals (both precious and functional), works of art, historical treasures, military and civilian ships, slaves, anything and everything would be taken. Whole factories would be dismantled and transported to those worlds which the Kzam had designated to become industrial planets, powerhouses of the new Kzamate.

And the key to this great treasure house of the Empire was Tolon. Its resources were essential. It was populous, industrialised, developed and strategically placed. It was the first great stepping stone on the path to the heartland of the Empire.

If a straight line were to be drawn from Akkadis to Tolon, it would not of course pass directly through the solar system of any inhabited Imperial planet. But it would pass very close (in astronomical terms) to several such planets. The first of these was New Wessex, a temperate world which was already well on the road to prosperity.

Ozim demanded its surrender. His orders were to conquer, to crush all resistance without mercy and to leave no Imperial toeholds behind the advancing line of Atkoi control. His father had told Ozim how much depended on his success.

Ozim did not intend to disappoint his father. He would impress him with his diligence and ferocity. He would make his father want to name him as his heir. At the same time, he would enjoy his first command.

For the thousandth time, April Parsons tried to shut out the memories of the past few days from her mind, but try as she might the horrible images kept forcing their way back into her consciousness.

It had begun almost a week ago. The news reports said that the Atkoi fleet had demanded the immediate surrender of New Wessex. The planetary governor (who was appointed by the Emperor) and the Chief Minister (who was indirectly elected by the adult citizens) had both rejected the demand out of hand. An Imperial planet did not surrender to Atkoi raiders. The garrison would hold off any attackers until the Imperial reinforcements arrived. The Atkoi ships would be blasted out of space. They had offended the Emperor, and they would pay the price for their arrogance. The people of New Wessex were united in their defiance and proud of their resolve.

Then the torment began. The five largest cities on the planet were blasted from above. These were not the precise, controlled blasts of a civilised enemy aiming to destroy only military targets or strategic buildings. Each blast vaporised huge sections of a city, reducing it to dust. All the military bases were attacked, and most of the spaceports. New Wessex was unable to offer any resistance. With the capital city destroyed, no one was left even to surrender. As the blasts continued, the remnants of the civil authorities in the other cities and districts attempted to transmit their submission. They were ignored. Ozim would make an example of New Wessex.

Living in a suburb some miles from the centre of one of those large cities, April had seen the blasts. The blasts and the fires had lit up the sky that first night. Her family had considered fleeing. They had a landcar, but the news broadcasts advised strongly against travel. By morning, the blasts had stopped, but a thick grey cloud of smoke and dust covered the city, making it difficult to breathe even several miles from the blasted areas. The news broadcasts had stopped.

When broadcasts resumed, they were in the harsh tones of heavily accented Inglic. The Atkoi were in command. They had appointed a new planetary governor, called the Ul-Kzam, the Right Hand of the Great Kzam on New Wessex. The populace were ordered to stay at home. Anyone found out of doors would be considered guilty of sedition and executed. Those who stayed at home had nothing to fear.

But the Ul-Kzam had also decreed a havoc, to last for seven days. The doors to all properties were to be left unlocked. Anyone locking their doors would be considered guilty of sedition. Anyone offering resistance would be considered guilty of sedition. Several divisions of berserkers had landed on New Wessex and would deal with any resistance without mercy.

April's father, Jared, explained that a havoc was an Atkoi tradition. It was barbaric. It meant that for seven days, their soldiers could do anything they pleased. They could enter any property, seize any goods or persons they chose, and no one was allowed to resist.

April's parents considered it best to comply in every way with the decree. They must give the invaders no cause to take offence. It was unlikely the Atkoi would visit their house. Surely they could not visit every house on the planet; but if they did come, then the family would be polite and cooperative and give them everything they wanted. They would not try to hide or bury any valuables. They would not provoke them in any way.

For three days they waited nervously. Their doors were unlocked. They ate little. It would be necessary to conserve food. Nor could they waste water, as the supply had been cut off. Their power cells had recently been recharged and their electricity would last, provided it was used sparingly.

By the fourth day it was still quiet and they dared to hope that nothing would happen.

At nine o'clock that evening, horror beyond words arrived at April's home.

For the first time the Parsons family saw flashes of neutrino blasts in their own neighbourhood. They heard screams and shouts, and several houses nearby were burning. Then there were more screams, closer to their own home. It sounded like Mrs Medina next door, or possibly her daughter, Ellen, who was April's friend. Both girls were studying at the local university. Ellen was a pretty brunette studying to be a teacher. April was an attractive nursing student with fair, almost blonde hair.

Mr and Mrs Parsons looked at each other. Sally Parsons shook her head urgently. Whatever happened, they must not intervene. For the sake of their daughter April and their son Allan they must not intervene, despite fearing for the safety of their friends and neighbours.

Suddenly there was an intense, bright flash, visible through the darkened window. Jared Parsons crossed to the window to make it transparent, but Sally hissed urgently, "No! No!" and he stopped himself. They must not draw attention to themselves in any way.

At that moment they heard a noise at the door. Four men in dusty Atkoi berserker uniforms swaggered arrogantly into the living room. Jared thought one or two of them had been drinking. Three were armed with neutrino rifles. Their leader carried a pistol.

"All you, stand there. By wall," he said bluntly, in heavily accented Inglic.

"Good evening, gentlemen," Jared began. "God bless the Kzam. Welcome to our home." He had planned this speech. He wished his voice would not tremble so much. "How can…"

The Atkoi pointed his pistol at Jared and snapped, "You get on floor. All you." Then he said, "Where is money? You. Fetch." He indicated

Jared. Jared handed over the money. There was very little actual money in the house, only a few credits, but Jared cooperated fully. They searched the house and took everything of value that was small and portable. They also took food and liquor. “Leave land car in front,” said their leader. “Supply officer fetch later.”

Then to Jared’s dismay he added, “Now give me money you hide.” As he spoke, the Atkoi raised his pistol and pointed it directly at Jared.

They had not hidden any valuables. They had not dared to. But other families obviously had done so, and so now the Atkoi assumed everyone was holding something back. Desperately Jared and Sally shook their heads. April felt her heart thumping in panic. Suppose the Atkoi did not believe them?

The Atkoi leader gestured towards April and Sally. “Two women. You stand,” he said. He looked at them critically. The younger one was a real beauty, he decided, the best they had found tonight. He would get a bounty for her. Even the older one was pretty.

He grinned and said something in Atkoi to his subordinates. One of the grinning men stepped forward and firmly took hold of April. She screamed and looked to her parents for guidance.

Jared stood up. “Wait! We’ve given you everything we’ve got. The Ul-Kzam said that no one would be hurt if they…” but for the second time on that dreadful evening Jared’s sentence was left unfinished. The leader of the four Atkoi raised his pistol and blasted Jared, and then turned the weapon on April’s brother, Allan.

In those two intense blasts of light, Sally Parsons saw her world destroyed forever.

7: CRY HAVOC

The cities of New Wessex have been vaporised, their inhabitants slaughtered by the million, enslaved, or driven out of their homes to starve. Everything of value is being seized and transported back to the Atkoi worlds. Factories have been stripped of their machinery and hospitals cleared of equipment. Even the planet's food reserves are being commandeered and sent to Atkoi desert worlds where food is expensive. The work of generations, of centuries, is being destroyed.

Unnamed refugee from New Wessex quoted on an Imperial news channel in 3000.

The remains of both bodies slumped lifeless to the floor. Neither had screamed, although Jared had made a hissing, rasping sound as the heated air escaped from his lungs and past his vocal chords. The berserker's leader gave his men further instructions. They grinned. Sally and April seemed too shocked to scream. They were whimpering, until one of the men ordered them to silence. With a supreme effort of will, they controlled themselves.

"You. Both you. Take off your clothes," said the leader. April looked at her mother. "Else you get burnt like them, yes?"

Sally understood the point he was making. "Do what they want," she whispered urgently to her daughter. Somehow they had to survive this evening. Hesitantly, they removed their clothing until they were both wearing only their briefs. They stood, covering their breasts with their hands and burning with shame, terrified beyond words but unable to remove the final flimsy shreds of their modesty. All four men had stopped their search of the house to watch the humiliation of the women.

"All clothes. You waste time, I blast you."

There was no helping it. They obeyed.

"Put arms by sides."

Sally and April stood side by side, entirely bare. The berserker's leader had been correct in his initial assessment. They were both very attractive. Both were fair haired and nearly blonde, with straight shoulder length hair. Both were of medium height, with slim, attractive figures and curving hips. Sally, at thirty-nine, had full, round breasts. April's breasts were smaller, but firm and conical. They both stood still, looking downwards to the floor a few feet in front of them and glowing pinkly in their misery and shame.

One of the men said something in Atkoi, and the others laughed. Their leader explained for Sally and April's benefit: "You both no hairs on body. They think very nice." Again, they understood what he meant. Depilation was fashionable on many Imperial worlds, including New Wessex, and it was considered a usual beauty treatment. Sally and April were both depilated. Mortified, they stared at the floor in front of them. These Atkoi were peasants from Papegaai, unused to such a sight and fascinated by it.

One of the men reached out to touch April's breasts. Sally pulled her daughter back and said, "Please! Sir, please don't hurt my daughter. I'll do whatever you..." but her words were cut short as one of the men slapped her forcefully on the side of her head, seized her by the hair and stuffed a piece of cloth in her mouth. It was an embroidered, ornamental cover which Sally had made for a small coffee table. He pulled Sally's hands behind her back and snapped a tie around her wrists, fastening them firmly together.

He was standing behind Sally and he pushed her elbows together and gave her a little shake. She was an attractive woman and her full breasts bounced prettily. He grinned and called to the other men, and repeated his demonstration for their benefit. They found it quite entertaining.

Sally closed her eyes and tried to force herself not to panic. She felt her breasts bouncing again, and then the man was fondling her, squeezing and feeling her. *Whatever they do,* she thought, *I must endure it. For April's sake, I will endure. When they are sated, surely they will leave, and perhaps they will spare April.*

One of the other men fastened April's hands behind her back. He looked around the room and noticed the dining table. It was solidly made, with a crossbeam connecting its legs. He ordered April to kneel and he tethered her wrists to the crossbeam with another tie. She would not be able to slide her wrists free. For good measure he tied her ankles together too. Their leader, who spoke Inglic, turned to April and said, "You stay here, girl," as if she had a choice. "You not go nowhere. We come back later. We not forget you." He said something to his men, and they all laughed.

The four men led Sally stumbling along the hall to the main bedroom. April watched in horror. *They tied my ankles together*, thought April. *But they have not tied Mama's ankles.*

They did not shut the doors. From time to time, April heard the men talking and laughing and she heard Sally's muffled squeals and whimpers.

They took a very long time. They had taken several bottles of beer or wine with them, the contents of Jared Parsons' drinks cabinet. April tried not to look at the bodies on the floor. She pulled as hard as she could on the ties, but only managed to cut into her wrists. *The core must be made of fibresteel,* she thought. She concentrated on pulling on the tie, ignoring the pain and the intermittent yelps and screams from the main bedroom.

After a long time April heard another scream, louder and more frantic than all the others. She tensed, sensing that something was about to happen. Then she heard the spit of a neutrino pistol, and a flash of light was reflected down the hall and into the lounge. The screams and whimpers ended abruptly. Horrified, April froze. There was a second spit, and a second flash.

Then April heard a movement. *The men will return any second now*, April thought. *They will return for me*. Desperately, with all her strength, she tried to break the tie. It cut deeper into her flesh. She adjusted her hands and tried again.

Then the men returned to the room. One of them walked over to April and squeezed one of her breasts. She tried to twist away and said, “Please, no please.” He saw her bleeding wrists. He called to the others, who came to see. They spoke in their own language and laughed. It amused them, that she had imagined she could break a carbonite and fibresteel tie. Their leader looked at the cuts. They would not affect the bounty, he thought. With a tiny clipper, he cut the tie which fastened her to the table, and pulled her upright. Then he cut the ankle tie.

This is the beginning, thought April. *They're going to start on me now. I want it to end quickly. Perhaps if I struggle, they will kill me quickly.*

But the men did not molest April at all. Their leader spoke. “You going to honeypot,” he said. “Later we come to honeypot, maybe we use you,” he added. April had no idea what he meant. They pulled her stumbling out of the house to a military personnel carrier parked nearby.

April found herself in the company of perhaps two dozen other girls from the surrounding suburbs. She looked for Ellen, but Ellen was not there. From time to time the vehicle was moved and more terrified girls were ordered aboard.

It was light by the time they were taken to a large corrugated fibresteel building which looked like a factory. There were about two hundred prisoners, all female, already there. They comforted one another as best they could. One girl kindly gave April a garment to wear, a white underdress which became her only apparel.

As the day progressed, more groups of prisoners were brought in. The room, large as it was, became crowded. April was dismayed to discover that her twin cousins, Zoe and Chloe Brewster, had been seized too. The twins were blonde and very attractive. Mercifully, they said that their parents were alive, as far as they knew. Their mother was April's mother's sister. The three girls hugged and clung to each other for several minutes.

April also saw a group of six of her friends and acquaintances, trainee nurses from St Anthony's Hospital.

St Anthony's was the pride of the city's health service, large, modern and very well equipped. There had been thirty-two nurses and trainees staying there in the Nurses Residence. The soldiers had entered the hospital and demanded medicines, machinery and equipment, and seized twelve of the nurses. They had been taken to a police station, which the Atkoi had taken over, and locked in a cell overnight. During the night some Atkoi officers arrived and took away four of the terrified girls. They had not been brought back. The remaining eight girls were taken to the factory building the following day.

It was late afternoon before anyone thought to supply the girls with food or water. When they did, long queues formed for the water. Bread was supplied, but fear suppresses appetite and many of them at little or nothing.

The prisoners brought in later in the day had snippets of news about what was happening outside. The Atkoi had organised work details. Groups of men were being conscripted to collect the bodies of people killed in the attack, or killed by soldiers afterwards. The Ul-Kzam did not want disease to break out. They were going from house to house, loading the bodies unceremoniously onto trucks and taking them into the countryside to dump in huge piles to be incinerated.

One girl said that she had seen huge, horrible creatures, things called borbods, helping the Atkoi. Another said that this could not be right, because borbods were on their side.

A pretty dark haired girl named Emily described how she had been seized trying to leave the city. Her family had decided to try to escape, late at night, in their land car. The streets were deserted. They had travelled several miles when suddenly a very bright light shore on them. They were ordered out of the car by several Atkoi soldiers with rifles. Their leader seemed to speak quite good Inglic.

"What have we here? You thought you'd go for a little drive, did you?" he said. Emily was taken to a nearby police station and locked in a cell and brought to the factory the next day. She was terribly afraid that her family may have been executed. The other girls tried to reassure her. Not all the Atkoi were barbarians, they said. Her family had not tried to fight the Atkoi. They would surely not be killed for something as natural as trying to escape.

Then April met a young woman named Jinni. Jinni had seen a terrible sight: a stake embedded in the ground, on which a young woman had been impaled and left to die. The stake had eventually pushed its way up through her body and out of the front of her stomach. It was a punishment, Jinni had been told. It was what the Atkoi did. The girl had been sent to the honeypot. In the honeypot one of the soldiers had chosen her, but she had struggled. She was to be an example to all of them. The girls in the honeypot must never offer resistance to a soldier who wanted them.

April had no idea what Jinni was talking about. She remembered the name, though: *honeypot.* The Atkoi had mentioned the honeypot. With mounting dread, April listened as Jinni explained what the word meant.

Every Atkoi military or naval unit had a sort of club where the soldiers could go to be entertained by girls. This was called the honeypot, a translation of an Atkoi word. The girls were, in fact, pleasures slaves. During the days of havoc the Atkoi soldiers could simply choose any woman and do as the pleased with her, but when things settled down they would have to go to the honeypot if they wanted a woman. They did not even have to pay. They were each allowed one visit every two weeks, if they so pleased. The Atkoi believed it was good for morale. It kept soldiers happy. Every Atkoi garrison on New Wessex would have its own honeypot. The men expected it. It was one of their privileges, their perks. There was usually one girl for every two hundred soldiers in the garrison.

The honeypots required recruits. April, Jinni, Emily, Zoe, Chloe and all the other girls were being conscripted, procured to fill the honeypots. They had been harvested to stock the military brothels of New Wessex and perhaps later, other conquered planets, and for military bases on the Atkoi home worlds. They were camp followers. As the tide of Atkoi conquest swept forward, they would be moved with it. Others would be transported to different worlds in the Kzamate and sold as slaves. Soon the girls would be selected for different purposes and divided into groups to be sent to different destinations. The attack on New Wessex was not intended to be a mere raid. The Atkoi were not here simply to pillage it and despoil it and then make good their escape. It was to be a conquest, a permanent settlement.

April was silent. The horror of what was happening was beyond words. Some of the other girls groaned. Others quietly wept.

8: ACROSS A CROWDED ROOM

Travel light and you can sing in the robber's face.
Juvenal

This was the sort of crowd in which people might faint or even die, Rollo Troxellant thought, but still remain standing upright.

Rollo was waiting with his family in the crowded hall of the main spaceport on Chimaera Bis. They had been waiting for twelve hours. An enormous crowd now filled the huge hall and the lawns outside, pressing them from all sides. He glanced at his wife, Michaela, and their two daughters, Abigail and Theresa. All three were upright, but they had not fainted.

He wished people would stop shouting. Shouting achieved nothing. They would simply have to wait for the next shuttle and the next after that, and hope the shuttles kept coming. He wished they had begun their journey here a day sooner. That would have made a difference. He wished the regular passenger lines had not stopped their services to Chimaera. The small independents who still dared to come to Chimaera did not have the capacity to evacuate many people, and they charged astronomical rates. He had heard of one family of five who were charged ten thousand credits each for the voyage to Bodnant, twenty times the usual rate. But Bodnant was where they needed to go. It was deeper within Imperial space, and out of the direct path of the Atkoi fleet.

New Wessex had surrendered ten days ago, if indeed there had been anyone left there alive to surrender. The Atkoi fleet had not waited to consolidate their gains. They left a garrison on New Wessex and pressed on to Rhadamanthus. The governor there had been offered terms. If the planet surrendered, there would be no havoc, no movement of population, and no plundering or slave taking. Since the Imperial fleet was too far away to offer any kind of protection, the governor had accepted. It appeared that the Atkoi were keeping their word. Apart from a few unplanned violations, there had apparently been no major atrocities.

After Rhadamanthus, Magellan had also capitulated. Within ten days, Ctesiphon, Albany and Mulholland had also surrendered. It was rumoured that the Imperial Navy would not even defend Terminor, instead concentrating all their efforts on Tolon. No one had officially admitted this, but the rumour seemed plausible, somehow.

Rollo did not blame the planetary governments in the region for surrendering. Without Imperial Naval support, there was little point resisting. He hoped the governor of Chimaera would surrender. The alternative was too ghastly to contemplate. But either way, he did not want his family to be on Chimaera when the Atkoi arrived.

Perhaps the Atkoi would keep their word, at least at first. Perhaps there would be no atrocities. But they had a war to pay for and their subject peoples would be expected to contribute. And a subject people was precisely what they would be. Of that there could be no doubt. Abi and Trixi were aged nineteen and eighteen now. In a few years they might get married and have children themselves. Rollo did not want his children and grandchildren to have to live under the Atkoi yoke, and have to bow to Atkoi overlords and pay them taxes and learn their language, and perhaps one day be made to convert to their religion. They were citizens of the Empire. They would leave while they could.

Rollo was thirsty; thirsty and tired. He knew his wife and daughters were suffering too. He could sense that Michaela was weakening, although Abi and Trixi appeared to be coping. Both girls were slender, with dark brown hair, and both were very attractive. Rollo clutched the briefcase in front of him. It contained seventy thousand credits in cinerium bars. That would be enough to begin a new life on another world. They would go to one of the central worlds, as far as possible from the Atkoi, one of the old planets like Picamar, where his grandparents had come from. The Empire would never let the Atkoi get that far.

The briefcase was manacled to Rollo's wrist. Seventy thousand credits was all he had been able to raise at short notice. He had always worked hard and been reasonably successful in his business, but much of his wealth was tied up in property. If the Atkoi ever left Chimaera, they could return to reclaim it. That possibility was looking depressingly unlikely, in the short run at least.

Rollo knew though, that he had brought everything of importance with him to the spaceport. His family were what mattered. He had enough money for them to survive, even if rather more modestly then they were used to. That did not matter. Getting off Chimaera as fast and far as possible was the priority now.

Rollo heard someone in front of him complaining that Erebus Transport wanted fifteen thousand credits per person. The queue, if it could be called a queue, had moved a little, albeit slowly. Above the heads of those in front of him, Rollo could now see some of the crew of the tramp vessel whose shuttle they were hoping to board. A tough looking man, stocky, unshaven and bald although not old, wearing a scruffy boiler suit and a heavy gold ring in his ear, was shaking his head. A label on his suit read 'Erebus Transport.'

The usual smartly dressed spaceport staff had long since fled. The man from Erebus Transport said the shuttle was full. Rollo strained to hear snatches of his conversation. They would all have to wait. The shuttle would return in four hours.

A murmur of despair rippled through the crowd, tested beyond endurance. They simply did not believe that the shuttle would return. Angrily, several men surged forward, trying to leap over the counter. The bald man punched one of them with surprising force and he staggered back with blood gushing from his nose.

From nowhere two neutrino rifles suddenly appeared in the hands of two of the bald man's colleagues, one of whom fired a warning blast upwards. Rollo saw the tongue of white energy too intense to be called fire, spit upwards towards the roof of the building.

Michaela and the girls screamed. "Get back," said the bald man, sharply. The heaving crowd leapt backwards as one man. Chimaera was civilised. They were not used to seeing weapons.

"Excuse me! Excuse me! Seventy thousand, for four tickets, in cinerium, if we're on this shuttle!" Rollo made a desperate attempt to be heard.

Despite the noise the bald man did indeed hear him. He looked towards Rollo. "Have you got it? On you?"

Rollo showed him the briefcase. The bald man forced back the other prospective passengers, and helped Rollo, Michaela, Abi and Trixi to scramble over the counter. Some of the crowd objected vocally to this queue jumping, and Rollo was glad that the menacing neutrino rifles were on his side, to protect his family. He opened the briefcase and showed the bald man that he did indeed have the wherewithal to pay.

The man's name was Pitogo. Rollo had overheard it.

Pitogo nodded. "Standing room only, on the shuttle," he said. "You can relax properly when we get to the Erebus." He smiled. He seemed a reasonable man, Rollo thought, despite his greed. Pitogo did not take the payment immediately, nor did he issue a ticket. He smiled politely though, and ushered the Troxellants through the boarding gate from where they were escorted hurriedly across the plascrete apron to a boarding lift.

Once inside the already overcrowded shuttle, the Troxellant family stood watching while still more passengers were allowed aboard. It must surely be illegal to cram so many people aboard, Rollo thought, but presumably the crew must know what capacity the vessel could safely carry. Finally, one last passenger was admitted, an attractive but exhausted looking young woman, before the doors slid shut.

There were, indeed, a number of attractive young women aboard the shuttle, more than you might expect to see in a random sample of the population, Rollo thought. He wondered why. They were undertaking a very expensive voyage. Were the wealthier sections of the population physically more attractive? Did those of wealthy families marry more attractive spouses, over a number of generations?

Rollo felt the shuttle lift. He felt heavy as it began to accelerate. At last they were away from Chimaera. He was relieved. He looked at Michaela, Abi and Trixi. It had cost them everything they had, but Rollo had done his duty. He had protected his family, and that was the highest duty any man had.

It took seventy minutes for the shuttle to reach the Erebus.

Michaela, Abi and Trixi were a little disappointed in the vessel. The girls had never before been off planet and they had imagined the Erebus would be more glamorous, somehow. In fact it was not a passenger liner at all, but a tramp freighter. Rollo explained that this meant a vessel which did not follow a regular route. It had only recently been adapted to carry passengers. But that did not matter. It would carry them to safety. Then Rollo was asked to go to the purser's cabin to pay for their tickets. He took the briefcase with him.

Two hours later, Michaela was becoming concerned. She waited with the girls in their cabin. It was small, and crowded. She thought about going to find one of the crew to ask where Rollo was, but they all seemed very busy and she was a little embarrassed. Logically, he had to be somewhere aboard the Erebus.

At least there was no shortage of drinking water. The crew had provided an ample supply, guessing the passengers might be thirsty.

The toilets were some distance away, down a long corridor, and there was a very long queue. Michaela, Abi and Trixi had been hoping that if they waited long enough, the queue for the toilets would diminish. It did not. They joined the queue anyway. Oddly, an armed crewman allowed only one passenger into the toilets at a time. He apologised. The other toilets were being mended, he said. They saw no one leaving the toilets. They were told there was a separate exit, leading onto another corridor.

Abi went in first. Everything aboard the Erebus seemed rough and ready. Even the signs on the doors which said, 'Ladies,' and 'Gentlemen,' were hand written. After a minute or so, Trixi was allowed in.

She went through an outer and then an inner door. Both closed automatically, firmly. Trixi found herself in a small room with neither cubicles nor basins. Suddenly two crewmen appeared from behind her.

"Good evening, miss," said one of them. "This toilet is not yet operational. Please come with me." He gestured towards another door. Despite the hum of the extractor fan, Abi could faintly smell something burnt. Perhaps they were welding the pipes, she thought. She hesitated though, and the man added, "It's not far."

It was a peculiar thing to say, Trixi thought. Something was wrong.

"What do you mean," she began, "it's...ouch!" The other man had suddenly twisted her arm behind her back and forcibly marched her out of the small room. His colleague closed the door. They were in a hurry. The next shuttle was due in soon.

Michaela entered the room next. She sensed the two men behind her. She may even have glimpsed one of their neutrino pistols, as the man raised it and pulled the trigger.

It is said that a victim neither sees nor hears nor feels the bolt of neutrino plasma which kills him. It kills more quickly than the human senses or brain can function. The narrow beam cut into Michaela's head and boiled away the soft tissue of her brain. Her body flopped vertically to the floor. Two other men dragged it away, to pile it with all the other victims. The bodies would be ejected later. They would never be found. Even if they were, no one on Chimaera Bis would be in a position to investigate.

Pitogo considered his options. The Erebus was not going to Bodnant. It was going into Atkoi territory. The Atkoi were glad to pay for any cinerium they could buy. They were paying more than the Empire, because they were building more ships. Atkoi, building ships! That would have been laughable not so very long ago. And the Atkoi would not raise any objections if a few dozen slave girls were landed and sold without deeds of ownership, especially not if the slaves concerned were, from the Atkoi perspective, enemy citizens.

It would take a few weeks to get there. The Erebus was not a warship. It was a freighter, and relatively slow. But Pitogo and his crew need not be bored. They had entertainment readily available. The two sisters, for instance, Trixi and Abi he thought they were called, they were very pretty. And they seemed well educated, too. That always made it more fun.

9: A SOLDIER'S TALE

The great nations have always acted like gangsters, and the small nations like prostitutes.
Stanley Kubrick

In Akkad City, a new government appointed by the Kzam had taken office. Oligarchs and senators scrambled to collaborate with the new regime. With the Commission for Public Safety almost entirely wiped out, the police took responsibility for investigating Scamander's murder. The pleasure house known the Maidens of Nenuphar had not been damaged in the attack, and the police interviewed all its inmates, but learned nothing. Honey appeared to know nothing, either about the murder or her mother's whereabouts. Aimee, to her immeasurable relief, realised that whatever had happened to Amanda, she must somehow have kept her promise not to implicate her.

Most of the population drifted back to the city and business at the Maidens continued very much as usual. If anything, custom picked up. The armed forces of Akkadis were now part of the Kzam's war machine and were expected to fight under his banner. Young men were being conscripted into the Navy and Marines, and many of them, away from home, would visit the Maidens and similar houses while on leave, or before going off to war.

Despite his most strenuous efforts, Artur Thrux was no exception. He had been called up to a military unit known as the 4044th Light Armoured Division. The terrified youth had ingratiated and grovelled, begged and beseeched his uncle to use his senatorial influence to have him exempted, but to no avail. Artur had considered fleeing, but the probability of capture and punishment frightened him even more than the military service itself.

As the situation was not to be helped, Artur decided to make the most of his predicament. He appeared at the Maidens of Nenuphar as loudly and brashly as ever, boasting that his application to join the 4044th had been successful. Many men applied to join the 4044th, Thrux explained, but few were accepted. Most gave up or were rejected during the gruelling initial training. It was a crack unit, he continued, which would spearhead the Kzam's advance into enemy territory. Whenever Imperial resistance was fiercest, whenever swift and decisive military action was required, there the men of the 4044th were to be found. The Berserkers were all very well, of course. No one would question that; but the true elite force of the Kzamate was the 4044th. Artur was looking forward to it, he said. He had always said that the Imperials deserved a damn good hiding. Now he would help see to it that they got it.

Thrux's enthusiasm lessened only a little, later in the evening, when his friends, Danielz, Ottinger and Stobbins arrived and it emerged that they, too, had been conscripted into the 4044th. Having begun his boastful interpretation of military strategy he was unable to retract it.

Many of the girls at the Maidens were relieved to hear that Thrux and his hangers on would be leaving; none more so than Roxie, who hoped she would never see them again. She hoped that Thrux and his friends would all be killed.

This was not because she had any sympathy for the Imperials. The Empire had not lifted a finger to help the cause of reform on Akkadis. Indeed it was rumoured that their envoy, Scamander, was partly responsible for crushing the Reformist movement.

Roxana Keswick had been a trainee teacher when her parents were proscribed and killed. Roxie herself had been branded and sold unto the most degrading kind of slavery possible. She had endured the mortification of having to entertain her former students, Thrux, Danielz, Stobbins and Ottinger as a pleasure slave, when they discovered her serving at the Maidens. To make matters worse, those four had told their friends, and within days the entire student body of Akkad City State Senior School Number Eleven knew that the pretty ex-teacher was serving in a pleasure house. A number of them found it deliciously entertaining to have Roxie serve them drinks and dance naked for them, twisting and gyrating to the lively beat of an exciting Atkoi tune, and then if they could afford her fee, have her entertain them more intimately.

There were even several youths whom Roxana had considered good students, polite, hard working and academically promising, who had nevertheless chosen to visit her and made her serve them as though she were just another pleasure slave. To be fair, the school authorities had attempted to prevent their students from visiting the Maidens or any other pleasure house, but the very prohibition drew attention to the situation and there was little that could be done to control what students could do in their own time. Nevertheless Thrux and his immediate coterie of hangers on were Roxie's worst tormentors, and it was hardly surprising that she hoped they would not return from their military service.

After her mother's death, Alicia Carno had inherited Akkadis Leisure. Her grief at the loss of her mother was more than adequately compensated by the wealth, power and prestige which Akkadis Leisure afforded her. She was not an active owner. She allowed the company accountant to appoint a new manager for the Maidens, to replace Mrs Knott, who had been arrested and executed for blackmail. Alicia's contribution to managing the company was to visit its various premises and give unhelpful instructions to the long suffering managers. In time even this hindrance lessened, as she lost interest. Her thoughts were occupied instead by the arrangements for her forthcoming wedding to Jak Zadkine. It would be a grand occasion. No expense would be spared. Her friends would not know whether to be envious, or struck dumb with wonder by the elaborate arrangements which were to be made.

10: ERE THEIR TALE IS TOLD

A prince must take care to appear and sound like a person of integrity, honesty, kindness and humanity.

A wise prince cannot and should not keep his word when it is disadvantageous to do so.

Niccolo Machiavelli: The Prince

Meanwhile on Ziandakush, in the seraglio of His Dread Lordship Rurik the Third, Great Kzam of All the Atkoi, Kyra, Millicent and six other novices had been summoned to the private chambers of the Kzama Radmilla, the Kzam's senior wife.

They made obeisance to Radmilla, remaining perfectly still with their foreheads touching the floor at their mistress's feet. The Kzama was usually kind, but they could not afford to take her benevolence for granted. Since the attempt on the Kzam's life, Radmilla's moods had become unpredictable. Most of the girls all tried to avoid her now. At times she seemed quite dangerous to approach.

The Imperial authorities had denied any knowledge of the plot on Rurik's life. On this particular occasion they happened to be telling the truth. Though Princess Athanasia had never guessed it, it had been Radmilla herself who had supplied her with the poison, through an intermediary. Radmilla had then intervened to save the Kzam's life. She did not want her husband dead; at least not until her sons' inheritances were secured. Her only purpose had been to gain her husband's gratitude to increase her own influence.

For a while it had seemed as though war might be averted. The would-be assassin, Princess Athanasia, was being held in a cell beneath the seraglio awaiting the Kzam's judgement. Kyra had been given the task of taking the Princess a tray of food each day. The Kzama had told Kyra it was an honour, in recognition of her hard work.

Then Scamander, the Archpriest and Imperial Ambassador, had been murdered, sparking off full scale hostilities. For the girls in the seraglio, insulated from the outside world, the war seemed less important than the attempt on the life of their lord and master. The war would not affect them personally. It would be fought in Imperial space, and they would be in no personal danger. The Kzam would obviously win. The main effect of the war was that their master would be absent even more than had been usual before hostilities began.

Millie wondered fearfully why they had been summoned by the Kzama. She knew that her progress with the flute had been less than satisfactory. She tried her best in all subjects, but she was obviously not very musical. But then why had Kyra been summoned - Kyra, who everyone said was doing so well and who would probably be the first among the novices to walk the Golden Path to their master's bedchamber? Millie and Kyra were good friends, but Millie could not help but feel a little jealous of the Cormic girl.

The Kzama told the girls to straighten up. They looked at their mistress, wide eyed. "It's all right, don't be afraid," she reassured them. Radmilla always seemed to know what her girls were thinking and feeling. "I have wonderful news for you. You have all made excellent progress, both in your book subjects and in the graces." Millie felt some relief. The 'graces' included music, singing, dancing, deportment and physical training. Radmilla continued, "Your progress in physical training has not gone unnoticed." She caught Millie's eyes when she added that last comment and the novice blushed, embarrassed but delighted by the compliment. Radmilla paused for a moment. "I am therefore delighted to inform you that you are all to be presented to your lord and master the Kzam upon his return to the seraglio in three weeks' time."

Radmilla smiled as the girls tried without success to stifle their delighted squeals, so that the end of her sentence was hardly audible. Forgetting protocol, they hugged one another and thanked the Kzama enthusiastically.

Kyra also thanked the Kzama, though perhaps not as profusely as her friends. She would never have chosen to be trained as a concubine of an Atkoi Kzam, and yet she knew that her destiny was not in her own hands. The Kzam was the only man there could ever be in her life, and like all the girls, Kyra had wanted to be seen and be noticed by him. He was the object of their dreams and fantasies, their prayers and their natural feminine affections. Yet now that she was due to be presented to the Kzam, Kyra was nervous. All of this, the Kzama saw and understood.

It was in fact three weeks later that the Great Kzam returned to Ziandakush.

Rurik was reading a lengthy report, seeming to glance through it swiftly, yet digesting every detail. Akkadis had been pacified. Loyal Akkadisi - those sympathetic to the Kzam - had been appointed to the Oligarchy and the Senate. Akkadis would now be considered an Atkoi world.

On New Wessex too, progress was being made. Like many conquered planets it would be renamed to make it more attractive to Atkoi settlers and to remind the local populace that they were now Atkoi subjects. The planetary capital, Prendergast, was to be razed to the ground. Its site would revert to natural forest as soon as radiation levels subsided sufficiently. It would be a powerful gesture. The population were already being dispersed. A new capital, an existing city, had been selected and renamed Port Rurik. That, too, was being cleared of inhabitants to make way for Atkoi settlers. Port Rurik would also become the seat of a Provincial governor responsible for eight inhabited planets of the Kzamate.

Transports had already left New Wessex en route for the old Atkoi worlds, carrying machinery, metals, raw materials, manufactured goods, slaves and commodities of every kind. The planet's bank vaults had been emptied and their contents shipped back to the Kzamate. In return, the transports would bring the first wave of Atkoi settlers.

Word of Ozim's terror had spread before him. A number of refugees had escaped from New Wessex. That would do no harm. They would tell the other Imperials about the price New Wessex was paying for resisting the Kzam.

Rurik's son Ozim was ably advised and assisted by an experienced officer named Gaeta. Vice-Admiral Gaeta was an excellent commander, although disgusted by Ozim's cruelty. The Kzam understood this. He would have use for Gaeta long after Ozim had completed his task. Nevertheless the policy of terror was bearing fruit. Planet after planet was surrendering to the Atkoi. Soon they would reach Terminor. It was believed that the Imperials had already withdrawn their fleet from Terminor. The Kzam wanted its shipyards, both for his own use, and to deny them to the Empire.

Rurik had already dispatched a second fleet which was heading directly to Tolon. The Imperials would be taken unawares. It was under the nominal command of his son Khostrounil, who like Ozim was assisted by an experienced officer. Rurik was aware that his appointment of Khostrounil was deeply resented by his senior wife, the Kzama. She had wanted him to choose Ozart, her younger son. Khostrounil was Rurik's son by a more junior wife. He was a threat to Radmilla's plans.

The Kzam smiled. Radmilla would be angrier still when he replaced Ozim. He would deal with that problem later. The Kzama was not as indispensable as she imagined. Neither were her two sons. But Khostrounil had the makings of an excellent commander, and Rurik promoted talent.

The Kzam was not at all impressed by Radmilla's claim to have foiled the plot on his life. The conspiracy had been amateurish and doomed to failure. The murderous Princess Athanasia had proved useful though. In the months before hostilities began, the Emperor had made concessions which he would never have made if his daughter had not been a prisoner charged with a capital crime, in effect a hostage. Now that they were at war, Rurik could hardly expect any further such concessions, but Athanasia would still be useful. The execution of an Imperial Princess would demonstrate how helpless the Prendergast regime was to help even the Emperor's own daughter. They would be shown up as cowards too, for using her as an attempted assassin. Or perhaps as a gesture of magnanimity she could be spared and later exchanged for Atkoi prisoners held by the Imperials. For now, the Kzam would keep his options open. He would leave them guessing.

The Kzam had returned to the seraglio.

It was a time of great excitement. The girls had been assembled in a courtyard to watch his return. Screaming in excitement, one of them had fainted. Rurik pretended to be faintly amused by their hysteria.

Those chosen to be presented formally to him would each wear a beautiful white dress. No effort would be spared and Radmilla had gone to great lengths to make the presentation a success. She faced increasing competition for her husband's affection, from younger women who were well trained, beautiful, and eager. She faced this with dignity, helping the Chief Eunuch, the Klang Arak, to organise and manage the girls. She needed to keep her position as Kzama and to retain the Kzam's affection, at least until Ozim inherited the throne. Until then, her son must be protected from his own foolishness. Consequently, Radmilla made it her business to be indispensable.

The girls had been bathed, perfumed and dressed in preparation for their presentation. Kyra looked especially lovely in her gown. She was beautiful, sweet, intelligent and vivacious, the sort of girl who could win the Kzam's heart, and yet Radmilla felt she would not be a threat. Not while she could be controlled. Perhaps Radmilla could even use Kyra to deal with the little problem of Zoey.

The foolish upstart Zoey was now a concubine of the third rank. She had become dangerously arrogant. Zoey had discovered that she could influence the Kzam without asking Radmilla's advice first. The power had gone to her head. She did not even have the sense to realise the danger she was in.

But Zoey could wait. The Kzama made a final inspection of the girls. There must be not a hair, not an eyelash, not a ribbon out of place. Satisfied, she called the Klang Arak, who also inspected them. He too was satisfied. Outwardly graceful despite their thumping hearts, the girls followed the Kzama, who led them to an adjoining room to await their lord and master.

They stood in line in the richly appointed room, before a thick burgundy carpet on which stood two empty gilded chairs. One of the girls was unable to repress a squeak of excitement as the Kzam entered the room. Radmilla made a mental note to speak to her afterwards.

The Kzam and Kzama took their seats. The Klang Arak remained standing.

There was a clash of cymbals and the sound of flutes and lyres, and the girls began their dance. It was a modest dance, the eight beautiful young women moving in perfect harmony for just long enough for the Kzam to study each girl in turn while the Kzama leaned towards him, whispering her thoughts and comments on each of them.

The dance ended, the girls curtsied, and Radmilla invited Rurik to inspect them. He walked slowly along the line, occasionally stroking or pinching girl's cheek or feeling the texture of her hair. The Klang Arak told him each girl's name as he reached her, and she curtsied. With some, he exchanged a few words. Each girl spoke if and only if the Kzam first spoke to her.

When he reached Kyra, he lifted her chin and looked into her eyes, smiled and tickled her chin. Kyra giggled. "Now you don't look so nervous," the Kzam said. "I saw you swimming. You are lovely." Kyra blushed hotly and thanked him and curtsied, but he had already passed her. The Kzam had been referring to the seraglio tradition which Kyra, shy by nature, hated most: that of the novices swimming naked in the pool beneath their master's window. Kyra understood that she could not alter her destiny, but she still found the experience mortifying. And yet even Kyra's blush had been pretty and demure, Radmilla thought. Above all, the Kzam had noticed her.

Within minutes, the presentation was over. The Kzam departed. The eight girls were overwhelmed by emotion. Some, who imagined the Kzam had shown particular interest in them, were overcome by excitement. Others, whom he had hardly seemed to notice, were tearful and frustrated, particularly if they had already spent several years in the seraglio without having been summoned to walk the Golden Path.

Kyra, whom the Kzam had appeared to favour, received some black looks from her jealous peers. Her own feelings were mixed: she was excited and happy, but also nervous. Suppose she was chosen. Was she truly ready? And would the Kzam still like her?

That night the novices slept little. They lay on their mats on the floor of the dormitory discussing in hushed whispers the prospects for each of the eight girls who had been presented. Every word, every gesture of the Kzam was discussed, analysed and assessed. Eight hearts, so eager for love and the chance to give their love, beat in anticipation of the morning. They dared speak only in the softest whispers. The eunuch Baltazaro, the Deputy Keeper of Slaves responsible for novices, was a light sleeper. He lay in his room adjoining their dormitory.

The following morning, Kyra and her friend Daphne were on duty. It was their turn, according to the novices' roster, to rise a little earlier than the other girls and make a small pot of mint tea for Baltazaro. Later they would also be expected to make his bed, tidy his room, wash and iron his clothes, polish his shoes and clean and polish his urethrum, his most treasured possession, the tube through which he urinated and which had been a gift from the Kzam himself.

They knelt and served him the tea as they had been taught in their deportment lessons. When Baltazaro had finished, he told Kyra that she was to attend the Kzama immediately after breakfast.

Dizzy, Kyra nearly dropped the tray. She knew she would learn her destiny that morning. Within seconds of being dismissed by Baltazaro, Daphne told the other novices. By breakfast time the entire seraglio knew, and it was all they could talk about.

Kyra knocked on the door of Radmilla's private sitting room. She entered, curtsied, approached the Kzama and sank gracefully to her knees, her heart beating with a mixture of excitement and trepidation.

"Kyra my dear," Radmilla began, "I think you can guess why I have sent for you." Radmilla smiled, and paused. "Kyra, I am so pleased for you. You were lovely yesterday. I thought so, and your master the Kzam obviously thought so too. You have found favour with him. Tomorrow night the Kzam will dine in the Amethyst Room. After he has dined, you will dance for him."

11: TO PAINT THE LILY

Do not try to find out -- we're forbidden to know--
What end the gods may bestow on me or you.
Horace: Odes, Book I No 11

Daphne polished Baltazaro's urethrum alone that night.

Radmilla told Kyra to spend the remainder of the day practising her dance steps. She would not be returned to the novices' quarters. That evening she was given a draught to help her sleep. She slept on Radmilla's bedroom floor, to spare her from the endless questions of the other girls. The Kzama wanted her to get a good night's rest. Rurik liked his women to look healthy, with bright eyes, shining hair and smooth skin.

The following morning Kyra was sent to the seraglio beauticians. By mid-afternoon she had been bathed, perfumed, depilated and powdered. Her hair was shining. Her finger and toenails and eyelids were painted a tasteful shade of pale blue-green.

The beautician stepped aside proudly for the Kzama and Klang Arak to inspect Kyra. Narciso, the Klang Arak, nodded. She would do. Radmilla hugged her and said, "You look gorgeous, absolutely gorgeous. The Kzam will love you. Soon, Kyra, soon you will walk the Golden Path."

An hour before the Kzam was due to have his supper, the Kzama Radmilla personally escorted Kyra to the small room adjoining the Amethyst Room and waited with her.

By the time Kyra had been waiting a few minutes, she was on the verge of panic. She suddenly realised that she could not go through with it. The Kzama hugged her and encouraged her, but made it clear that Kyra had to perform her dance. To disobey the Kzam's express command could not be countenanced.

The Kzam ate alone. He sat on a cushion on the floor, at a low table. Often he dined with the Kzama or one or more of his sons, or a senior minister or official, but when he dined in the Amethyst Room, he dined either alone or in the company of a favourite concubine. Two pretty, smiling girls served his meal, while another two knelt, waiting to serve his tea. They were dressed identically in painted blue silk dresses with long split skirts. When the Kzam had finished his meal and was sipping his tea, he told one of them to ring a gong.

It was the sound Kyra had been dreading. Terrified, she turned to the Kzama for support. Radmilla squeezed her arm and whispered, "Relax. Just do what you were taught. He will love you. I know." In another alcove the musicians, trained concubines who played flutes, lyres and tiny finger drums, had already begun an introductory piece. Kyra straightened herself and stepped through the archway into the richly appointed Amethyst Room. She curtsied, and stood with her hands above her head, back to back. That was the signal for the dancing music to begin.

She was dressed in a short bolero of deep blue-green silk, and a wraparound skirt of the same colour, which was fastened at her hip with a silver clasp, but which left her right thigh and leg visible. She would never have dared choose such an ensemble herself; the wardrobe mistress and the Kzama had selected it for her.

When she began to dance, Kyra found that it was not as difficult as she had imagined. She tried not to think about the Kzam watching her. She concentrated on the music and the movements she had learned and practised day after day until she could repeat them almost without thought. The training of novices in the Kzam's seraglio was thorough. There was little else for them to do. She remembered to smile throughout the performance. The Kzam liked his girls to smile. She let the music flow through her, responding to it as though it was the music, rather than her own mind, which controlled her body.

As the music reached its crescendo, Kyra suddenly realised that she had nearly finished, and she had not made any mistakes, and that she had put so much energy and feeling into the performance that she was certain the dancing mistress would have approved. And that meant that maybe, just maybe, the Kzam would like it too.

Suddenly her smile broadened. She had finished her dance. The ordeal was over and she felt she had done well. She heard the final clash of cymbals and the final notes of the flute, and she sank gracefully to her knees and made obeisance.

Kyra remained with her forehand touching the floor for several seconds. She would remain so until the Kzam spoke to her, or until someone told her to lift her head. She had finished her part. It was out of her hands now. The decision rested with the Kzam. Would he wish to see her again, to talk to her, and eventually summon her to walk the Golden Path? Or would she simply be transferred to the Reliquary, to live out her days in monotonous, meaningless sterility?

Kyra did not have long to wait. “That was very good. A charming performance,” the Great Kzam announced. Kyra smiled nervously.

“Your name is Kyra, isn’t it? Come here, Kyra and sit with me. I’d like to talk to you.”

To have the Kzam call her by name was an honour which Kyra had not expected. It made her feel important; wanted, somehow. The Kzam spoke to Kyra for perhaps half an hour. At first she was nervous and simply agreed with whatever he said. After a while she relaxed a little. He gestured to one of the girls serving tea, who smiled and poured a cup for Kyra too. He asked her about her family and her home on Coromandel. She was surprised by his detailed knowledge of her home world, insignificant as it was.

The Kzam stood, and Kyra stood too. He held her upper arms, and slowly kissed her. Kyra had never been kissed before, by a man. It made her feel almost dizzy. He cupped her face in his hands and kissed her a second time. “I have enjoyed talking to you, Kyra,” he said. “I am leaving now. I am obliged to go away for a while. When I return, I will send for you.”

Kyra sank to her knees to make obeisance once more, but the Kzam had already turned to leave. He would see her again! He would send for her! Did that mean she would walk the Golden Path? Kyra hardly knew whether to feel excited or afraid.

When the Great Kzam was in residence, the girls lived in hope of being summoned to his chambers. But since the war had begun, he was absent more often than not and they were limited to writing him letters expressing their love, or shyly hinting at it, which they would take to the Kzama’s chambers to give to one of her maids in the hope that they would be transmitted to their master.

Usually they were, once the Kzama had read them. The chief exceptions were the letters from Zoey, which the Kzama invariably destroyed.

Radmilla had found that her husband’s long absences could be very useful. She used them to consolidate her position. The time had now come to deal decisively and permanently with Zoey.

Zoey was certainly beautiful. Radmilla understood entirely why the Kzam had become so enamoured with her. She had lovely dark hair and a very pretty face, smooth pale skin and a slender figure. Her breasts were not particularly large, but they were firm, shapely and thrusting. She was charming, witty and vivacious. She was still only twenty-two. In four years she had risen to the third rank, a rise of unprecedented speed. She had danced for the Kzam on countless occasions. She had walked the Golden Path and been mentioned in the Blue Book over a hundred times; Radmilla had counted them. Many of the women of the seraglio speculated that Zoey might one day be appointed to the coveted position of Ankh-il-Wath, the Preferred Concubine of the Seraglio, a position which was currently vacant.

But Zoey had made enemies along the way. Several of the more senior concubines considered her a threat to their own positions. Worse still, she had attempted to meddle in matters above her station. One of the Kzam's eight wives, a lady named Helma, had a son serving in the Kzam's navy. Helma had approached Zoey to ask the concubine to use her influence with the Kzam to have Helma's son promoted.

Zoey felt as if her heart would burst with pride. A wife of the Kzam had approached her, a mere concubine, as a supplicant! Zoey decided to test the limits of her power and show off her influence. Instead of discretely raising the matter with the Kzama, she chose to ally herself with Helma and approach the Kzam directly with her request.

Unfortunately for Zoey, her request was successful. Helma's son was given command of his own vessel. It was a small vessel, to be sure, but a vessel, nonetheless.

Naturally Radmilla discovered the truth. Never had the Kzama felt her monopoly on influence so directly challenged. It did not help that Helma was a daughter of the Longuiz clan, traditional rivals of Radmilla's own Pandulfis clan.

Radmilla decided Zoey's fate then and there. Her fall from grace would be as meteoric as her rise.

It was easily achieved. Zoey was accused of gross indecency, of trying to seduce one of the other women. There were many women, grateful and loyal to the Kzama, some of whom Radmilla had even saved from the Reliquary, whom she could have asked to act as witnesses. Radmilla chose just two. It was better not to overstate her case.

The Klang Arak heard the evidence while the Kzam was away. It was damning. Narciso was livid. For such a thing to happen in the seraglio brought his competence into question. The girl's guilt or innocence was, in a sense, irrelevant. If the Kzam even believed such things might be possible, his confidence in Narciso would be diminished.

Narciso would make an example of her. The rule relating to lesbian misbehaviour in the Kzam's seraglio was an ancient one, but a simple one. For the first offence, the guilty woman was flogged and cut. The procedure involved complete circumcision, the removal of the labia and clitoris. For a second offence the miscreant would be destroyed altogether. Rurik placed complete confidence in his Klang Arak to hear such cases, pass judgement and order sentence to be executed. The Kzam did not wish to be bothered with the minutiae of seraglio administration.

Zoey had fallen to her knees and begged and pleaded for mercy. There had been a terrible mistake, she said. The allegations were not true. She loved her master devotedly and she was certainly not a lesbian. She had beseeched the Klang Arak to take pity on her.

He commanded her to silence and sent her back to her quarters. This was not because of any indecision on his part. Narciso had decided on her punishment the instant he heard the allegations. But it would do no harm to give the other concubines the chance to speculate about Zoey's fate, and to leave Zoey to anticipate her punishment for a little longer.

Three days later, after breakfast, an apprentice eunuch brought Zoey a message. She was to attend the eunuch Bastinak immediately.

Zoey knew what the message meant. Bastinak was the eunuch responsible for branding new slave girls and for piercing any girl's flesh if the Kzam wished her to wear rings in her nipples or labia. But it was Bastinak's third responsibility which was pertinent on this occasion. If a girl was to be circumcised, it was Bastinak who performed the operation.

Sick with fear, she followed the apprentice to Bastinak's quarters.

In the event it was the apprentice, Irtuk, rather than Bastinak himself who performed the circumcision. The boy needed the experience, and Zoey was a good subject for him to practise on.

Anaesthetic was not necessary for circumcisions. The girl being cut was strapped so firmly to the cutting table that very little movement was possible. Disinfectant was used, however. Irtuk used Bastinak's scissors and tweezers, although he worked rather more slowly and methodically than his master and mentor.

Two days later Zoey was summoned to the Klang Arak's office.

It was a large room, but crowded now with the Klang Arak, the Kzama, the Kzam's other wives except for Princess Athanasia, and several senior concubines, women whom Zoey had taunted with her rise to greatness. At Baltazaro's command, the novices were all present. They would stand at the back of the room, while their betters sat nearer the front. They were gathered there to witness Zoey's disgrace. The upstart concubine was to receive the second part of her punishment publicly.

Zoey saw no sympathy in the faces of the higher ranking concubines or the Kzama. She dared to glance at the Klang Arak. She saw the fury in his eyes and looked away quickly. Even Helma, the indirect author of Zoey's fall from grace, showed no sympathy. She guessed the true reason for Zoey's punishment but she was powerless to intervene. She knew better than to question the Kzama's decisions. At least her son's promotion had not been rescinded.

Zoey was wearing a gown of thin silk, fastened with a cord. The Klang Arak ordered her to disrobe. She was beautiful, with a slim, toned body, fine breasts and sweetly curving hips and buttocks. She stood gracefully, straight and still with her chin up, her toes together, her hands at her sides and her shoulders back. She stood very straight, blushing beneath the scrutiny of her former rivals.

Narciso could remember when Zoey first arrived in the seraglio. He had been struck by her beauty even then. It was a waste, he thought; a criminal waste. The girl could have had anything but she had chosen to ruin her own future, either by her perversion or her breath-taking stupidity in challenging the Kzama's position; it hardly mattered which. Both were inexcusable, and inexcusably stupid.

The Kzam's wives and higher ranking concubines watched in silence, but several of the novices could not help themselves from gasping in horror. They had never before seen a girl who had been recently cut. The experience would be instructive for them, Radmilla thought. The wound was still red and raw, with a deep red scab. Zoey had been plucked of body hair before the operation and the wound was clearly visible. She had also been recently caned. Half a dozen raw stripes were clearly visible across her breasts.

Radmilla had been told that the girl had made a dreadful fuss in Bastinak's chambers. She had been screaming and trying to wriggle the whole time she was on the cutting table. That would explain the six stripes of the cane across her breasts. *The girl has no strength of character,* the Kzama thought. *No will power.*

Zoey did not waste time pleading her innocence or begging for mercy. She had already exhausted that route. She could better appease the Klang Arak's anger by submitting herself obediently to her punishment.

She knew that from here she would be escorted directly to the Reliquary. She had been warned not to complain or protest her innocence. If she made a fuss, she would find herself accused again, of a similar crime. With her record for unnatural behaviour, no one would believe she was innocent. If she was accused of repeating her crime, she would simply be destroyed.

In the Kzam's seraglio, that meant that she would be tied or sewn into a sack weighted with rocks and dropped into a well in the grounds of the seraglio. It was a deep well, noted for its bitterly cold water. Zoey would accept her punishment obediently.

When the Kzam returned to the seraglio, he would find Zoey missing. If he enquired about her, Radmilla would show him a letter which Zoey had been ordered to write, confessing to her unnatural behaviour and apologising for it. Radmilla would divert the Kzam's attention with a newer girl, a novice who was more pliable, more loyal, and just as beautiful, if not more so. Radmilla had the ideal candidate in mind: Kyra. Kyra would be perfect for the Kzama's plan.

The Klang Arak unfastened Howler from his belt. The whip was made of bull hide, stiff and inflexible. It was a yard long, with a thick handle tapering to a narrow tip.

Zoey stood perfectly still while the Klang Arak announced the sentence. "For polluting our lord and master's seraglio with unnatural conduct, sixteen strokes."

Several of the novices gasped again, but only quietly. It was not wise to appear to question those in authority. The usual seraglio flogging consisted of twelve strokes, and even that was rare.

Helma was burning with embarrassment, but said nothing. The Kzama and the Kzam's other wives and senior concubines also remained silent. Zoey herself tried to say, "Yes, master," but was so terrified that the words emerged only as a little whimper.

The Klang Arak gestured her towards the frame and Zoey dutifully stepped forward, ascended the step and bent herself over it with her wrists and ankles ready to be strapped into place. An apprentice eunuch stooped to fasten first her ankles and then her wrists into place. Zoey's hips were resting on a horizontal beam, so that her buttocks and the backs of her thighs were raised, ready to receive Howler's attentions. Although her hands and feet were held securely, Zoey would still be able to move her head, and some limited movement would be possible for her hips and buttocks. The apprentice stuffed a rag into Zoey's mouth to muffle her screams. He stood and nodded to the Klang Arak.

The Klang Arak raised Howler and brought it down ferociously across Zoey's buttocks. Zoey began urgently squealing and clenching and unclenching her buttocks and twisting them alternately left and right.

She continued to squeal and wriggle until well after the Klang Arak had finished the flogging. Radmilla had been right to suppose that the display would be instructive for the novices. Even the Kzam's senior concubines and his other wives had learned a new respect for the Kzama and her authority.

12: CRIME AND PUNISHMENT

10 Kzams and Judges, you shall suffer neither a maiden nor a faithful wife to be set upon the stake: 11 but the adulteress shall end her days on the skewer. 12 For it is not seemly that wickedness shall go unpunished in the Worlds of the New Covenant. 13 She will face judgement unshriven. 14 She will seek entrance to the Valleys of the Righteous, but she will be turned away. 15 She will knock upon the gates of Jerusalem, but they shall not be opened unto her. 16 She will be cast into the space between the stars: 17 and she will wander until the end of the Ages.

The Third Book of Milos, 12: 10-17

"My name is Satkisant." The speaker was a lugubrious man in a dark grey suit. "I am the High Executioner of Ziandakush."

A month earlier, Rurik had reached a decision concerning his wife and would-be assassin, Athanasia. It had been transmitted to Ziandakush and conveyed to the Klang Arak. Or perhaps the Kzam had reached his decision six months or a year earlier and merely waited for the right moment to execute it. Either way, Athi had been given a week's notice of her appointment with Mr Satkisant.

Princess Athanasia Otheris at Otheris (to use her married name, which in practice she did not) stood in the preparation room adjacent to the Chamber of Execution in the grounds of the palace of the Great Kzam, on Ziandakush. She appeared tired, pale and strained, but none of those could disguise her beauty.

"As you are aware," Satkisant continued, "Your despatch is scheduled for sunrise. The preparatory procedures are fairly lengthy. As I am sure you are also aware, they are hardly pleasant. They are not intended to be.

Nevertheless they are the requirements of the law and therefore represent His Dread Lordship's express wishes. You must not imagine that anything which is done to you tonight is done out of malice. It is in no sense personal. My advice to you, for your own benefit, is to cooperate to the best of your ability with all instructions that I and my men will give you." At this point the High Executioner indicated his three subordinates. "This will mitigate your suffering to a limited extent." His voice hardened as he added, "Nevertheless I must warn you that I will not tolerate any recalcitrance, nor any disrespect to my men. I will not have it. Do you understand me quite clearly?" Satkisant's mournful expression did not disguise the hardness of his determination.

Athanasia glanced at the men but did not answer. She hoped her silence conveyed her contempt. *He looks like an undertaker*, Athi thought. *I am conversing with my own undertaker. Not many people do that.* His three subordinates, though also wearing suits, looked like thugs, except perhaps for the youngest.

The executioner continued. "Your preparation is scheduled to begin at midnight. Since it is a little past midnight now, we will begin at once. There is nothing to be gained by delaying." Despite her week's foreknowledge, Athi was shocked by the immediacy of his words.

"There is a small glass of medicinal liquor on the table. I strongly recommend that you drain it. You will not find the taste especially pleasant, but it is drugged. It will mitigate your suffering to some degree. You will of course still be very much aware of what is done to you. You will then remove all of your clothing," continued the executioner. "Fold it neatly and leave it on that table. You may wrap the towel around yourself. We will wait in the adjoining room, to spare your shame." He nodded to his men, who began to move towards the door.

"No," Athi spoke at last. "I will not do that. I am an Imperial Princess and I insist that I am treated as such." Athi knew that this was her last opportunity to make a stand. She had been warned that the executioners would try to make her grovel and make obeisance like a slave. That, she would never do. Never. “If my father the Emperor knew you were ... oh! Ouch!”

Athi’s words were cut short as the speed of the executioners took her by surprise. They had been told that she might be difficult. Athanasia found herself suddenly seized, her clothes unceremoniously jerked from her, and a wide collar wrapped around her throat and buckled shut. The collar must have had two smaller straps attached at the back, Athi realised, as first one wrist and then the other was pulled behind her neck and fastened in place. She could no longer struggle to any effect. Around each of her ankles they fastened another strap, to each of which was attached a ring, several inches in diameter, shaped like a capital letter D so that they looked rather like stirrups. The executioners did not explain what these were for, nor was Athanasia in a position to ask. Events for Athi were moving so fast that she gave the stirrup like rings little thought. One of the men pulled her head back and pinched her nose shut, while another poured the tiny glass of fluid into her mouth. He held her mouth and nose closed until Athi had swallowed at least some of the foul tasting fluid. As Athi gasped for breath, another of Satkisant’s men thrust a wad of cloth into her mouth and taped it in place.

Unable to cover herself with her hands, Athi attempted to curl up, facing away from the men. She wished she had simply disrobed when they ordered her to do so. She wished she had never proceeded with her foolish assassination plot at all.

Athi understood her position in Atkoi law, now. It had been explained to her. A wife who murdered her husband was to be reduced to slavery and impaled. There were no exceptions. It was a terrible crime, a rebellion against the natural order ordained by God, a betrayal of the man to whom she owed absolute loyalty. A failed attempt was punished as severely as the murder itself; it was the attempt which was criminal, the motivation, as much as the outcome. Hence Athi had been ordered by a mere functionary to respect and obey his men. They no longer considered her a princess, but a slave.

Satkisant picked up Athi's scattered clothes. To his eyes, they appeared to be of no better quality or value than ordinary clothes within the reach of ordinary people. He had never seen the sense in spending hundreds of karats on expensive clothing. Nevertheless he knew that people like Princess Athanasia habitually bought items which were expensive simply because of who had made them. Athi's short jacket and long skirt looked as if they might have been garments of that sort. The blouse, with some sort of colourful beads sewn on it in patterns, and even the underwear, might be worth saving. Traditionally, the executioners were permitted to keep for themselves anything found on the person of the condemned criminal. Satkisant would take the things to a dealer he knew.

Jakob Satkisant did not know much about *haute couture*, but he was right to imagine that even second-hand, these items would be valuable. Athanasia had dressed expensively in clothes from some of the most exclusive couturiers on Nenuphar. Princesses, Kzamas and senator's wives wore such outfits if they could afford them. On Akkadis, Mrs Carno had liked to imagine that her clothes were of similar quality. Athi's costume was intended to make a statement, to proclaim that she was to be treated with respect.

Her strategy had failed. Satkisant put the clothes on the table, and addressed Athanasia again. "You will be made ready in this room, and taken into the neighbouring chamber shortly before sunrise." He nodded to his men, who stepped forward to begin their assigned tasks. One had scissors. Another carried a pair of bellows and a branding iron.

The youngest of the High Executioner's men was named Mikal Satkisant. He was the nephew and apprentice of Jakob Satkisant and he was an ambitious young man. His uncle Jakob had no son, and hoped that Mikal would one day succeed him. The title of High Executioner of Ziandakush had been in the Satkisant family for over a hundred years and Jakob could not bear to think of the position passing out of his family. Mikal had been delighted to be offered the apprenticeship. It was an excellent career, offering both status and prospects. He had now helped his Uncle Jakob on several jobs.

Mikal was in fact a little nervous, though he would never have admitted to the fact. The law required that as part of her preparation for the skewer, Athi should be thoroughly and repeatedly debauched, as Uncle Jakob rather formally described it. To an outside observer this might sound like congenial employment, and Mikal's friends had teased him mercilessly about it while drinking in their favourite public house, The Kzam of Malitbog. They were jealous. Mikal's chosen profession would allow him to give the Imperial Princess what Mrs Knott at the Maidens of Nenuphar would have vulgarly described as 'a damned good ruttocking.'

But Mikal himself realised that in many cases a condemned woman was not especially attractive. Far from it: many were doubtless quite repugnant, but as an executioner he would be expected to perform his duties professionally, thoroughly and above all, completely impartially in all cases. Mikal was therefore both relieved and delighted when he saw Athanasia. She was a beauty, and Mikal's task tonight would be a pleasure and a delight.

Athi was branded and prepared for the skewer, and then the men took their turns with her in order of seniority. Michael was obliged to wait in the adjoining room for several hours for his turn. He was, after all, the apprentice and most junior of the men. His Uncle Jakob, professional as always, showed him no favouritism, although Jakob had advised Mikal to make the most of this aspect of their evening's work. Relatively few women were impaled on Ziandakush, and few indeed were so presentable as this one. Mikal waited, listening to the occasional yelps and whimpers emanating from the preparation room.

When at last it was his turn, Mikal was not disappointed. Athi sank to her knees, clumsily but with alacrity, touching her forehead to the floor at his feet three times before kneeling upright, perfectly straight. It was obviously difficult with her wrists fastened behind her neck, but she performed the obeisance quite adequately. Mikal's Uncle Jakob had just given Athi some instruction in how to comport herself, and he had emphasised his instructions with a rattan cane.

Athi's dark hair, now crudely trimmed into a slave cut with kittentails, framed her pretty face beautifully. She had a slender figure, long legs and full, round breasts now lifted prettily and thrust forward helplessly by her raised arms.

Seeing her so unexpectedly compliant, Mikal considered for the briefest instant removing her gag and having her serve him on her knees, but he dismissed the idea instantly. She might cry out. Mikal valued his career too much to jeopardise it foolishly. He also respected his Uncle Jakob. The elder Satkisant had said that Mikal was professional, thorough and talented and had the makings of an excellent executioner. Mikal valued his uncle's esteem.

Instead, Mikal ordered Athi to stand. She struggled to her feet and Mikal reached out slowly and squeezed her breasts firmly. She looked at Mikal, wide eyed, but did not attempt to resist or back away. She winced when he touched the two purple welts which now crossed her breasts, the evidence of the rigour the elder Satkisant's chastisement.

"Lie down," said Mikal. "On your back." Athi obeyed, clumsily but quickly enough. Mikal lay beside her. Athi winced again as he traced the shape of her new brand, still fresh and raw, with his finger. It was the bar and circle, used to mark much of the Kzam's property. "Spread your ankles apart," he added. "Further. Much further. Good. Now bend your knees. Lift your ankles up. Higher. Yes, good girl."

Mikal enjoyed the next part of the evening's proceedings to the full. Eventually, fully sated, he grinned in satisfaction. When he next saw his friends in the Kzam of Malitbog he would tell them that the Imperial Princess had been a beauty and a delight. He would have told them that anyway, but since it was in fact true, his words would carry added conviction. He would say that she had squealed for more. Even this was partly true. She had indeed whimpered a little, though perhaps not in pleasure.

Athi crawled to his feet to make obeisance again. She was aware of Mikal looking at her breasts, and she made sure her elbows were pulled back. The High Executioner had told her to keep her back straight and her elbows back, and Athi did not want another stroke of the rattan for slovenliness. Mikal reached out to give her breasts a final squeeze before he left the room.

It was still several hours until sunrise. The others would take their second turn, now.

13: TIME'S WINGED CHARIOT

31 Nor shall the prisoner suffer upon the stake during the hours of darkness. 32 But you shall end their torment at the setting of the sun. 33 For the Lord Almighty is merciful, and you must (imitate) Him.

The Third Book of Milos, 12: 31-33

"Stand up," said Satkisant. Athi struggled to her feet. "Stand straight. Feet together. Head up, elbows back. That's better." Athi wondered how long it was until sunrise. Not long now, she guessed. It had seemed to take ages, but eventually the men had tired of her and left her curled up on the plascrete floor of the small room. Her eyes were red from crying. Satkisant wiped her nose with a rag.

"A word of advice to you, Athanasia," he continued. He did not use her title, but he did not sound impertinent. If anything, there was a hint of kindness in his voice: kindness, but not pity or weakness. "I understand this evening has not been easy for you," the High Executioner continued, "But the worst is now over." That final remark was a lie, but a well intentioned one. "It is time now, to go to the other room. Conduct yourself with dignity. There will be two witnesses, and both of them will be personages of some importance. I cannot at his stage tell you how long the procedure will last, but I can assure you that my men and I will not prolong it unnecessarily. Now follow me."

Athi followed the High Executioner into the larger room. The floor was of cobbled stone, marked with brown stains. It sloped down to a channel which ran along the centre of the room, leading to a drain in the floor. There were no windows, but above their heads was a skylight. To her dismay Athi saw that it was no longer entirely dark outside. The pale light she saw was too bright to be either of Ziandakush's two small moons. She had been right in her guess. It was not long until sunrise.

"Kneel here," said Satkisant. She knelt where he indicated. "Upright," he added, and Athi knelt with her thighs and torso in a straight line, instead of allowing her buttocks to rest on her heels. It was an uncomfortable position to hold. Satkisant checked her bonds. Her hands were still held firmly to her collar, behind her neck. Her gag and her stirrups were still held tightly in place.

"Kneel back," said Satkisant. Athi gratefully lowered her buttocks to the floor, taking the strain off her thigh muscles. Satkisant and his men were fully dressed again now. They brought two chairs and placed them several feet in front of Athi, facing her. They placed a tiny table between the chairs. Mikal placed a sheet of paper on the table. It was the death certificate, ready for the witnesses to sign.

Then Athi saw the skewer. Satkisant's deputy was carrying it. He walked over to a point between Athi and the two chairs. There was a small hole in the stone floor. He carefully positioned the rod above the hole and slid it in. It slid perhaps two feet into the hole. The man tested it for steadiness. It fitted tightly.

The sight of the skewer shocked Athi. For the first time, she saw the implement of her own destruction. It was not especially high. It did not need to be. Now that it was set vertically in its socket, it came up to shoulder height. It was a little thicker than a man's thumb. It was made of fibresteel, black or dark grey in colour. At the top it came to a sharp point.

Athi saw the youngest man, the one they called Mikal, smear something shiny or greasy over the top foot of its length. 'Greasing the skewer,' as it was called, was an act of mercy, she knew. The sides of the skewer were fluted. Athi did not realise this, but the grooves were intended to make it easier to withdraw the skewer from her body after use. Finally, three stout wooden boxes or blocks were arranged on the floor around the base of the skewer. Again, Athi could not imagine their purpose.

The preparations were complete. Satkisant and his men sat on a bench at one side of the room to await the witnesses. Mikal made tea, which he brought them. The men talked quietly while they waited, sometimes laughing at a private joke. None of them addressed Athi. Her brand was burning. She was sore, she was thirsty and she was very afraid. The light from above was growing steadily brighter.

Then Athanasia heard a sound behind her, and the men stood. Athi dared not turn her head but she realised that the first witness had arrived. The men bowed. Mikal tapped Athi with the cane. "Kneel straight up," he said.

She heard the witness's voice, and realised it was Lord Nardilic, the Lord Provost of Ziandakush, responsible for administering the planet's civil and criminal judicial system. He exchanged pleasantries with the executioners and went to sit in one of the chairs. Mikal fetched a tray with a small pot of mint tea, and poured a tiny cup for Nardilic. The executioners' own tea cups had already been removed. The men stood respectfully at one side of the room.

Athi had seen Nardilic in formal meetings in the Throne Room, and even spoken to him briefly. She was mortified to be seen by him now, like this. "Make obeisance," said Mikal. Athi crawled forward, knelt lower and touched her forehead three times to the floor, at Nardilic's feet. She raised herself and crawled backwards to her original position. She performed the obeisance a little clumsily. Unlike novices in the seraglio, she had never benefited from Baltazaro's tutelage. Besides, it was difficult to balance with her wrists strapped behind her neck. But Lord Nardilic did not appear to mind. "Head up!" said Mikal. "Back straight! Elbows back!" Athi did her best to kneel perfectly straight. She was aware that with her elbows pulled back, her breasts were lifted and thrust forward.

She seemed obedient enough, thought Nardilic. He knew that Athanasia had been somewhat self-willed and poorly brought up. Oiku did not know how to teach their women, he knew. She was also extremely attractive. He had known she was beautiful. He had seen her at court, but he had never before dared to look at her closely. She had been a wife of the Kzam, after all. To see her displayed like this was a pleasure he had never anticipated. Satkisant's men had obviously prepared her properly. Her hair was arranged in kittentails, as the style was usually known, although the correct term was a 'slave cut.'

Nardilic looked at her breasts. They were firm and thrust forward proudly. She had been caned, he saw. Perhaps she had struggled or answered back at some point. Satkisant would have dealt with any such nonsense very sharply, he knew.

Nardilic tried not to look at Athi or her breasts for too long. He was conscious of his dignity as the head of the judiciary. He did not wish to be seen obviously enjoying the sight of the naked pretty brunette displayed before him. Athi dared only once to glance at his features. He looked severe and angry, and she looked away quickly.

Nardilic had seen the stains of blood on Athi's thighs. The rumours were true, then. She had been a virgin. Satkisant and his men had been thorough in all respects. Religious law stated that a woman could only be skewered for adultery. That requirement had been fulfilled by the executioners during their preparation of Athanasia. She had chosen to commit her crime. That led directly to this punishment. Part of the punishment included being debauched by the executioners. In that sense, the condemned woman was, logically, guilty of adultery.

Technically, the executioners were also guilty of adultery. But they could seek absolution afterwards, at any shrine, if they were religiously inclined. They would have to bathe themselves ritually beforehand, recite the appropriate prayers and give the priest a sum of money in atonement for their sin. The minimum sum was twenty karats, although they could of course donate more if they so chose.

Nardilic himself was not especially religious, but he understood the benefits of religion for society. The Arian faith taught good moral conduct. Deterrence was also necessary. People were naturally corrupt, and the tendency had to be discouraged.

Nevertheless he was not without mercy. He saw that Athi was struggling to hold her position, kneeling upright. “You may kneel back, girl,” he told her. Athi gratefully lowered her weight again.

Nardilic sipped his tea, wishing the other witness would arrive. She was late. Nardilic was an articulate man though, and he chatted politely with the executioners. He had a talent for conversing with anyone, of any social rank, and making them feel at ease. They discussed the progress of the war, rising prices, and rising rents in particular. Mikal was hoping to rent a home of his own soon, and Nardilic offered him some useful advice.

Then the second witness arrived, and Athi’s humiliation was complete. It was the Kzama Radmilla. She had dressed expensively, smartly and beautifully, as if to emphasise Athi’s nakedness. Her clothes were not as expensive as Athi’s had been, but her taste was if anything more refined. She sat down beside Nardilic.

Radmilla was accompanied by Kyra, who carried the Kzama’s purse for her. Kyra was dressed modestly, but not expensively. She wore a long skirt and tunic and headscarf. It was the first time Kyra had left the seraglio since she had arrived there, although the Chamber of Execution was still within the grounds of the palace. Kyra knelt to the right of her mistress and a little behind her, as befitted her rank as an attendant handmaiden.

Athi was told to kneel straight up again. Kyra was shocked to see the Princess like this, prepared for execution. She had seen Athanasia almost every day over the last few months, and got to know her a little. It was not that the Princess was an especially nice person. She seemed surly, haughty and ill-tempered. But Kyra understood that she had been waiting to learn her fate, and obviously allowances had to be made.

Then Kyra saw the skewer, stark and straight, narrow and pointed, with its tip already greased. A cold hand of fear and horror seemed to clasp her heart. She nearly cried out loud, but suppressed the urge. She closed her eyes for a moment and breathed slowly. She was glad she was kneeling. It would make her less likely to faint. She put her hands on her knees to steady herself. She forced herself to look again at the skewer. It was still there, still real and still as horrible as before.

Radmilla spoke to Nardilic. "Oh Odo, I do apologise for keeping you," said Radmilla. "Something cropped up. One of the girls had a little upset, and I had to sort it out. But how are Emelza and the children? Of course, they're not really children any more, are they?" Radmilla greeted the executioners too, and sipped her tea. Naturally Kyra was not offered tea.

Athi made obeisance to Radmilla, as she had done to Nardilic.

"You look quite different, with your hair like that," said the Kzama to Athi. Radmilla turned to Nardilic and remarked, "The slave cut alters a girl's appearance completely, doesn't it, Odo?" Nardilic agreed.

The Kzama looked at Athi carefully. The condemned woman was beautiful, Radmilla thought. The Kzama was a good judge of beauty. *If the girl had not been so stupid, she might have learned to exercise real influence in the Kzamate,* Radmilla thought. *And if she had had any sense she would have used some of the poison to kill herself, after her attempt to kill the Kzam failed. At least it would have been a quick death.*

After Athanasia's failed attempt to kill her husband, Radmilla had retrieved the tiny bottle and helped herself to half of the contents. She had transferred it to a different container and left the original bottle for the police to find. Radmilla had plans of her own for the little bottle of perfectari she had secreted away. There was not much of it; only a few drops, but that would be enough for her purposes.

"Are you thirsty?" asked Radmilla.

Athi nodded urgently, desperately. She whimpered emphatically, unable to speak through the gag. She was very thirsty.

But Radmilla merely nodded. "Yes. New slaves often mention that. After they're branded, they feel thirsty." Her words were carefully chosen to humiliate Athi further. Radmilla continued, "And I see Mr Satkisant has had to discipline the girl. Was she... difficult, then, Mr Satkisant?"

“A little, my lady,” he replied.

“Yes. She always was rather self-willed, I’m afraid,” Radmilla mused. “Well, it’s past sunrise. We’re due to begin, aren’t we, Odo?”

Nardilic nodded. “Before you begin, Mr Satkisant, a few words, if you please.” He placed four small but thick discs on the tiny table. “The former Princess Athanasia wishes to express her most sincere gratitude for your patience and forbearance last night and this morning, and she apologises profusely for any wilfulness, discourtesy, or hesitation to obey you or your men. She does not seek to excuse any such shortcomings, but assures you that they were entirely unintentional on her part. She is new to servitude, and naturally fearful. She prays that you will understand her situation and accept her sincerest apologies. She further prays you will accept these small gifts, and she beseeches you most earnestly to afford her as swift a despatch as is possible.”

“My men and I thank the lady for her gift, my lord,” replied Satkisant, addressing Nardilic without glancing at Athi or at the small pile of coins.

Mikal did glance at the coins, though. This was better than he had dared hope. Unless he was mistaken, the large coin must be a two thousand karat piece. That would be for Uncle Jakob. The three smaller coins must be one thousand karat pieces. One of them would be for Mikal. The condemned prisoner often tipped the executioners. If she was a woman and from a poor family, the gratuity was typically twenty karats for each of the executioners. This was sufficient for them to pay their atonement offering at a shrine or temple. It was, in a sense, the prisoner’s fault that the executioners would have to spend that money. They should not be out of pocket merely for doing their duty.

Richer prisoners, or those who had pretensions of high status, gave larger gratuities. They did not wish to lose face. But never had Mikal heard of such a generous gift as this. The new coins now in circulation no longer contained any real cinerium, and there had been substantial inflation, but the gift was still extremely generous. If Mikal’s uncle allowed him to keep the thousand karats, it would be the equivalent of several months' salary.

Nardilic spoke again. "His Dread Lordship sees no purpose in a lengthy impalement, and therefore instructs you to render the tug of grace immediately."

Athi was listening carefully. She knew that sometimes an impalement lasted for hours, the stake pressing slowly upwards through the prisoner's body as he or she twisted and writhed. Eventually gravity would do its work. A light woman might survive longer than a heavy man. If the prisoner was still alive at sunset, the executioners were supposed to pull both legs to force the body down and end the suffering. This was known as the 'tug of grace'. In Athi's case, the tug of grace was to be applied straight away.

Radmilla spoke. "Did you hear that, girl? Your lord and master is merciful. We welcomed you into our home as a stranger and you tried to kill our Dread Lord and cause immeasurable suffering to his people. You would have ruined the lives of his children, his wives and his concubines, and millions of his people. Billions! But still he is moved to compassion."

The Kzama nodded to Nardilic, Nardilic nodded to Satkisant, and Satkisant nodded to his men. Athi saw the nods, and understood.

Satkisant addressed Athi. "Thank the lady and gentleman," he said. Athi crawled forward and touched her forehead to the floor in front of the Lord Provost and then the Kzama, and then crawled awkwardly backwards.

Satkisant too, was not without mercy. He preferred the tug of grace to be given immediately. It was kinder, and it gave the executioners the opportunity to demonstrate their skill and speed.

As soon as Athi had returned to her position, Satkisant recited a brief prayer commending Athanasia's soul to the Almighty. The witnesses, executioners and Kyra all uttered their 'amens.' At that instant Mikal slipped an elasticated hood over Athanasia's head.

The moment had arrived, she knew. She emitted a startled whimper or wail, and wriggled as she felt herself lifted by her arms and thighs and carried forward. She heard the men step onto the wooden blocks to lift her higher. Satkisant positioned her carefully over the skewer and Athi squealed as they lowered her slightly so that the greased tip of the skewer entered her like a phallus. They stepped off the blocks and kicked them away. In that instant, Athi's full weight pressed down upon the skewer and her whimpers were replaced by a prolonged, urgent shriek.

Athi was pressing the soles of her feet against the stake as though she could get sufficient grip on it to lift herself up. Satkisant saw this, but was not concerned. It was an instinctive gesture which all prisoners condemned to the stake made, no matter how intelligent or courageous they had otherwise seemed. Satkisant did not even bother advising against it. There was no point.

Instantly, two of the men had each placed a foot in Athi's stirrups and pressed down with all their weight, jumping in unison to force her down the skewer quickly. This was the tug of grace. Satkisant himself, holding Athi's waist from behind her, lent his own weight to the effort. Athi's shriek, though intense, was brief.

Radmilla, though accustomed to cruelty, had to suppress her shock to maintain her composure. Kyra leant forward, desperately trying not to be sick. She could not bring herself to look at Athi, but the condemned woman's shriek seemed to bore into her mind. Nardilic had witnessed executions before and was more prepared for it. Blood trickled down the grooves of the skewer and into the drain.

It was over. From the moment the hood was placed over her head, to the moment Athi had fallen silent, no more than five seconds had elapsed. The witnesses commended the executioners for their efficiency, signed the death certificate and left. Kyra followed close behind Radmilla.

"Well done, lads," said Satkisant, when the witnesses had gone. "That was good work. She's done." He stood behind Athi, checking her neck for a pulse. There was none, but the High Executioner always made doubly certain. He hefted a club, short but heavy, and forcefully clubbed the back of Athi's limply hanging head. "Get the hose, Mik," he said. "Let's get her bagged up." The High Executioner sounded pleased.

Mikal was pleased, too. He was elated. He went to fetch the hose and a carbonite bag. The more he considered the question, the more convinced he became that Uncle Jacob would let him keep the thousand karats.

There would be free drinks all round at the Kzam of Malitbog that night.

14: IN WHICH WE SERVE

The budget should be balanced, the Treasury should be refilled, public debt should be reduced, the arrogance of officialdom should be tempered and controlled and the assistance to foreign lands should be curtailed lest Rome become bankrupt. People must again learn to work, instead of living on public assistance.

Marcus Tullius Cicero

It would have been better by far for the Empire if the Atkoi War had been fought years earlier. Every passing week had strengthened the enemy in some way.

There had been a major battle at Tolon. Both sides were evenly matched. The Atkoi fired first, without warning or preliminary manoeuvres.

A modern battle was fought without any need for human input in aiming or firing weapons. Electronic systems identified friendly and enemy vessels faster than any human soldier could do. Coded signals, transmitted automatically and constantly by every Imperial ship, identified it to all friendly vessels. Every ship, friend and foe, left behind it a trail of radiation from which the size and type of its engines, its speed and even its mass could be estimated. Each Imperial warship could identify enemy targets and calculate their speed, direction and distance, even making allowance for its own movement and rotation, before firing its weapons.

These weapon systems could even identify which targets posed the greatest threat, firing first at targets closer to friendly vessels and targets which had not already sustained serious hits themselves. This entire process required a mere fraction of a second. Weapons systems on any given vessel could operate independently and yet share information with weapons systems on other friendly vessels, transmitting coded signals across space, although this would take valuable time. A Class 'A' Imperial warship had typically two hundred cannon, with primary and backup targeting systems, capable of firing sustained bursts of high energy neutrino plasma. The Atkoi fleet naturally had equivalent systems.

Given these facts, one might imagine that naval encounters were decided within seconds. They were not, partly because vessels on both sides were programmed to suddenly and randomly alter their speed and course, to confound enemy weapons guidance systems; and partly because of the distances involved.

Such a battle had to be fought within a very small area. The Battle of Tolon was fought within a roughly spherical volume of space, scarcely ten million miles in diameter. Beyond this distance it was impossible to score a direct hit. Travelling at the speed of light the radiation would take about a minute to reach its target. Even if it were possible to score a direct hit, neutrino radiation was ineffective beyond this range. Over such a distance it could not be focused into a sufficiently narrow beam to provide an effective weapon.

Centuries of military research had focused on making cannon more powerful, their plasma beams tighter, the targeting systems faster and more accurate, and evasive manoeuvres more effective. Attempts had even been made to create defensive shields, energy fields capable of deflecting plasma weapons, but so far no such innovations had proved effective.

The weapons systems were at least durable, though. Successive blasts of neutrino fire might tear open a ship so badly that every deck was compromised and all crew who were not already inside sealed compartments were killed, but the weaponry could continue to locate and fire upon the enemy. The weapons control system was located so deep in the ship, it had so many sensors and so many cannon, that it continued to live after the rest of the ship was dead. Human intervention in the weaponry during an exchange of fire was neither necessary nor desirable. A ship's commander could override the system, but seldom chose to do so.

Although the Atkoi were expected to attack Tolon, they dropped out of hyperspace and appeared together rather closer to Tolon's sun than an Imperial fleet would have chosen to do. In so doing they took a risk, but it was a risk which the Kzam considered justified, and in the event it paid off. Their unexpected appearance gave them a momentary advantage. Both sides were approximately evenly matched in terms of their number of ships and their weaponry. Both succeeded in destroying several enemy vessels within the first few minutes. Admiral Hric, who commanded the combined Imperial Fleet, expected the exchange of fire to continue until one side began to lose more of its ships than the other. If either side gained such an advantage, the imbalance would usually increase to the point where the losing side would withdraw, rather than face total annihilation. Hric knew he had the advantages both of Imperial training and equipment. He had every reason to hope for a decisive victory.

But at Tolon, events had suddenly taken a turn for the worse. When the positions of all Imperial vessels had been identified by the Atkoi, a second Atkoi fleet had suddenly and unexpectedly appeared. Naval intelligence was not usually so poor, but the monitoring stations at Cidenas and Terminor had been destroyed or captured and the Imperial Fleet had been obliged to rely upon outdated estimates of Atkoi strength. This second fleet had not fought in any previous engagements; it had arrived directly from the Atkoi worlds. The ships were untried in battle although thoroughly tested in regions of space where Imperial intelligence could not observe them. They incorporated the most modern advances, including techniques either stolen from the Empire or freely given during the time when Rurik had been an ally of Aethelstan.

Hric had planned for his fleet to approach the enemy in the form of a bowl which would wrap itself around the Atkoi, surrounding them. Suddenly he realised that a second enemy fleet was approaching from the side, obliging every Imperial vessel to divide its firepower, aiming some weapons forward and others to the side. The Imperial Fleet passed through the Atkoi formation and both fleets turned to regroup, but the tide of battle was beginning to turn. The Atkoi appeared to be winning.

Hric did not consider withdrawing at this stage. Too much depended on saving Tolon. Every Atkoi vessel they could destroy now was one less that could continue on to Nenuphar, and Hric knew that it was the Imperial capital that was the eventual target of the Atkoi. With such force available to him, with his enemy so weakened, why should Rurik stop at Tolon? If he did stop, it would only be to build up his strength again. Hric also dreaded that the people of Tolon would pay the price of defeat if the Atkoi were successful that day.

The second Atkoi fleet had turned and were firing on the Imperial Navy from the rear. Hric's original thirty cruisers were now reduced to twenty-four. The Atkoi had lost five ships, but with twice the original number available, they could afford to. Rupert Hric did not lack courage, but neither was he wasteful of men or materiel. Men could not be trained, nor ships built, during the time that this war would last.

A screen showed two more Imperial ships as lost, and there was no reason to suppose the balance would alter in the Empire's favour. This was the threshold. Hric had always known that if he was outnumbered to this extent, he would withdraw.

He gave the signal. Close though they were to Tolon's sun and its gravitational field, the Imperial fleet accelerated anyway and disappeared into metaspace.

On the bridge of his flag ship, the Atkoi fleet Commander, Prince Khostrounil Otheris at Otheris, felt almost dizzy with pride, joy and relief. The Imperials had gone. Khostrounil fought to control his voice before speaking: "Notify His Dread Lordship that the enemy navy has fled Tolon. Vessels of the Kzamate are now moving into orbit over the planet. The planetary governor will be invited to surrender. The peacekeeping force is prepared for landing."

In the Imperial palace on Nenuphar, Arbuthnot-Samar and Aanrud remained silent, waiting for the Emperor to speak. Aethelstan gave no sign that he had heard what Aanrud had said.

The Princess Athanasia was dead. The Atkoi had captured Terminor. The shipyards on Terminor had already been destroyed to keep them from falling into enemy hands. That was the only crumb of comfort. And now the Kzamate had captured Tolon and decimated the remaining fleet. The two Atkoi fleets were now advancing separately but were both heading in the direction of Nenuphar. Five whole divisions of borbod mercenaries had mutinied, turning on their officers and joining the enemy. Every day, reports were received of more planets surrendering to the advancing Atkoi. Bellerophon, Picayune, Hermanus, Rhodoria, Solva, Isodia, Antipolo, and Greenwood had all fallen, to name only some of the more developed, populous worlds. On the borders of the Empire, the whole Sardanapalus Province had declared independence. Its Viceroy had declared himself Emperor and announced that he would remain neutral in the war. The Kzam had recognised Sardanapalus as an independent polity. It would be spared the ravages of war. It was possible that other outlying provinces might also break away. Doubtless the Kzam was even now encouraging them.

Aanrud at least had a plan. Admiral Bazan had been summoned, with his fleet, back from the Nizami Marches. It would take him months to arrive, Aanrud knew. Bazan had spoken of his plans in case the military situation ever deteriorated this far. They would send a powerful fleet behind the Atkoi lines and attack Atkoi planets. They would be as brutal as the Atkoi themselves. The Kzam would be forced to bring back his fleets to fight them. It would give the Empire time to rebuild and prepare a counterattack.

Individual warships would also work separately, attacking Atkoi planets and swiftly moving on, forcing the Kzam to divert much of his navy to policing his home worlds. To have Bazan in command of the fleet would inspire confidence, not just in the navy but among the population as a whole. Bazan had that effect on people. There had been too much talk of defeat, as though it were inevitable. Arbuthnot-Samar agreed with Aanrud. They waited for Aethelstan to reply.

"They've killed Athi," said the Emperor.

"Yes, Your Majesty," said the Lord Chancellor.

"Where is Sigismund? He should be here, with his mother and me. Where is he, Thomas?"

"Your Majesty, an aircar has been sent for the Crown Prince. About Admiral Bazan…."

"No, no, it won't do. It would take Bazan ages to get here. I know what I will do. I will move to Old Earth."

"Earth? Your Majesty, you are needed here. Your presence here will show people that--"

"The Atkoi will be here before Bazan could possibly be. Earth was the capital of the Empire once. It's the home of civilisation, the cradle of humanity. The Empire was founded to protect Old Earth. Old Earth, and its neighbouring planets, those are what matter. We think of Nenuphar as the centre of the Empire, but it's not. Not really. Earth is the true centre, and Nenuphar is on the edge. Let the Atkoi have the rest. If people don't like it, they can come to the Central Planets. They would be welcome. They would make us stronger. With a smaller area to protect, we could keep the Atkoi out. We could keep everyone out. We're spread too thin, don't you see? We're over extended. A smaller Empire would be easier to defend. That's what the Centralists have always been saying. And really they're right, you know."

Aanrud and Arbuthnot-Samar exchanged a glance. "Your Majesty," began Aanrud, "we could not defend such a small region. If the Atkoi take Nenuphar, they could be on Earth in ten days. It's not--"

The Emperor shook his head. "I've made up my mind. Transport is already being arranged. My family will be with me. I've lost one child, Edward. I can't lose any more. Where is Sigi? You'll like Earth, Edward.

It's the cradle of humanity. Besides, this Atkoi attack will fizzle out. They always do. Then we can come back here."

15: STRANGER IN A STRANGE LAND

Memnon Quat: Earth type planet, fourth planet of Memnon in the Petwen Province, 335 light years from Nenuphar. Discovered 2399 and settled from Petwen. Population 350 million humans, (estimated: the exact figure has been declared a state secret). Political status: since 2835, it has been the personal fiefdom of the Emperors. Fewer than one hundred thousand of the inhabitants are free citizens, the vast majority being held in feudal serfdom.

New Galactic Encyclopaedia (Infopress: Nenuphar)

Jemima Firth was seventeen when her mother sold her to the Emperor's factor.

It was not that Elaine Firth did not love her daughter; far from it. But she knew that Jemima would be far better looked after by her new master than if she had remained on Memnon and married a local man. Life was hard on Memnon Quat for any poor family, let alone a widowed mother of two children. Arthur Firth had died a year earlier, having laboured all his life on their tiny farm.

Two centuries earlier, all the land for miles around had belonged to the Firth family, and the nearby village had been a thriving little town. It had been in the time of Arthur's great grandfather that the Firth lands, along with all other fixed property on the planet, were forfeited to the crown. Now the Firths were merely tenants on a tiny portion of their original estate.

Memnon Quat, which meant Memnon Four and was usually called simply Memnon, had now been under direct feudal rule for almost one hundred and sixty years. Life was not easy for its people. They were in fact serfs, little better than chattels of the Emperor, unable to own property outright or even to move from one district to another without the permission of their local baron. They were obliged to pay a poll tax. Most could work only in agriculture, or certain specified occupations.

Their mistake, or rather the mistake of their ancestors, had been to lend support to the losing side in the last of the civil wars which had divided the Empire. Felix Prendergast, Duke of Memnon and Iturbide, had quite possibly had a better claim to the throne than his second cousin and rival, Konrad; but Konrad had greater support in the Navy, and that had proved decisive. It was Konrad who had ascended the throne. Felix himself and many of his supporters had fled to independent worlds and had mostly escaped the new Emperor's justice, despite determined attempts to extradite them. Those less fortunate had faced summary trials and execution. In several cases, whole planetary populations were punished with enormous fines. Memnon's punishment was the severest of all, because its popular support of Felix had been both widespread and enthusiastic.

All land and fixed property was seized. Memnon's people were stripped of their citizenship and liberty. Legally, they were reduced to serfdom. Much of the land was sold to Konrad's loyal supporters. In a stroke, Konrad had punished his enemies, rewarded his friends, created a new source of income and paid off many of his debts. Now, generations later, Memnon was still the personal fiefdom of the Emperor. Imperials suspected of disloyalty were still on occasion banished there, sometimes in perpetuity, by Imperial decree.

Arthur's rented farm had been scarcely large enough to generate a living. He lived all his life in the fear that his son would one day be a mere labourer on the land that their forefathers had owned outright. He died leaving Elaine deeply in debt and his son Roland too young to manage alone. The ideal solution would have been for Jemima to marry a wealthy man, who could help their family. She was certainly very attractive, but such men were scarce.

Then a lifeline appeared. The Emperor's factor, or business agent, was due to visit the chief town of the district where the Firth family lived, with the object of selecting several girls or young women to be sent to the Emperor's seraglio. The factor made a tour of Memnon every three years for this purpose, and a generous bounty was offered for every girl selected: five thousand credits, more than enough to solve all the family's financial difficulties.

With a heavy heart, Elaine took Jemima to Government House to present her to the factor. They waited with a number of other girls in a large lobby or corridor, on the appointed day. Many hopeful applicants were turned away, being deemed unsuitable, and left tearfully, their hopes of escaping poverty dashed. The girls who were actually admitted to the waiting room numbered perhaps fifty, and Jemima noticed that they were all beautiful and beautifully dressed and beautifully made up. Many had clearly visited professional beauticians before attending the interview.

That was good, Jemima thought. With so much competition, of such quality, it was surely unlikely that she would be chosen. Perhaps she would be spared after all. She was a good daughter and she would try her very best to be successful, but if despite her genuine efforts she was not chosen, it would not be her fault.

Eventually, Jemima and her mother were called into a small office. Jemima realised that somehow she had jumped the queue. There were girls who had been waiting longer than her, who had not yet been seen.

The factor introduced himself. His name was Mr Bubug. Jemima curtsied, politely and nervously. A lady called Flavia was also present. She was perhaps fifty years of age, and Jemima guessed she must have been very beautiful as a young woman. She had come from the Emperor's seraglio on Nenuphar, the Imperial capital world, to advise the factor in his choices.

Flavia and Mr Bubug asked Jemima a number of questions, glancing at her application form. Flavia seemed kind and friendly. Mr Bubug seemed businesslike, but friendly too. After a few minutes, Jemima began to relax a little. Flavia smiled at her encouragingly as she answered the questions. Eventually Jemima noticed Mr Bubug and Flavia exchange a glance. She tensed.

It was Flavia who spoke. She invited Jemima and Elaine into another room, where Jemima was to be examined by a doctor.

The doctor, (Jemima was thankful that it was a female doctor) explained that she was going to examine Jemima, to ascertain that she was a virgin and in good health. Jemima was shocked that her purity might even be questioned. She looked to her mother, who nodded in encouragement.

Flavia remained in the room and watched carefully while Jemima undressed. The girl was lovely, Flavia thought, with long blonde hair, slim, with firm breasts and attractive legs. She was definitely the best she had seen in this district, Flavia decided. Jemima lay on the couch and submitted herself to the humiliating examination. Flavia saw her wince. The doctor was satisfied. Jemima dressed again, grateful that the ordeal was over. Jemima and Elaine were shown into another room where they waited. There were no other applicants present. Jemima knew that her future was being decided.

After only a few minutes, they were called back into the office. Jemima could feel her heart beating. She could see a document on the factor's desk. She knew it was a legal document, from the peculiar script and the red ribbon attached to it. Jemima was intelligent, with excellent results in her high school diploma, and her father had once asked her to help him make sense of their tenancy agreement. That had been written in a similar script. Jemima could see what was written on the first page of this document. She could not help herself from reading it.

'Deed of Indenture,' it said, 'entered into between and by Mistress Elaine Arcadia Firth,' (her mother's name had been hand written into the blank space) 'hereinafter referred to as the Transferor, being the parent and or legal guardian of Jemima Sonya Firth,' (Jemima's name was also hand written) 'hereinafter referred to as the Indentured Party, and James Anilat Bubug, factor, for and on behalf of His Imperial Majesty

Aethelstan IV, hereinafter known as the Transferee. In consideration for the sum of five thousand credits….' Jemima understood the document so far. She knew what indenture meant. It meant slavery, or concubinage.

She read on: 'notwithstanding that the transferor is not liable under any covenant implied by this transfer concerning the condition of the indentured party in the title below referred to…' This part was beyond Jemima's understanding. It could have been Ancient Inglic for all she could make of it.

Then the factor spoke. Jemima had been accepted. Elaine received the news with mixed feelings. Roland's future was secure now. With five thousand credits they could pay off all their debts, repair the farm buildings and the roof of the house, pay the rent and all their taxes for years to come, buy new equipment and hire labourers and still have a sizeable sum left for emergencies. Perhaps they could even rent extra land. And yet Elaine could not help feel a sense of shame, and fear for Jemima. *Was this what Arthur would have wanted?* she wondered.

Elaine thanked the factor profusely for his kindness in choosing Jemima. Her family were undeserving of such an honour, and Jemima would serve her master the Emperor faithfully, loyally, obediently and gratefully all the days of her life, she added, relieved that she had remembered all of her prepared speech.

The factor nodded and congratulated Elaine. "And congratulations to you too, young lady," he added to Jemima. He explained that Jemima would be very well cared for. The Emperor's concubines were never branded, although she would have a tiny slavemark tattooed behind her ear, and a microchip implanted in the back of her neck. These were for her own protection, so that she could never be stolen. Her future was secure. She would have a good life. If she had children, they too would have wonderful, privileged lives.

Elaine knew it was her last opportunity to ask her daughter whether she was really willing to go to the seraglio. Jemima hesitated only a moment. “Yes, I will go,” she said clearly. She would not destroy her family’s only hope of escaping ruin.

Elaine was relieved. She had not forced her daughter to accept. Jemima had made the decision herself. “I’m glad, Mimi,” she said. “You will have a much better future, for you and your children, on Nenuphar than you ever could have had here with us,” she added.

Jemima nodded, unable to speak. Her mother had not called her Mimi for years. It had been her mother’s childhood nickname for her, and Jemima was suddenly overwhelmed by emotion and close to tears. Flavia and Bubug both smiled, as if to reassure both mother and daughter.

Elaine signed the deed. The sum of five thousand credits would be paid promptly, the factor explained, less a tax of twenty per cent and less his finder’s fee of fifteen per cent. Elaine had not been expecting the deductions, but she dared not complain. The factor could still change his mind.

Bubug glanced again at Jemima. She was a gorgeous creature, he thought. He saw a great many attractive women in his job, and this girl was one of the finest. For a moment he imagined what it might be like to own such a creature himself instead of merely buying her for the Emperor. Perhaps his eyes lingered on Jemima a moment too long because she blushed prettily, as if sensing his thoughts.

The owner of a pleasure house on Nenuphar had once asked Bubug, only half joking, if he could recruit girls on Memnon, pretending they were for the Imperial seraglio, but actually sell them to the pleasure house. It was an interesting thought, but the factor had merely smiled. Mr Bubug was in a position of trust. For defrauding the Emperor he could be sent to Niflheim, or sentenced to incarceration for life in a nerve disruptor on Undane Six. Bubug would make do with his salary, his percentages, and the various other emoluments which grateful Memnonites sometimes gave him for favours he was in a position to grant.

Bubug and Elaine exchanged documents. Only then did Jemima speak again: "But what if the Emperor doesn't like me?" she asked, wide eyed. The enormity of what had just happened was beginning to sink in.

It was Flavia who replied. She hugged Jemima and said, "Jemima my dear, of course he will like you. He will love you. I know what our master likes. He will care for you, and the seraglio will be your new family and you will be happy there. I promise. And the Emperor will look after your mother and brother too. He is the father of his people everywhere. Now come with me." Somehow Flavia's kind words had released Jemima's emotions and she could no longer keep herself from weeping.

Elaine and Jemima were left in an adjoining room to make their farewells. Flavia returned after only a few minutes. She was not unkind, but she knew that lengthy farewells were painful for all concerned. She remembered the day over thirty years before when she herself had been purchased for the seraglio. Aethelstan had been young then, in his thirties, and Flavia had been eighteen. She had borne the Emperor a daughter who was now grown up and married to the governor of Trull Minor, a planet in the Zimisces Province.

"Come with me now, Jemima dear," said Flavia, taking Jemima's arm, "and meet the other girls who are coming to Nenuphar with you. They are your new sisters, now. They're all nice girls, like you. You'll like them."

16: CAT AND MOUSE

The end came quickly, when it came. It came faster than anyone expected it to come, so that even those who thought the end was near were surprised by is suddenness.

Itchenor, E: The Causes and Consequences of the Atkoi War, Vol. 7 (Cornubium University Press: Nenuphar, 3020)

Chief Eunuch was dead!

Jemima ran lightly through the deserted halls of the palace, her heart beating in fear and horror at what she had seen.

It was a year since she had arrived in the seraglio, and she had never felt so afraid. Chief Eunuch had told the soldiers they could not enter the seraglio. It was not allowed. The soldiers did not argue. One of them simply raised his rifle and incinerated Chief Eunuch with a single blast. The other eunuchs and Jemima and her friends had fled.

In the past year, Jemima had been trained in everything a concubine needed to know. Flavia herself had instructed the new girls in what to expect and how to behave when they were summoned to the Emperor's bedchamber. Jemima had still been waiting for that summons, nervous but excited, when Aethelstan had chosen to leave Nenuphar.

Jemima could recite the Emperor's forebears back to the mythical ones on Old Earth. She could recite every winner of the Megabowl Trophy since the competition began. Aircar racing had been a particular interest of Aethelstan as a young man, and the Chief Eunuch had insisted that the girls should be able to converse knowledgeably about it. She could translate small passages of the classics from Ancient Inglic, and she understood the basics of mathematics, astronomy, physics and logic. She knew the Bible in some detail. She could dance and play the flute. She could play chess and thunderball, and was physically fit.

But now the Emperor was gone. If only her master had remained on Nenuphar, the whole Empire would have stood together and fought. Everyone said that. Now, everyone could see they were losing the war. There were even rumours that some ships' crews had mutinied and deserted because they did not want to fight. For weeks the girls and women of the seraglio had heard the rumours of the advancing enemy, but they had known that of all places in the Empire, the Radiant Palace was safest.

Then the Emperor had fled.

No one had dared use the word 'fled.' The girls had been told the Emperor was on a diplomatic mission. But with Aethelstan gone, everyone knew that Nenuphar could not be defended. The girls had listened fearfully to news broadcasts and exchanged horrified gossip about what the Atkoi did to young women when they captured a planet. But Chief Eunuch said they would all be safe. They were the personal property of the Emperor himself, and no one could touch them. No one.

Chief Eunuch's certainty gave them confidence. No one had ever dared defy Chief Eunuch. Jemima had feared him, naturally. All the girls did; but it was a fear borne of respect. He performed a function for the Emperor similar to that which the Klang Arak performed for the Great Kzam. Any seraglio, whether it belonged to an Emperor or a Kzam, a governor, senator, satrap or any wealthy man, required someone to govern it and to plan and supervise the training and daily routine of its inhabitants.

That did not mean that the rules and systems of Rurik's seraglio were identical to those of Aethelstan's. There were significant differences. Aethelstan, though he had almost two hundred concubines, had only one legal wife, although several of his concubines were daughters of families of senatorial rank. These ladies were considered to be of vastly higher status then ordinary slave concubines. Their families considered it an honour to be so closely linked to the crown. Aethelstan's daughter Demetra, for instance, was the daughter of one such exalted lady. Demetra, like all the Emperor's children, had now been evacuated to Old Earth.

In Cornubium the streets were empty, now. After the Emperor and his family had fled the city, the senators and the rich had also left, quickly. Then anyone else who could afford to go, followed them. When ships stopped calling at Nenuphar, the flow of refugees heading out of the city did not stop. If anything, it increased. They headed towards smaller cities, towns, and villages in the hills.

Those who remained behind placed their hope in Admiral Bazan. Day after day passed. Surely, of all places, he would rush to save Nenuphar. But still there was no news of the Imperial Fleet.

Then it was too late. The Atkoi had arrived.

They arrived suddenly. It was around midnight. The girls had awoken in their dormitories and watched from the windows of the upper floors of the palace. They saw the skies light up with plasma fire so bright it hurt their eyes. They saw the landmarks of the Imperial City destroyed. The Temple, with its huge dome, was hit. Jemima wondered whether the Patriarch of Nenuphar was safe. She said a silent prayer for him. Perhaps he was at home in his palace. The Imperial Library and the Baldwin Memorial were both destroyed. The Senate was hit badly. Some bright flashes from behind Porlock Hill and Mount Pleasant must mean that the naval base and marine headquarters were under attack.

The girls were told to go down to the cellars. That was the safest place in the whole palace. An earlier emperor had built them in the time of a civil war, centuries ago.

Chief Eunuch arrived to lead them to safety. It was a pity they were not dressed more sensibly, he thought. It would have been better if they had looked less… attractive. With the Emperor in the provinces, they did not need to look their best all the time, but almost by definition their clothes were beautiful. These were girls whose sole purpose and function was to be decorative. They existed only to serve and entertain their lord and master.

In any case, there was no time for them to change now. The twelve girls from Jemima's dormitory hurried after the Chief Eunuch in a group, but a serious of blasts prevented them reaching their place of safety. Instead, they scattered in all directions. Jemima found herself in the courtyard near the Maidens' Gate, the entrance where newly acquired girls were led into the seraglio. It was an impressive edifice built by Osiander II, who had extensively redesigned the Radiant Palace.

Jemima saw the soldiers' uniforms, with a red stripe across their chest and their faces, and her heart turned cold with fear. She had heard about this kind of soldier. They were called berserkers. They were the worst kind of Atkoi, terrible, terrible men who were mad with a frenzy of killing. They took drugs to make them strong, and fearless, and violent. Jemima had heard what berserkers did when they invaded a city or a planet. She had heard what happened to women who were captured.

The Chief Eunuch stood calmly and solidly in the gateway. He simply told the men that they were not allowed in without his master's permission. Perhaps he hoped to delay the invaders, or shock them into reconsidering their actions, but it did not work. Without hesitation, one of the berserkers simply lifted his rifle and blasted the eunuch. Shouting wildly, the berserkers rushed forward. They had seen the girls. There was another eunuch in their way. The berserkers did not even bother shooting him. One of them simply smashed the butt of his rifle in the eunuch's face so hard that Jemima heard his bones break. The eunuch flopped lifeless to the ground.

Jemima and her companions hardly had time to flee. One of the Atkoi seized Jemima's friend Lydia, clenching his fist firmly in the girl's hair.

Lydia's hair was short and dark and she was beautiful in face and figure, slim and well proportioned. Like Jemima she was a virgin, from Memnon. She was wearing her physical training outfit, a white tee shirt and dark blue jogging shorts, both close fitting. She had thought this would be quick to put on and practical if they had to run.

Lydia squealed, twisting wildly. One man, grinning, held her while several others ripped the clothes from her. Within seconds Lydia was naked. Jemima could hardly see her friend as the men, howling with delight, fell upon Lydia and pushed her to the floor. She was still squealing frantically. The first man began to loosen his belt. Powerless to help, Jemima fled.

The authorities in Cornubium had already surrendered. The berserkers knew that the palace would not be defended. Their commander had proclaimed a havoc, to last for three days, limited to the Old City, the most ancient quarter of Cornubium which contained the Radiant Palace and its grounds, various government departments, and the broad tree lined avenues with the splendid homes of some of the Empire's wealthiest and most powerful citizens. Those houses were empty, now. Even the servants had fled. But the houses would be plundered. The palace itself contained treasures accumulated over the centuries.

In the confusion, Jemima and several other girls fled screaming across a courtyard and down a corridor. Then Jemima had an idea. Above the eunuchs refectory there was a loft. The Atkoi would not look there. Not yet, anyway.

Two other girls had also fled to the refectory. Their names were Dawn and Strawberry. They reached the tiny ceiling hatch by placing a chair on top of a table. They climbed up and wriggled into the roof space. Jemima, the last of the three girls to scramble up, kicked away the chair so that it fell to the floor as if knocked over by the looters. They replaced the hatch and crawled quietly along the dark, dusty loft. Then they stopped and listened, trying to remain silent and still. All three girls were blonde, with lovely figures. Strawberry's hair was elaborately braided; she was a favourite of the Emperor's.

They waited for perhaps two hours, crouching silently and listening to the sounds of mayhem, the shouting of soldiers, blasts of neutrino fire, and the unceasing screams of women and girls who had already been caught. Jemima tried not to think about what must be happening to some of her friends. *We are the fortunate ones,* she thought. *But how long before we too are caught?*

Eventually they heard voices, much nearer. They realised to their dismay that there were Atkoi in the room below. They heard something heavy being dragged across the floor. The girls hardly dared breathe. Eventually it went quiet again.

"I think they've gone. Do you think they've gone?" whispered Strawberry.

"Shsh," hissed Dawn, urgently. They remained in silence for several more minutes.

Then Strawberry coughed, several times. "It's smoke," she whispered. "It's fire!"

Strawberry was correct. The refectory and many of the other buildings were burning. The smoke was becoming thicker. "If we stay here, we'll suffocate," whispered Dawn. She left the alternative unspoken: if they left the loft, they would be caught instantly. Faced with this dilemma, they did not move. Jemima tried to breathe shallowly as the smoke grew thicker. She found herself coughing uncontrollably and her eyes streaming. To go down was impossible, but at one end of the dark loft was a skylight. They crawled quietly towards the faint flickering glow of its light.

The skylight was hinged, but had not been used for a century or more and the latch had rusted shut. The three girls pressed the duraglass as hard as they could, all together, but still it would not budge. They pushed until a fit of coughing forced them to stop.

They tried again, with strength born of desperation. This would be their last opportunity. The skylight opened with a loud thud. They looked at each other in indecision. Had they been heard? Would they be visible, once outside? But they no longer had any choice. One at a time they scrambled onto the roof, gasping in the fresh air, and slid down to a valley between two sloping roofs. The roof was made of Udankean slate. More precisely it was imitation Udankean slate, since the genuine material was quarried only on the remote airless world of Udanke and was prohibitively expensive.

The three girls could see the flickering light of plasma blasts and flames from behind the buildings, and the pale light of Nenuphar's single small moon glowing pinkish-white above them. They would be safe here for a little while, but the fire was spreading and soon it would be dawn and they would be easily visible. They had to press on.

They crawled to the end of the roof and then dropped to the ground. It was a single storey building and Jemima landed lightly, hurting her bare feet but managing not to cry out. They were in a courtyard. It was cloistered, with a fountain and a statue in the middle. The fountain was no longer working. They huddled together in the shadows. They could still hear shouting and screaming and the blasts and explosions of plasma fire, but they could not see any Atkoi or indeed anyone at all in the flickering light. There was a risk they would be seen if they crossed the courtyard, but that compared to a certainty of capture of they remained where they were.

Together the three girls dashed across the courtyard, hoping against hope they would not be seen.

At that moment the sky was illuminated by a blast brighter than all the others. Had it not been for that sudden flash of light, the three girls would probably have made it to safety.

17: AND THEN THERE WAS ONE

The Prendergasts had done immense good for humanity. They had made the Empire, and made it safe. But the dynasty had exhausted itself. If ever proof of that was required, then Aethelstan IV provided it amply.

Itchenor, E: The Causes and Consequences of the Atkoi: War Vol. 2 (Cornubium University Press: Nenuphar, 3020)

The flash illuminated the courtyard, the broken fountain, the pillars, the arches, and three pretty, scantily clad girls dashing across the flagstones with their blonde hair flowing behind them as they ran. A harsh, guttural voice was added to the noise of the dreadful night. “Stop! Else I fire!” it shouted. The three girls ran all the faster. One of them squealed in terror as she headed for an archway opposite.

There was another flash of light, but Jemima sensed that neither of her companions had been hit. They entered a corridor, and Jemima ran into the first open door she saw. It led into a small anteroom, which led in turn into a wide, rather formal dining hall. Jemima had never been in this part of the palace before. It was forbidden to her, being part of the State Chambers rather than the seraglio proper. In the circumstances, that rule no longer applied. Tonight, no rules applied.

There were thick, deep red carpets beneath her feet and an enormous, long table with gold candlesticks and chairs with deep red padded cushions. On the walls there were paintings of old emperors and their wives or favourite concubines. This was one of the palace banqueting halls, where earlier emperors, more sociable than Aethelstan, used to entertain their favoured guests.

Suddenly Jemima realised she was alone. Dawn and Strawberry must have taken a different route. Then she heard a noise in the corridor, and a voice, a man's voice.

There was nowhere to hide. At the far end of the room was a pair of huge, thick, carved wooden doors, closed. Jemima hurried lightly to them. Like all the girls in the seraglio, she had been kept physically fit. She was grateful for that, now. Mercifully the doors opened immediately. Jemima hurried through and tried to close them quietly behind her.

Then the screams began. This time they seemed louder, and Jemima realised to her horror that she recognised the voice. It was Dawn. One of the soldiers must have caught Dawn.

Or perhaps more than one.

Jemima saw that she was now in a much larger hall. She had never seen it before, but she had heard it described and guessed what it must be. It was the Hall of Maximilian.

Built by the Emperor of that name but now little used, it was of impressive size. It was forty yards long and perhaps half that in width. Its lofty ceiling was hung with huge chandeliers made of crystal from Sepulveda. Its floor was made of aram wood, imported from Syphax IV, an uninhabited world in the Rhodopea Province. The wood was noted for its hardness, durability, beautiful grain and prohibitive cost.

Jemima ran lightly towards the huge doors at the far end of the hall. Somewhere, Dawn was still screaming. Jemima reached the doors and pushed the handles. Nothing happened. Desperately she wasted precious seconds pressing down the handles with all her weight, but they were locked, and solid. She heard a sound from the room she had just left. The man must know which way Jemima had gone. He would be here in seconds, and there was no exit. She looked around desperately for somewhere to hide. There was no furniture in the Maximilian Hall.

But there were places to hide. Along the entire length of the hall, on both sides, were high windows. There were perhaps a dozen arched windows on each side of the hall. Each window stretched from the floor up to above head height. Thick, beautifully embroidered curtains hung over each window, and they were all pulled shut. Without further thought Jemima dashed to a nearby window and slipped behind the curtains, making sure they were pulled tightly closed.

She found herself in a tiny recess. The walls were two feet thick, giving her sufficient space to stand between the curtains and the duraglass window.

Jemima heard the door rattle as a man entered the room. He activated the chandeliers, bathing the room in light. She heard the man's footsteps as he hurried to the other doors and tried the handles. She heard his laugh as he discovered that the doors were locked. He could easily open the doors. He had a rifle. But there was no point. He knew that Jemima was locked in the room with him.

"Come here, little birdy," he said in a mocking, singsong tone in heavily accented Inglic. There was only one man, Jemima thought, but he was armed, and strong. All the berserkers were strong. "Come here, my lovely birdy. I will not hurt you." Jemima was trapped, and the man knew it. He was enjoying the hunt.

"Come to me, little birdy," Jemima heard. She stood perfectly still and tried to keep the sound of her breathing under control. She listened to each unhurried, heavy footstep, as he walked slowly to the first window on her side of the hall.

Jemima tried to picture the hall, to work out how long she had before she was discovered. Literally discovered, she thought. Uncovered. She thought there must be perhaps ten or twelve windows on each side of the hall. Jemima was about half way along. She thought she was probably at the fifth or sixth window. The thick embroidered curtains were hanging in the ancient style from large aramwood rings on a pole, also of aramwood.

Jemima heard the berserker give a sharp tug to one curtain. The rings slid along the pole and snapped together audibly when they reached the end. He tugged the other curtain, and again Jemima heard the rings slide and then snap together sharply.

He walked slowly to the second window. Again he opened the curtains with two brisk tugs, and Jemima heard the rings snap together. “Come out, little birdy,” he said in the same mocking tone. “I will not hurt you, if you come to me now. But if I have to come and find you, I will be very angry. Do not make me angry, little birdy.”

He walked to the third window. Again he opened the curtains with two brisk tugs, and Jemima heard the wooden rings snap together. “Come to me, my little birdy,” he said.

Dawn was silent now, Jemima realised. She looked at the windows. They were high and arched, but did not open. The panes were of thick duraglass, strong enough to protect those within from a blast of neutrino fire. There was no escape that way. She had heard that the Maximilian Hall had beautiful views of the Palace gardens, but it was still too dark to see anything but the dim outline of trees.

The man’s footsteps stopped and Jemima heard the fourth pair of curtains briskly jerked open. If only Jemima had run to the other side of the hall, she would have had a little more time, she thought: but only a little. The man was methodical. He was in no hurry.

Again she heard footsteps, slow and deliberate, but closer now. “I’m coming for you, my little birdy,” he said. He walked slowly to the fifth window. Perhaps he tugged the curtains harder this time, because Jemima heard the pole and the curtains crash to the floor.

With dismal certainty, Jemima knew that the next curtains to be pulled open would be hers. Should she run for it now and at least have the advantage of surprise? Perhaps if she bolted for the door he would blast her and kill her instantly. A quick death would be better than what they had done to Lydia and Dawn.

Then it was too late. Jemima heard the slow, firm tread of his footsteps. Then he stopped. He must be just inches away from her now. She dared not breathe. She felt her heart thumping, and wondered whether it was possible for him to hear her heartbeat. Why did he not simply pull the curtains?

He did. He grinned. He looked at Jemima, and grinned. She was a beauty, with long blonde hair and a slim flat waist and nicely curved hips. Her breasts were small but firm, pressing against her short thin pyjama top which left her waist bare. Her pyjamas were a pale blue-green. The trousers were thin and low cut. Her feet were bare. She was wide eyed, standing pressed against the window behind her, as far away from the berserker as she could. She stood very straight, with her hands crossed over her breasts as if to protect herself from what he was going to do. She was everything he had hoped for when he had first caught sight of her fleeing in the pale light. The Emperor had good taste, and the money to indulge it.

The berserker's name was Katto. Katto knew that the war could not last much longer. The Imperials were retreating as quickly as the Atkoi could advance. When it was over, the Kzam would reward him with land. Katto had already chosen the world where he would settle. It was called Tungstall.

Tungstall was an Earth type world, with rolling green hills and valleys and rivers. To Katto, who came from the semi desert world of Envermeil, Tungstall seemed so green it scarcely seemed natural. When Katto had first seen Tungstall, he knew what the Valleys of the Righteous must be like; and he could live there now, in this life. Katto had been part of the invasion force which had conquered Tungstall. There had been very little resistance. The inhabitants had heard of what had happened on New Wessex. After the war, Katto would claim his land, send for his family, and settle on Tungstall. Many of the lads who had been with Katto said they would settle there too, if they survived the war.

Katto thought he would survive, now. He had survived this far, and soon it would be finished. With the loot he found on Nenuphar, he would return to Tungstall a wealthy man.

But the others would be here, soon. They would all want their turns with this girl. Katto would satisfy himself with the little birdy first, and then go looking for more valuables.

Katto grinned, drinking in Jemima's beauty. Then he said, "Take your clothes off."

Jemima stared at him, too frightened to run, or speak, or obey him, or move at all. Like all berserkers he had a red stripe across his face and tunic. He looked horrible, terrible. Two gold candlesticks hung from his belt, leaving his hands free to hold the rifle.

Katto raised the rifle and pointed it directly at Jemima. "You do like I say, else I blast you. Top first, then trousers."

Jemima belonged to the Emperor. No other man was allowed to see her naked. For that matter no other man was allowed to see her clothed. She tried to say, "Please…" but no sound came from her mouth.

Then something happened which Jemima did not at first understand. There was a flash of light so bright that she could not see. She heard a brief shout or gasp and then screaming. It was a blast of neutrino plasma fire. *Why am I still alive?* she wondered. Then she realised the screams were her own. She felt a hand over her mouth, and a voice urging her to silence.

When Jemima could see again, she saw the remains of the berserker smouldering on the aramwood floor. The head was still attached to the shoulders and arms. They were on the floor, but separate from the legs and waist. The body parts were black and charred. The berserker's chest and stomach were gone, burnt entirely away by the blast. *Did his own gun explode and kill him?* she wondered. The floor was black and scorched too, except for a distorted but clearly man shaped pale shadow where the berserker's body had protected the floor in the instant of his incineration. Even the curtains each side of Jemima were burnt to ashes.

Then Jemima realised it was Gaspar, one of the junior eunuchs, who was holding her. He had blasted the berserker from one side. Jemima was unharmed, protected by the thick walls of the window recess. He picked up the berserker's rifle and told her to follow him.

They ran down a corridor, through a side door and into the gardens. Gaspar pointed towards a small copse. “Keep going that way,” he said. “When you get to the wall, follow it, to a small gate. If it’s still locked, blast it with this,” he said, handing her the pistol. He kept the rifle for himself. Jemima would have struggled to carry the heavier weapon.

“That’s the trigger. Just point the thing and pull the trigger. No! Not at me! Point it at the ground if you want to test it. You’re on your own now. I’m going back. There may be other survivors. You’ll have to hide. Hide in the city. Find an empty house. Here, take my jacket. Put it on. You can’t go around town dressed like that.” He paused for a moment. Jemima was shaking. “Jemima, if it looks as if there are going to catch you, kill as many of the bastards as you can, but don’t let them take you alive. If they catch with that pistol, they’ll skewer you.”

18: IF YOU SEEK HIS MONUMENT

Where Troy once was, are fields now.
Samuel Johnson

Giorge Bazan stood on a green hill a few miles north of London, on Old Earth. *Earth!* he thought. *The birthplace and birthright of man. The cradle of humanity! Earth, where the grass is green because it is meant to be here, because it belongs here, and not because the very molecules of the world have been forced to accept it.*

Earth! The very name was heavy with emotion. In many ways the Emperor had been right. By moving his capital here, Aethelstan would have reminded people of their origins, of the glorious past of the Empire. And if the Empire's capital was on Earth, then the Empire's enemies would be, by logical extension, the enemies of humanity itself.

But now was not the time for such a move. The Emperor was reviled now, for fleeing Nenuphar when the Empire needed him most. Aethelstan was not expected to be a great orator or tactician or leader of men. As a constitutional monarch he could have served the Empire well, simply by doing nothing except remaining on Nenuphar. Mere inertia could have guaranteed his place in history as the Empire's saviour.

But it was too late now. Aethelstan had fled Nenuphar, and now he had fled Earth. The Emperor and Empress and their two sons were gone. Officially, the Emperor was going in person to the Autarchy of An-Nizam, to appeal for help. Aethelstan believed, or said he believed, that the Nizamis would not want an aggressive Atkoi Kzamate on their borders. It was in their best interests to create a human buffer state, effectively a protectorate, between An-Nizam and the Atkoi. Aethelstan would be its head of state. He would even retain the title, Emperor, and a certain degree of autonomy. But it would be a shadow of the former Empire, a pretend Empire.

Bazan and many in the Navy and Marines and at least some of the senators had a different idea. They still believed it was possible to fight and win. The Nizamis were the ancient enemy of Man. To invite them now, into human space, was an idea loathsome to Bazan and many others.

The truth was that the Great Kzam, like Bazan himself, possessed a remarkable instinct for understanding and influencing people. Perhaps Rurik had sensed that executing the Princess would send the Emperor out if his mind not merely with grief or anger, but in sheer panic.

The war was progressing poorly. The borbod divisions had mutinied, turning on their own officers and fellow Imperials at a critical moment and siding with the enemy. They had been intended as the Empire's shock force, to inspire terror in the enemy, to be more than a match for the Atkoi berserkers. Now they had betrayed the Empire together, as if it were planned in advance. None of the so called experts in borbod behaviour had predicted that. No one truly understood how their minds worked.

Several planetary and provincial governors had declared themselves independent, and the faction who called themselves Levellers were seeking to abolish the Empire altogether and replace it with a Republic around the Central Planets. More than a third of the Empire's inhabited planets were now under Atkoi rule, including Nenuphar, many of the Central Planets and important industrial or strategic worlds such as Terminor, with its shipyards, Tolon, a vital strategic centre, Ratisbon, a major industrial world, Antiochus, a provincial capital and seat of a Patriarch, Lucaris and Ximines, prosperous industrial worlds, Ambergris, with its naval base, and wealthy, populous provincial capitals like Konigsmark and Aegina. Everywhere the Empire was in retreat.

Earth itself had not yet faced a full scale attack. A single Atkoi vessel on its way to rejoin the enemy fleet had dropped out of metaspace to fire upon the Viceroy's Palace in London, which Aethelstan had made his official residence. Several naval and strategic targets had also been attacked. Damage had been minimal, but as with Cornubium on Nenuphar, many people had simply left London. They knew that it was only a matter of time before the Atkoi returned in force.

London was an ancient city. It had been ancient before the Nizamis came. It had been a national capital when humanity was limited to Earth alone. In ancient times, Bazan had read, it had been home to over a million inhabitants.

Then the Nizamis came. They had no use for large cities. As the population fell and people moved to the country or small towns, thousands of houses were abandoned and fell into disrepair. The great river Thamesis was allowed to flood when its embankments crumbled, and much of the land to the south and east had reverted to its original swamp and forest. Concrete, brick and tarmac had crumbled as ancient forests reclaimed the land. Rivers that had disappeared centuries before flowed once more. Old Earth did not require geoengineering like man's new colonies among the stars. The mere absence of people gave it the respite it required to recover.

Only when London became a provincial capital within the Empire did the city begin to grow once more. Broad, straight, tree lined avenues were built, with gracious, spacious homes and buildings. By the late 2900s London was home to almost a quarter of a million people, if the outlying suburbs and villages were included. Near the river, the ancient domed temple was still the seat of one of the twelve Patriarchs of the Holy Orthodox Church. It had been rebuilt three times over the centuries – roughly twice every thousand years. London's university attracted students from throughout the Empire.

It was early spring and the day was cool but comfortable and bright. Bazan wanted to clear his thoughts. His driver would arrive in an hour to take him to see the Chancellor.

It was not Bazan's first visit to Old Earth. He was well travelled. It felt good to stand once more on real, solid ground and feel the Earth beneath his feet. *Literally the Earth*, Bazan thought. He was walking on Primrose Hill, looking southwards down the valley. In the distance he could see the hoverrail which threaded its way through woodlands and past cottages which had stood for a thousand years or more. Beyond the horizon, he knew, it passed the ivory towers of the University. He wondered if that was where the expression 'ivory tower' came from.

Beyond this was the city proper, which stretched all the way to the broad river. The hoverrail ran across the river and south through the Forest of Surre and past scattered clearings and villages, to the coast. Other hoverrails ran northwest to other cities, and southeast to one of the main continental land masses.

Bazan needed to know where the Chancellor stood and what his intentions were. The Atkoi had organised their forces into three fleets, each steadily advancing into Imperial territory. The Navy had been fighting rearguard actions and sending small squadrons to harry enemy bases within Atkoi held space. Their orders were to create as much damage as possible, to fight only when they outnumbered the enemy and then to move on to a new target. The speed of the Atkoi advance had slowed a little. Bazan was preparing to lead a larger fleet deep into Atkoi space, but he feared that there were those in government who lacked resolve. They might try to seek some accommodation with the Kzam.

He saw a movement and looked up. It was his aircar, approaching from the south. He suppressed some momentary irritation. Rawlings would not have come early without good reason.

The car landed, and Rawlings ran over to Bazan and handed him a piece of paper. "Sir, Admiral Salazar said you should read this immediately," he said, breathlessly. Bazan took it without a word and read it.

"Are you aware of what this says, Felix? he asked.

"Yes sir."

"All dead? Are we certain?"

“Yes sir. The Admiral said the source was reliable.”

Bazan took barely a second to digest this. Then he said, “I think we’d better go straight to the Residency, Felix. You may ignore the usual speed restrictions."

19: RULES OF ENGAGEMENT

A crisis like this brings forward new leaders, new talent. The Empire needs new talent. It's the most important resource we have, and probably the scarcest.

Thomas Arbuthnot-Samar

The Emperor was dead. So were his sons Sigismund and Roderic. Crewmen of the Imperial yacht Warrior had mutinied and put the Emperor on 'trial' for cowardice and dereliction of duty. Needless to say they had found him 'guilty'. Aethelstan and his heirs were murdered and their bodies cast into space. The atrocity had been committed somewhere in the vicinity of the planet Antalcidas in the Torrelaguna Province, en route to the Nizami outpost at Uartuuguch.

Bazan hardly needed to be told that Levellers had been responsible. The Viceroy of Torrelaguna, a man named Edmund Ayala, had condemned the outrage and then promptly proclaimed the abolition of the Empire and its replacement with a Commonwealth. A hastily appointed Parliament had elected him acting Lord Protector of the said Commonwealth. Ayala had further invited all civil and military authorities to pledge allegiance to the Commonwealth.

Arbuthnot-Samar, Aanrud and Bazan met in the Cabinet Room of the Residency. The building had not been seriously damaged in the Atkoi attack, although one wing was now boarded up. No repairs had yet been undertaken.

The problem was not that the Levellers were strong. It was rather that the Empire was weak. They could not afford to fight both the Levellers and the Atkoi at once.

Aethelstan had been a weak Emperor, but now they had no leader at all. People needed a figurehead. The Emperor's elder son Sigismund had fathered no children. Gossip suggested that he kept a seraglio only for the sake of form and that his true interest was in boys. His younger brother Roderic had also been childless, because of his youth rather than any lack of interest. Aethelstan had had numerous sons by his concubines, but those were not considered as possible heirs to the Radiant Throne. A law excluding them had been passed four centuries earlier, in the time of Otto I. Too many Imperial princes by different mothers were a recipe for civil war when their father died, and Otto had decreed that only the children of an Emperor and his legal wife could inherit the throne.

True, the law could be changed, the Lord Chancellor conceded. He was a lawyer by training. The Imperial Senate could meet in emergency session and pass an Act of Succession to name a new heir. Most senators would accept a candidate who had sufficient support in the Navy and the populace generally to unite the Empire and deal with the Atkoi threat. One ambitious young man, the son of Aethelstan and one of his most favoured concubines, had already approached the Chancellor and offered himself as a candidate. His name was Joachim, but he had expressed the wish to rule under the name Justinianus II. His mother Felicia was by birth a member of the Immelmann family, of senatorial rank.

The Lord Chancellor paused. He had already discussed the matter at length, not only with the Minister of War but with other ministers and leaders of various factions in the Senate. It was generally felt that neither Joachim, nor any of his brothers or half-brothers, were very impressive candidates. The Senate would only approve Joachim if no better candidate could be found. The late Emperor had no surviving full brothers, and none of his nephews were particularly popular.

"Our late sovereign also had a number of daughters by different concubines," the Chancellor continued. "The law could also be changed in favour of one of them. Provided that she had sufficient support in the Senate."

"A sovereign, ruling empress?" enquired Bazan.

"It's happened before. Constantia Prendergast-Rana ruled in her own name after her husband died. She wasn't even of the Imperial line, but she is considered a great ruler. I was talking to that fellow Itchenor, from the university, you know. He thinks Empress Constantia ranks along with Baldwin I as one of our greatest rulers. But never mind that now. The point is, a daughter of Aethelstan might be just the figurehead we need. It all depends on who she marries. In a case like this, it might be the husband who ends up as the real Emperor. Or at least a joint Emperor. A joint emperor in fact, even if not in name." He paused, as if waiting for his implications to sink in. Bazan sensed they were waiting for him to reply.

"Of course," continued the Chancellor, "In a sense, all of this is academic. You hold the real power, Giorge." It occurred to Bazan that the Chancellor had never used his first name before. "You command the Navy. And you're a popular admiral. You can stop people defecting to the Levellers. And if you can beat the Atkoi too, you'll stay popular. People don't forget something like that in a hurry. And the Senate will support anyone who can get them out of this mess."

The Chancellor paused. Aanrud said nothing. His silence spoke volumes. It proclaimed his agreement, which in turn implied the support of a sizeable faction in the Senate.

"Are you an ambitious man, Giorge?" asked the Chancellor.

"I am ambitious," Bazan replied, equally carefully. "My ambition is to serve the Empire." He saw the barely perceptible glance exchanged by the two others, and the slight nod.

"The Empire needs ambitious men," said the Chancellor.

Aanrud picked up the conversation. "Have you ever considered marrying again, Giorge?"

Bazan already understood what was being offered. From the moment he had read the message Rawlings gave him, he had guessed what might happen. He had a talent for anticipating other people's moves and quickly deciding his own response. “As a Naval officer, I seldom saw my wife. That’s why she divorced me,” he said.

“I know. It’s different for an Admiral, though. After this war it’ll be different,” Aanrud corrected himself. “But in principle, you have no objection to marrying again?”

“No. I presume you have a specific…suggestion to make?” The Chancellor noticed Bazan’s bluntness. It was a good sign.

“The Lady Demetra Prendergast. The Late Emperor’s daughter. She’s very intelligent. Very witty. Attractive, too, if that makes any difference. Impeccable pedigree. Her mother was an Andrieux. Her grandmother was a Quintero-Paget.” The Chancellor spoke and waited for Bazan to reply.

“She sounds utterly charming. What makes you think she would be agreeable?”

“She is agreeable. I have asked her. Naturally she is in mourning for her father; but she is also romantic. She considers you her saviour. And she is patriotic. She wants to help. And she wants to be an Empress. She was disappointed when Aethelstan didn’t give her to the Kzam. But you can discuss this with the lady yourself.”

“Discuss it? You mean….”

“Yes. I will introduce you. She is waiting for you in the Rose Garden. Have you seen the palace gardens? They’re lovely at this time of year. I believe the lady ordered some tea to be brought out for you both.”

20: OF HUMAN BONDAGE

Plan! Plan before your enemy even knows that a plan is needed. Strike before your enemy has a plan of his own.

The Great Kzam Rurik III (Attributed)

How would it feel to spend the rest of your days regretting what might have been, if only you had acted decisively and in good time? Would the pain, the regret, fade as the years passed? Or would the sense of loss for greatness so nearly achieved but so carelessly lost, remain forever?

The Kzama Radmilla Otheris at Otheris: Diaries

Radmilla was going to have to kill her husband. There really was no alternative. And it would have to be done that night. Timing was everything.

Radmilla knew what had to be done. She had known for a very long time that she would have to act decisively to save her sons' inheritances and preserve their futures. She had deferred the dreadful moment for as long as possible in the hope that it would prove unnecessary. But now, if she hesitated a moment longer, she and her sons would lose everything.

The Kzam had sidelined Radmilla and her sons. His navy had been organised into three fleets, each progressing independently and steadily into Imperial space. Each fleet was divided into squadrons. More squadrons were held back in reserve and to patrol the Atkoi home worlds. But neither Ozim nor Ozart would have command of any of the fleets, nor any squadron nor even an individual ship. After everything Ozim had done for his father, he had been put aside. Khostrounil would command the central fleet whenever Rurik himself was not present. *Khostrounil!*

Two other sons of the Kzam by his more junior wives would command the two other fleets. Various other sons by wives and concubines were trusted with squadrons. But for Ozim and Ozart, his sons by the Radmilla, nothing. The humiliation, anger and sense of betrayal forced all thought of caution from her mind. Rurik had promised to make both of her sons planetary governors. Ul-Kzams! The sons of the Great Kzam's senior wife! The insult was intolerable. The son of a lowly concubine might aspire to greater heights.

Radmilla had considered speaking to Rurik, to plead her sons' cause and urge reason upon him. She rejected this option. Firstly, she knew that once his mind was made up he would not alter it. The Kzam made decisions quickly once he knew all the facts, and once made, he did not alter them. Secondly, if she raised the subject with him at all, he would be warned. He would know that she was dissatisfied. *Strike, before you enemy has a plan.* That was what Rurik said. Well, a kzama could be quite as ruthless as a kzam. She would act tonight.

It had to be tonight, or not at all. Just as Aethelstan had retreated with his entire headquarters, Rurik was planning to advance with his. His ultimate plan was to move the capital of the Kzamate much closer to the centre of the old Empire. He had considered and rejected Earth, Nenuphar, Tolon and several other possible choices, and instead selected the obscure world of Abercrombie III, which he had renamed Rurikshaevn. Its population was small, but it could sustain many more. New settlement would be encouraged: Atkoi settlement. New cities would be built. It was not a major industrial centre, but it was within easy reach of several strategic planets and it was situated on the crossroads of several vital trade routes.

There was a mood of hysteria among the girls. Most hoped above all else to be chosen to join their master in his move to his new capital. Where their master went, they naturally wanted to follow. None wanted to live out their days as failed concubines on Ziandakush, but none knew for certain who was going and who would stay; none except Radmilla, in whom the Klang Arak had confided.

The transfer of an entire headquarters, palace and seraglio was of course a major undertaking which had been months in the planning. Everything the Kzam might require had to be shipped to Rurikshaevn. The Kzam had appropriated the former governor's Residency; it would have to be extended, of course. Rurik himself would be moving in two days' time. Most of the Kzam's personal effects were packed. All of his favourite concubines as well as the Klang Arak and the most proficient eunuchs would travel with him.

But today, Radmilla had discovered one vital fact which would force her to act immediately or not at all. Only five of the Kzam's wives would travel with him. These were the mothers of those sons he had recently promoted. Radmilla was not to be among them. The Kzama herself would remain on Ziandakush. The palace and the seraglio would be maintained as the Kzam's official second home. Radmilla would retain her title of Kzama, at least for the present. She would be in charge of a houseful of failed wives and older concubines: a reliquary in all but name. Whether she would ever see the Kzam again, she did not know. Certainly she would be excluded from any kind of power or influence.

The Kzam had sprung his trap. He had planned it and struck before Radmilla had known that the danger existed. And Radmilla had only a day and a half to execute her own plan.

"Oh Kyra, my dear little dove, you mustn't be frightened." Radmilla cupped Kyra's face in the palms of her hands as she spoke. "Kyra, the Kzam will love you. I know his tastes. You are blessed. Let me tell you a little secret, Kyra dear. The Kzam nearly summoned you months ago, after you danced for him, before he went away. The Klang Arak thought you were ready to walk the Golden Path even then. He is very pleased with your progress. Very pleased indeed. There are many beautiful girls in the seraglio, Kyra, but you are the most beautiful, talented, intelligent and charming. No, I mean it. And now I think you are truly ready to please your master. He is going away again, soon. He has not summoned anyone to his chambers. Tonight you will serve him at dinner. If he asks for you, you will walk the Golden Path soon. Very soon indeed."

The fact that Kyra had known this day would come in no way lessened the shock of the Kzama's words. She nodded and said, "Yes, ma'am," or at least she tried to. Her words were barely audible.

By the time the beauticians and the wardrobe mistress had finished with Kyra, her hair and skin shone. Her eyelids were shaded pale green and her cheeks were powdered so subtly that the Kzam would not even realise why she looked so lovely, Radmilla assured her. Kyra's hair was fair, a dark blonde. Radmilla had chosen against dying it a brighter shade, preferring instead its natural look. It was parted and tied in two kittentails, one each side of her head, and hung down to her breasts. Her toenails and fingernails were varnished a subtle, translucent pale green. Her body hair had been plucked. These and a hundred other preparations had been made.

Radmilla herself had selected Kyra's dress for the evening. She was to wear a short cropped bolero top, pale green in colour with a pattern of gold thread and a row of tiny gold coins hanging from its lower edge, and a wrap skirt which came to her calves, also pale green, fastened with a gold clasp. Her right thigh was visible when she walked. Around her neck and her right ankle were golden chains, also with gold coins attached. Underneath she wore a white patang, but no bra. Kyra was terrified to be seen by her master so scantily clothed, but the Kzama reassured her. The Kzam would love her, she said. The green and gold set off her hair and eyes beautifully and the skirt enhanced her height and her slim waist and figure. Finally, Kyra was sprayed with perfume, a scent which the Kzam favoured.

At last the Kzama was satisfied. She dismissed Dora, the beautician, and Bella, her assistant. They curtsied and said, "Thank you, ma'am." Dora squeezed Kyra's hand and whispered, "Good luck." Dora and Bella giggled and left, but Kyra hardly felt like smiling.

The Kzama glanced at the clock. "It is time," she said.

The Kzam dined, giving last minute instructions for the forthcoming move as he ate, and asking questions about the readiness of the palace. The Kzama sat beside him, and the Klang Arak stood. Rurik was apparently satisfied with the arrangements, and turned his full attention to the food.

While Kyra was not serving, she stood at the edge of the room, on the marble tiled floor. The Klang Arak stood on the carpet, as was his prerogative. Kyra would not have dared to stand on the carpet. She stood very straight, with her toes and heels together and her hands crossed behind the small of her back, with her palms flat. She could maintain this position for two hours, if required. Indeed, during her training it had been required.

Once, the Kzama caught her eye and smiled reassuringly. Kyra was grateful. Another time, the Kzama discreetly gestured to Kyra to adjust her hair. One of her long kittentails had fallen behind her back. Kyra flicked it to the front, hoping the Kzam had not noticed. Radmilla smiled again at the novice.

Only when matters of state and his meal had both been dealt with did the Kzam finally turn his attention to Kyra. He looked at her, and Kyra felt cold with fear. "Come here, Kyra," he said.

He remembers my name, thought Kyra. She curtsied and tried to smile, stepping forward. This was the moment when her future would be decided, Kyra knew. She would have been surprised indeed to realise that the Kzama was as nervous as she was and that the rise and fall of Empires would depend on what happened next.

Rurik scrutinised the slave girl. Then he addressed the Klang Arak. "Is this girl to be sent to Rurikshaevn?"

"No, Dread Lord," replied Narciso. "Her name was not on the list."

"Add it to the list," he said simply. To Kyra, the Kzam added, "I have not forgotten what I told you, Kyra. Matters of state have conspired to keep us apart, but I will see you again. Soon. Now, fetch me another glass of that red wine." Kyra curtsied and hurried to obey. For a little longer, it seemed, she had been saved.

Radmilla felt her heart thumping. Where did this leave her plans? *In shreds,* the Kzama realised. *The Kzam likes the girl, but not enough to summon her tonight. Send her to Rurikshaevn! That's no use to me. It's disastrous.*

The Kzama wondered whether she could persuade her husband to have Kyra walk the Golden Path the following evening. No. He would suspect something if the suggestion came from her. It must seem to be the Kzam's own idea. And yet this would be Radmilla's last ever opportunity for decisive action. Her mind swirled with indecision. Radmilla was still trying to resolve her dilemma when Kyra returned with the carafe.

Then Rurik spoke. "On second thoughts," he said, "have her sent to the Low Chamber. In one hour. Radmilla, would you see to it? I wish to speak to Narciso first."

"At once, Husband," the Kzama replied, like a dutiful Atkoi wife.

21: WITHOUT A PADDLE

What I have done, I have done to preserve the Kzamate for posterity. My *posterity.*

The Kzama Radmilla Otheris at Otheris: Diaries

Kyra was going to walk the Golden Path.

She was in the Maidens' Chamber, the small preparation room where the Golden Path began. Radmilla had sent for Dora and Bella. She had less than an hour to prepare Kyra. They would be able to do very little in that time, but little needed doing. The Kzama hugged Kyra and congratulated her warmly. The two beauticians were equally excited. Both had briefly been concubines of an earlier Kzam and both understood only too well the importance of their task.

Radmilla ordered Kyra to remove everything. Dora was not entirely satisfied with her make-up. Kyra looked a little pale, and Dora added a hint of blush to her cheeks. She also outlined Kyra's labia in red. Kyra looked at the effect in a full length mirror, and her blushes then owed nothing to the make-up. The Kzama reassured her: "The Kzam will like it," she said. "It is our tradition. Even brides have it done, on their wedding night." Then she added to Dora, "Do the nipples, too."

Dora selected a tiny bottle and painted a clear liquid onto Kyra's nipples. It felt very cold, and then it began to tingle. "Now, don't touch your nipples at all, Kyra dear," warned the Kzama. "You'll spoil the effect." Kyra knew the liquid was to make her nipples stand out. The Atkoi considered prominent nipples to be highly attractive. A bride or a virgin slave girl was often given ice cubes to press against her nipples to make them firm and pointed, shortly before she was led to her husband or master's bed. The chemical which Dora was using must be a mild irritant which would last a little longer. It would help Kyra to give a good first impression.

The Deputy Klang Arak, the wardrobe mistress, and Kyra's friend Millie were also present. The wardrobe mistress adjusted Kyra's costume and gave her a different necklace and anklet to wear. This time, beneath the costume, Kyra was entirely bare. Satisfied at last, the wardrobe mistress glanced at the Kzama for her approval. The Deputy Klang Arak also scrutinised Kyra and seemed satisfied.

Radmilla nodded to the Deputy Klang Arak, who turned to leave. The wardrobe mistress and beauticians also left. "You're gorgeous," Dora told Kyra. "Absolutely gorgeous. You'll knock him dead, you will."

Kyra, Radmilla and Millicent were left alone in the Maidens' Chamber. There were chairs, but Kyra stood looking at the clock, and Radmilla stood too, out of choice. Millie stood out of necessity. She could not sit in the Kzama's presence unless invited to do so, which she had not been.

Traditionally, a novice could request two friends to accompany her on the Golden Path, for moral support. At least one of these two companions was usually herself a novice. If the chosen girl for some reason displeased her master so completely that he sent her back to her quarters, he might then choose to have the other novice serve him in her stead. In practice, such an outcome was unknown in Rurik's seraglio.

Usually when a novice was summoned to walk the Golden Path, there were several days or more in which to prepare her. Within hours of the Kzam's decision, the entire seraglio would learn of it. The excited girl's friends would congratulate her, and her enemies – for everyone had enemies in the seraglio – would cast jealous looks at her. Kyra had not had the luxury of knowing in advance that she was to be chosen, but she asked the Kzama herself and Millie to accompany her. Millie was nervous, but delighted to be chosen. To be glimpsed even briefly by the Kzam might benefit her. He might remember her, and send for her on another occasion. Even the Kzama seemed pleased that Kyra had asked her.

At one end of the Maidens' Chamber was a pair of huge golden doors. It was through these doors that Kyra would pass into the corridor known as the Golden Path. Above the door was a clock, and Kyra seemed unable to drag her eyes away from it.

A minute before the appointed time, the Kzama glanced at the clock. "It is time," she said. Kyra, with Radmilla and Millie on either side of her, began her short walk along the Golden Path. The Kzama instructed Millie to open the doors wide, and they began.

The Golden Path was not a particularly long corridor, Kyra saw. It measured perhaps sixty feet from the Maidens' Chamber, to the Low Chamber. The Middle and High Chambers must be a little further on, she guessed. Perhaps one day she would be summoned to the Middle Chamber. She would never, as a slave, see inside the High Chamber.

The corridor was wide. Its walls were decorated with gold leaf and its light fittings were golden. Kyra walked slowly, with Radmilla on one side, reassuring her, and Millie on the other, now suddenly almost as nervous as her friend.

They reached another pair of golden doors. This was her destination, Kyra realised with mounting fear. Her destiny. This was where the Kzam would take her virginity. Without hesitation, the Kzama knocked loudly. There was no reply. *What does that mean?* Kyra wondered. She felt her heart thumping.

The Kzama opened the doors wide and entered the room. Kyra and Millie followed. For the first time, the two novices saw the sumptuously decorated room.

Radmilla sat on a chair. "We will await your master in silence," decreed the Kzama. Kyra went to kneel at the foot of the bed, with her buttocks resting on her feet and her back as straight as a rod. Millie knelt beside her in a similar pose.

A concubine did not enter her master's bed at the side, as a wife entered her husband's bed. A concubine was a slave. She knelt at the foot of the bed, and when commanded she lifted the cover and crawled beneath it, up to the pillows. When her master dismissed her, she would crawl backwards and lie on the floor at the foot of the bed to sleep, or await his command.

Minutes passed. Kyra waited to reach out and hold her friend's hand, but she remembered her lessons in etiquette and knew that she was expected to remain perfectly still. The novices had all been trained to remain kneeling for hours, if necessary.

Kyra wondered if the Kzam would hurt her. Those concubines who had already walked the Golden Path sometimes delighted in telling the virgin novices that it would be painful when they were deflowered. But the Kzama had told Kyra that the Kzam was very patient and gentle with new girls in particular. This had encouraged Kyra to some extent.

In reality, both points of view contained at least some truth. In his own way the Kzam did try to be gentle; but he expected to enjoy the use of his seraglio, and he was thorough, and forceful. New girls were always warned to expect some discomfort, and strongly advised to try their best not to cry out.

When it seemed to Kyra that they had been waiting perhaps an hour, she heard a little noise from the door which led to the Kzam's private apartments. Her heart began thumping in panic. The door opened. Kyra and Millie both touched their foreheads to the floor and remained in that position, perfectly still.

Radmilla stood and curtsied. "Dread Lord," she intoned, "may I present your maidservant Kyra, prepared for you pleasure?"

"You may. Thank you, Lady Radmilla," replied the Kzam.

Radmilla hesitated. "Dread Lord, the girl is nervous, but she prays that you will be kind. If she seems reticent, it is not through any lack of love for you, but simply…"

"Yes. She is shy. I understand. You may go now, Lady Radmilla."

Radmilla seemed about to say something more, but she curtsied and turned to leave. Millie rose, curtsied and hurried after her. The Kzam seemed not to notice her. Kyra heard the doors click shut behind them.

I'm on my own now, thought Kyra, *with my master.*

"Stand up, Kyra. I want to look at you." The Kzam spoke not unkindly, but as one who expected obedience. Kyra rose gracefully to her feet. The Kzam loosened the ribbons in her hair and ran his fingers through her tresses. He slid his hands through her hair to the back of her head, and pressed her lips to his. Then he simply looked at her. Kyra looked back, wide eyed.

After a few moments, he unfastened the clasp on her bolero and slid it down. Kyra blushed as the Kzam scrutinised her, gently squeezed one of her breasts, and then kissed her again, on her lips and her neck. He removed the clasp which fastened her skirt, and let the thin fabric drop to the floor. Utterly exposed, Kyra blushed deeper. "Go to the bed," said the Kzam.

Kyra knelt at the foot of the bed, and then climbed on it, crawling as a slave. Burning with shame, she wondered if her parents would ever learn what had become of her. Or Simon. *Simon, forgive me*, she thought. *Do not think ill of me, Simon. I would have been faithful to you for all my life, but I did not choose my destiny. I am no longer your fiancée. I am not Kyra Welbeck now, only Kyra, an Atkoi slave girl.*

She felt the Kzam's hand slide down, over her waist, her hips, and trace the outline of her brand, the brand that proclaimed to both Kyra and the Kzam that she belonged to him. She felt his hand slide down to her intimate parts. Her eyes were closed. "Oh," she gasped. Strangely, she felt less ashamed now. It did not feel unpleasant.

He kissed her on the mouth again. Then he kissed her nipple, and gently sucked. "Master," she whispered. She felt less afraid now. He seemed patient and kind.

Suddenly everything changed. Kyra felt her master's teeth sink hard into her nipple, so hard that they must surely meet through the soft flesh. She knew that she should not scream. She was his property and if he chose to use her like this it was his prerogative entirely, but she was unable to help a whimper from escaping her lips. His hands, too, were squeezing her uncomfortably and his whole body had arched upwards.

Only gradually did he seem to relax. Kyra gasped again. The pain was less now, but it seemed to return in waves. A tear trickled from her eye as she blinked. The Kzam was lying on top of Kyra, but unmoving. Kyra too, remained still. She must do nothing to spoil her master's pleasure. She waited. Was he asleep? Was this usual behaviour for the Kzam? Surely there would have been rumours, if it were. For a long time, Kyra remained still, before she quietly whispered, "Master?"

There was no reply. It was not her place to wake her master. A terrifying thought occurred to her. Might he have had a heart attack? But he was in good health. What should she do? Paralysed by indecision, she did nothing for several minutes. She whispered to him again, and again there was no reply. Something was not right. She forgot the pain now. Very carefully she tried to adjust her position beneath him. Then his head rolled to one side and fell to an unnatural angle.

Kyra saw the face of her master and began screaming.

The eunuch Baltazaro was on duty that night. He heard the screams. These were not the squeals or yelps he sometimes heard, of a concubine put to some painful use or discipline, nor was the Kzam usually a deliberately cruel man. These were the prolonged screams of a girl in hysterical terror. Baltazaro rushed from the Maidens' Chamber to the Low Chamber and ran in. Alone of anyone in the entire seraglio, the eunuch on duty had the authority to enter the Kzam's chamber when it was occupied. He saw his master's body, naked on the bed, and the screaming slave, and commanded her to silence.

The habit of obedience was instilled into Kyra and she was able to stifle her screams to a quiet whimper. She was sitting on the bed beside her master, clamping the bed sheet to her mouth with both hands.

Baltazaro examined the body. His master was dead. He reached for the bell pull. The Klang Arak and the Kzama must be informed.

The Kzama arrived first. Kyra knelt on the floor now, still clutching a crumpled sheet and quietly keening and shaking. Radmilla turned straight to the terrified novice. “How could you?” she demanded. “How *could* you? He trusted you. We all trusted you.”

By now more of the eunuchs had arrived. Radmilla ordered the room to be searched for anything out of the ordinary. She ordered Kyra to be showered immediately, given a dress, and taken to a cell.

Word of what had happened had escaped. Despite the thick walls Kyra could hear the howls of lamentation as they spread throughout the seraglio. Some concubines were genuinely distraught, screaming and sobbing hysterically. Others were terrified of what would become of them, as concubines of a former Kzam. Would they simply be destroyed, as had been done in earlier centuries? Everyone knew the Kzam had admired the ancient Atkoi traditions. Did that extend to destroying his concubines when he died? Did his will specify their fate, or would his successor decide? And who was his successor? Those women who had never borne the Kzam a son were fearful because they were now of no use or relevance; and those who did have sons were fearful because they and their offspring might perish at the hands of an ambitions rival such as the Kzama or her sons.

The women who were neither grieving nor frightened howled too, and tore out their hair like the others. It was important to be seen to do the right thing. Hysteria feeds on itself, and the lamentation grew. Only the eunuchs and the Kzama were calm.

Baltazaro himself led Kyra back along the golden Path, through the Maidens’ Chamber and into the main corridor, where the hysteria was at its worst. Upon seeing Kyra, the women surged forward, screaming out their loathing for the woman who had murdered their lord and master. Baltazaro’s assistants whipped them aside, forcing a path through the crowd, but Kyra still felt her hair pulled and her face scratched. Suddenly she saw the face of Millie, her friend, but it was contorted with hatred. One of the girls spat at Kyra. All of her former friends now hated Kyra, she realised. Kyra was glad when they reached the corridor which led to the underground cells.

This was the corridor where Athanasia had been incarcerated, where Kyra had brought food and clean clothing and personal effects for the condemned princess. Now the wrought iron gates slammed shut behind Kyra. She felt relieved, almost grateful for the tranquillity of the place. She was protected now, from the women who hated her so much.

22: AN INSPECTOR CALLS

"And what will historians say of me, when I am dead and buried? If I lose this war, they will say I was a savage, a barbarian without compassion. But if I win I will be called a saviour, a conqueror, a law maker who created order out of chaos."

The Great Kzam, Rurik III (Attributed)

Chief Inspector Adriaan Voragine of the Kzamate Police Intelligence Branch (Ziandakush Division) knew that something was not right. A great deal was not right at all. His Dread and Sovereign Lord, Rurik, was dead. Voragine had a girl in custody, very pretty and very frightened, with one nipple half bitten off, who insisted that she had killed the Kzam.

Kyra maintained that the bottle of poison had belonged to Princess Athanasia, who had hidden it before she was arrested. Kyra and the Princess had become quite friendly while Athanasia was incarcerated. Kyra had been responsible for taking the Princess her meals. The Princess had told Kyra where the bottle was hidden, in case Kyra ever needed it. After Athanasia was executed, Kyra had retrieved the bottle. The Princess had told her that a tiny dose of the poison would act as a sedative. Kyra had not wanted to kill her master, she explained. She only wanted to make him sleep. She did not want to be his concubine. She had hoped to preserve her virginity, just for a day or two, after which the Kzam would move to the new capital, Rurikshaevn, and Kyra would remain safely on Ziandakush.

Voragine did not believe a word of it, of course. He was highly experienced, with an excellent understanding of people. Most suspects lied to deny responsibility for their crime, or at least to minimise their culpability. This one was innocent, pretending to be guilty. Why? Who was she covering up for? Someone powerful, surely. Who would gain by Rurik's death? The Imperial authorities? Or someone closer to home?

Voragine had no personal love for the late Kzam. He had been a highly successful police officer ten years before, when Rurik had seized power on Ziandakush and made it his capital. Voragine had been allowed to keep his job. He was a good policeman, but he belonged to the wrong family and clan. He did not have the right connections. Twice he had been passed over for promotion. He no longer bothered applying.

Nevertheless he would investigate this murder thoroughly. It would be dangerous not to. Voragine know that he was dealing with dangerous people, about as dangerous as anyone could be. People would be looking for traitors even where none existed. He would follow procedures to the letter. If he did not, he would lose at least his career (which though blighted was all that he had) and perhaps his life as well.

Voragine had been called to the palace around midnight. He interviewed the Klang Arak, an arrogant little toad who had refused him access to any other witnesses. Voragine had been forced to threaten him with a court order even to make him hand over Kyra. He had also been given a written statement, signed by Kyra, confessing her guilt. It gave the same unconvincing story that Kyra still insisted on repeating. The eunuch had also given Voragine a tiny bottle which had been found among Kyra's possessions. Voragine had already had its contents analysed. It did indeed contain perfectari, the poison Athanasia had used. Nevertheless Kyra's story was full of inconsistencies.

It was now late afternoon on the day after the Kzam's death. Voragine looked at Kyra across the table in the interview room. They had been joined by Sergeant Amber Yendys. Kyra appeared tired and drawn, close to exhaustion and pale with fear. Her eyes were puffed up from crying and her hair was untidy. None of this could disguise her beauty. She was without question the most beautiful woman Voragine had ever seen.

Kyra had never felt so alone in her life. Everyone thought she was a traitor, guilty of an abomination. The friends she had made in the seraglio all loathed her now. So universal and intense was their hatred that she had scoured her conscience in case she had done something wrong, but she could genuinely think of nothing. She was going to die on this foreign world and her family would never know what had become of her. She was glad they did not know she was here. They would think she had died a quick death, on the Evening Star.

As it was, Kyra knew she would be impaled if the Kzama did not save her. She had to convince the police that the story in her statement was true.

Kyra was confused. At first Radmilla had blamed her for killing the Kzam. It looked so obvious that Kyra was guilty. Who could possibly believe she was innocent?

Then the Kzama had offered her a way out. If she confessed to using the poison because she thought it would make the Kzam sleep, she would be spared. But she had to sign the statement and make the police believe her, otherwise she would be impaled. But what if Radmilla was wrong? What if the police believed her, and she was executed anyway?

The thought of being debauched and impaled made Kyra sick with fear. She had watched how Athanasia had died. It would be much worse for Kyra. She was a slave. They did not grease the skewer for a slave. Nor would they give her a tug to end it quickly. It might last all day. Kyra was light and slender. For a concubine, that was a very good, but for a condemned woman on the skewer it was terrible. It meant that she would survive longer. Her weight would not be enough to push her down. If she were still alive at sunset, they would club her. The Kzama Radmilla had explained all of this to Kyra.

Radmilla also explained that some victims stayed very still on the skewer, so that it pressed its way upwards only slowly. Others in their torment could not help themselves from writhing about. This made the pain worse, but killed them more quickly. Radmilla asked Kyra which she would do: writhe, or try to keep still?

Kyra was still wondering. Her mind kept returning to the dilemma. She wanted to see her family, her mother especially. More than anything, Kyra wanted to see her mother.

Writhe, or keep still?

Amber squeezed Kyra's hand and gave her a cup of mint tea. Kyra was grateful for the friendly gesture. "Kyra," began Voragine. He liked to use the suspect's name, to appear friendly. "Kyra, this absurd story, this ridiculous fiction, is simply wasting my time." He gestured at Kyra's statement. "I cannot believe you want to be impaled for a crime you did not commit."

Amber squeezed her hand again. "Kyra, please tell Mr Voragine what really happened. He knows you didn't really kill the Kzam. He can help you, but you have to tell him everything."

Kyra looked at Voragine. "I only used a tiny drop of the poison. It was painted on my…skin. I thought it would make master sleep," she said. It was the same explanation she had given a dozen times before.

"I don't believe you for a moment, Kyra. I think you are an honest and truthful young woman. That's why you are such an unconvincing liar. But whatever you've been told, you'd better understand this. For killing the Kzam, even by accident, you'll be impaled. Drugging him would be an assault. For a slave, that means the skewer. Besides which, whoever really killed him will need a scapegoat. Someone's got to be blamed, and right now that's going to be you. And if you take the blame, you will have to be silenced. They can't possibly allow you to live. And when you're executed, it will have to be the skewer. I'm very sorry, but you have to know. Do you understand me?"

Kyra looked from Voragine to Amber. Amber squeezed her hand encouragingly. Should Kyra tell him what Radmilla had told her to say? Or what really happened? She was tired, tired beyond endurance, and afraid.

Writhe, or keep still?

Kyra subsided into tears.

Over the following two hours, Voragine pieced together the story. At first, Kyra herself found it difficult to believe that the Kzama was guilty. She had grown to trust the woman like a second mother. But Voragine was in no doubt, and when she put the pieces together, Kyra knew too.

It's a pity about Kyra, Voragine thought. *She seems a nice girl. Obviously, she'll have to be skewered. She knows too much. What a waste.*

But what if they decided Voragine knew too much now, too? After the first ten minutes, he sent Amber out of the room. There was no point putting her life at risk too. Voragine himself would have to consider his options. He could pretend to believe Kyra's original statement and send her back to the palace. He was not an evil man, but neither was he a hero. He could publicly state everything he knew; but he did not know if it would be believed. He was tired. He needed to sleep. He ordered Kyra returned to her cell. He would decide what to do in the morning.

Despite his exhaustion, Voragine could not sleep that night. When at last he dozed off he was woken again by the buzzing of a videocom. Unwilling to wake up, he tried to force the sound from his mind.

Then he realised it was not his ordinary communicator, but a second, unregistered device which he kept for reasons of his own. Suddenly awake, he switched it to 'accept.'

"Message for Jimmy. This is Perkin," said the voice. Voragine did not reply, but his heart sank. His name was not Jimmy. Jimmy and Perkin were code names intended to confuse anyone who might be listening in. "You've trodden on someone's toes. You investigated the murder too well. It's terminal. I'm sorry."

"How long I have I got?" asked Voragine.

"A day, perhaps," came the reply. "They don't know you've been warned. Goodbye. Good luck."

The call terminated. It was deliberately short, too short to trace. Unlike Michael and Amanda Alba, and Roxana Keswick's parents,

Voragine was a trained and experienced officer in the Intelligence Branch of the police, and had been able to set up an effective early warning system. He had known for years that he might be in danger one day from someone in a position of power, and he had friends who had also felt under threat. Therefore they shared information. If he was right and the Lady Radmilla had killed the Kzam, she was an amateur, but an amateur with very powerful friends. They were also extremely dangerous. They had probably also framed the Imperial Princess, so they would not hesitate to eliminate Voragine, a commoner.

But Voragine had a chance to escape. He had known this might happen, and he had a plan.

Damn the bastards. *Damn the bastards!* He had worked his whole life to serve Ziandakush and this was his reward. Voragine went to a hiding place and retrieved a heavy pouch of cinerium bars. They were worth more than they used to be, but the passage off planet would be costly. Radmilla and her fellow conspirators had already cost him everything he had. They had stolen his career, his security, his worldly goods and his pension. And what could be he take from the Kzamate? Nothing.

No. There was one thing, one thing of theirs he could take. He could go to the police station first, and fetch Kyra. He had the authority to remove her from the headquarters. Why should she be skewered, if he could save her with no additional risk to himself? She was a beauty, a virgin, and trained to serve a Kzam. He was fleeing the Kzamate anyway. If he could reach Imperial territory or a neutral world, he could sell her for a tidy sum. Whoever bought her would look after her. And Voragine could begin a new life with the proceeds.

It was still several hours until sunrise. Voragine went to the intelligence branch first. He sent a sergeant to fetch Kyra and take her to the interview room. He signed to accept responsibility for her. It was best to follow procedures. Then he led the terrified girl outside. She was wearing a knee length khaki dress with short sleeves, and the cool night air outside helped to refresh her despite her obvious exhaustion.

Voragine used his land car. He had the authority to take a police air car but it would arouse suspicion. Besides, some of the people he was going to see were not particularly fond of the police. On the way he explained that he was helping her escape.

Despite her lack of sleep Kyra instantly understood why they were going and why he was helping her. They went to a little used private spaceport, a hundred miles or so from the city. Voragine had already made a number of calls and made the necessary arrangements. It was almost dawn by the time they arrived at the modest cluster of unlit sheds and the plascrete field which comprised the rudimentary spaceport.

Voragine abandoned the car and Kyra hurried to keep up with him. Then in the pale light before dawn, she saw the outline of a small spacegoing vessel on the pad.

Voragine caught sight of the man they were looking for. The two fugitives were shown aboard. They were the only passengers. Kyra expected a long wait, but the doors were closed and the vessel lifted immediately. It was a small vessel. Kyra thought it looked rather old.

The crew did not know why their passengers were fleeing the Kzamate, nor did they care. Voragine had warned Kyra not to mention the Kzam's death. At the Kzama Radmilla's insistence, it was not yet public knowledge. Kyra nodded. She realised the crew were probably involved in some kind of illegal activities, but even they would not dare to help anyone connected with killing the Great Kzam.

No identification was required. Voragine did in fact have two fake identity documents, in the names of Jenkins and Tubod, but he was not required to show them. Naturally Kyra had no papers at all. In the event, the agreed weight in cinerium was the only documentation necessary. It was an expensive trip, Voragine thought, but at least he was not being charged extra to bring Kyra along.

Kyra realised that Voragine knew the ship's captain. The captain seemed respectful to Voragine. He owed the inspector a favour, and

Voragine's contacts with Intelligence were sometimes useful to him. It was an acquaintance they had both cultivated.

Kyra was glad Voragine was with her. She knew he had a pistol. She had seen the way some of the crew looked at her and she suspected they would have had their own plans for her if Voragine was not there to protect her. The captain was particularly frightening, Kyra thought. He was a thickset man, with a shaven head and a gold ring in one ear.

His name was Andreas Pitogo.

Pitogo's vessel was known as the Princess of Atkonium. It was a small ship, capable of landing on a planetary surface. It did not require a shuttle. It was much smaller than the Erebus, which he had used for slave trafficking from Chimaera Bis. Pitogo would not have dared bring the Erebus to Ziandakush during wartime. It was too conspicuous. The Princess was much more discreet.

Alone in their tiny cabin, Kyra made obeisance to Voragine. Then she said, "Master, may I ask a question?"

Voragine grinned. "You can ask," he grinned. "But I'm having the bunk. You can sleep on the floor." He was in a good mood. He felt relief now that they were off Ziandakush. He would feel better still after they had shifted into metaspace and they could no longer be traced.

"I saw your pistol," said Kyra. "If the Kzam's men catch us, what will you do?"

Voragine became serious again. "If the Kzam's men catch us, we're both dead, Kyra. I will kill as many of them as I can, first. I will sell my life dearly."

"And will you… you see, I don't want them to catch me again. Not alive."

Voragine nodded. "I understand. I won't let them catch you. It will be very quick. And only if I think we can't escape."

"Thank you, master."

"Kyra, you seem very courageous. After everything that's happened, how can you be so brave?"

She thought for a moment. “I suppose it’s because I thought I was going to die. I think the rest of my life will seem like a bonus, something I never expected. It hardly seems real. It’s as if I were on the outside of my own body, watching someone else. It’s an adventure.” She smiled, and then tensed as there was a knock on the door. “Shall I open the door, master?”

Voragine stood within easy reach of his pistol, and nodded to her.

It was Pitogo, the captain. He handed Kyra a bag of clothes. “For you,” Pitogo said. “I saw you had no luggage. Some of these might fit.” Kyra took the bag hesitantly, looking at Voragine. “It’s all right,” said Pitogo, and he grinned. It was an ugly grin. “A lady passenger left them on board. It seemed a pity to throw them away.”

23: HELLO AND GOODBYE

Which brings me to my conclusion upon Free Will and Predestination, namely - let the reader mark it - that they are identical.

Sir Winston Churchill: My Early Life.

The Princess of Atkonium shifted out of metaspace somewhere in the vicinity of Hyrcanus IV to take its bearings, before continuing on towards Imperial space. While in normal space they were able to receive news bulletins from Hyrcanus.

Between lengthy interludes of discordant Atkoi funeral dirges, they picked up snippets of news. The Great Kzam, Rurik III had been assassinated. The finger of suspicion pointed to his son Khostrounil, who was denounced as a patricide and regicide and traitor of the worst kind. No stone would be left unturned in the hunt for the Kzam's killers. Rurik's eldest son Ozim had been proclaimed Kzam and anointed by the High Priest. He would travel to Asphodel in the ancient heartland of the Atkoi for his coronation, as soon as more urgent duties had been attended to. In the meantime all of his brothers had been summoned to attend the Great Council. A small group of naval officers and ratings loyal to the traitor had mutinied, and their disloyalty would be punished speedily. A year of official mourning had begun, with most memorial services to be held forty days after the Great Kzam's death.

Voragine read between the lines. Ozim's faction clearly controlled Hyrcanus. 'A small mutiny' must mean a sizeable mutiny. The mutineers had not yet been punished, which meant that Ozim's faction were not yet able to impose their authority everywhere. All of Ozim's brothers and half-brothers were expected to prove their loyalty by coming to

Ziandakush and putting their heads in the noose. If they turned up, they might or might not face execution. If they stayed away, they would certainly be considered enemies. Voragine did not envy their dilemma; it was too similar to his own.

The Princess of Atkonium continued its voyage, shifting out of metaspace near Acheron, then again at Pittacus, then Aegina and then Sibour, within the old Atkoi Kzamate, and then on towards Ozanan, Richmond, and Trebizond, Imperial planets now occupied by the Atkoi. Pitogo had some profitable scheme of business he intended to pursue within what remained of the Empire, and he had agreed to drop Kyra and Voragine on a world that still had regular links with the rest of the Empire, perhaps Pagerie or St Juvenal, if the Kzamate had not yet captured them.

As the weeks passed, Voragine could not help but become fond of Kyra. She had a ready smile and a quick intelligence. Sometimes in conversation she would reach the end of a sentence and smile and flick her head barely perceptibly to one side. Voragine wondered whether she was aware that she did it and whether she knew the effect it had on a man. *Can such gestures be entirely instinctive?* he wondered.

Kyra understood that when they reached one of the prosperous Central Worlds she would be sold to the highest bidder, but Voragine had been correct in his observation that she was facing her future with courage. She asked Voragine once, whether the Imperial authorities might simply return her to the Atkoi as part of a peace deal to appease the new Kzam. Voragine said he thought that was extremely unlikely. But she was not an Imperial citizen, and she could not hope to be freed upon reaching Imperial space, as some of her friends aboard the Evening Star would have been if they were returned to the Empire.

There had been a time when Kyra hoped that she would be rescued and Simon would marry her, but in her heart she realised that Simon was unlikely to want a wife who had been a slave for two years; and worse, the property of an Atkoi, marked with an Atkoi brand. Yet she could not stop herself from hoping. If as seemed most likely she was sold as a slave, her dearest hope was to be bought by a man she could love, a man who would keep her only for himself, forever. She did not want a succession of masters who would each keep her for a few years, tire of her, and then sell her on to successively less discriminating owners, at ever lower prices, until eventually she was little better than a whore, and later perhaps actually a whore. She preferred a swift death to that kind of slavery.

Kyra knew that as a slave she could never become a wife, but she wanted to be as loving and loyal as a wife should be. She was glad Voragine had not chosen to take her virginity. He seemed a kind man, but she knew he did not want to keep her.

Voragine looked at Kyra as she was sleeping. She was beautiful. There was an unsophisticated innocence about her. She did not consciously use her beauty to influence him. She could have been the Kzam's favourite concubine, he thought. And she belonged to him, to Voragine. It was tempting.

If they did manage to reach a safe Imperial planet, Voragine would need money to begin a new life. No one was going to employ an Atkoi ex-policeman. Voragine had nothing. Nothing except Kyra. Her sale, as a virgin, would not perhaps make him wealthy, but it would certainly give him the wherewithal to survive. He could start again.

In retrospect Voragine's life had been a series of wrong decisions, of opportunities missed. He had given the best years of his life to employers who would never promote him and who now wanted him dead. The Atkoi might still board the vessel, and he would lose his life and lose Kyra too. Perhaps he should live each day as it came and simply enjoy the girl while he still had the chance. They could never take that away from him. Life was short. It might be shorter than he imagined.

Suddenly Voragine reached a decision. The girl belonged to him. He wanted her. He deserved her and he would have her. Today. The vessel was due to shift out of metaspace again in less than an hour, at Bajimond. He would be allowed on to the bridge with Kyra, to watch. Afterwards he would take Kyra back to his cabin and take her virginity. He had waited too long already.

Bajimond was a remote, uninhabited system now within Atkoi held space, only eighteen light years from the front line. It was an ideal position from which to cross the frontier, far from any strategic or inhabited worlds, and not in a direct line between Ziandakush and the Central Worlds. No interstellar state or empire could possibly police every square light year of its borders, and Pitogo knew that in a time of war, the Kzam's vessels would be deployed more usefully than patrolling somewhere like Bajimond.

If anything, the Atkoi had probably advanced even further into Imperial space by now, but Pitogo would take no chances. The Princess would verify its position and shift back into metaspace at Bajimond, and then continue to St Juvenal, which they believed to be well within Imperial space. But they would take nothing for granted and approach St Juvenal with extreme caution. Then finally, Kyra and Voragine would be free of the Kzamate: free, and no longer at risk of a horrible death.

Kyra was nervous. Voragine had woken her and told her to come with him to the bridge to see the shift out of metaspace. She sensed something different in his mood, and it made her afraid. She dared not ask what was on his mind, in case that precipitated the very danger she was trying to discover.

Pitogo's first officer was looking at a screen. It portrayed a three dimensional map of this region of space, shaded in different colours representing political allegiances. The Empire was shaded in purple, the Kzamate in green and various independent planets were marked in red, blue and yellow. Five colours were all that were required for a three dimensional map in which no region bordered any other region shaded in the same colour. For a two dimensional map, four colours were sufficient.

The external shutters were open, so they could look out of the duraglass panels directly at the blackness outside. There were no stars visible. “Any second now…” said the officer. Nothing happened. Just when Kyra began to wonder whether the machine had gone wrong, the stars of normal space suddenly appeared.

But something else had also appeared. Pitogo and the first officer looked from one screen to another on what appeared to be a sophisticated monitoring and detection device usually available only to military vessels. For an independent tramp freighter, the Princess of Atkonium was remarkably well equipped. Voragine pretended not to notice the equipment.

Pitogo swore and a number of his crew rushed into action. “Warships”, said Pitogo. “Fifteen of them. They shouldn’t be here. No, sixteen. Dammit, they shouldn’t be here. We’ve dropped into the middle of the whole ruttocking fleet!”

“An Atkoi fleet?” asked Voragine, and instantly wished that his dry throat had not made his voice sound so frightened.

“They’ve seen us,” said the first officer.

Kyra’s blood ran cold.

24: ARMS AND THE MAN

The problem with hereditary rulers is this: a truly great monarch might be followed by a good one, and then an adequate one, and then a fool, and then a dangerous fool, a spendthrift or a murderous tyrant. Nor is democracy the answer: if elections are held every five years, senators will make decisions which benefit the Empire for five years, or at best ten. But long term measures, such as the settlement of new worlds, or a first class defence or education system, or stabilising the currency and paying off the Imperial Debt - measures which require generations to reap any reward - such policies are shunned by elected politicians. They do not win votes. Instead, to buy themselves popularity, they run up huge debts which impoverish future generations.

Itchenor, E.: The Causes and Consequences of the Atkoi War, Vol. 1 (Cornubium University Press: Nenuphar, 3020.)

As if in answer, a voice in Inglic made itself heard over the ship's outercom.

"Hailing unknown vessel at 323.623.888." The first officer glanced at a screen. That was indeed their location. "This is the Imperial flagship, Emperor Otto. State your name and registration number. Do not attempt to activate your weapon systems. Do not begin procedures to enter metaspace. You are locked into our targeting system."

The threat was needless. For the Princess to fire upon a military vessel would have been suicidal. Instead, Pitogo recited a series of numbers and gave his vessel's name as The Princess of Nenuphar.

There was a long pause. Kyra looked at her master. Voragine looked strained. He was naturally relieved that the vessels were not Atkoi, but he could not help but feel nervous.

Then they heard the reply: "That registration number and name does not match with your radiation trail. We believe you to be the Princess of Ascham, registered in Ascham. As an Atkoi vessel, you will be boarded and searched. We believe you to be carrying two passengers of interest to us: an escaped concubine who belonged to the late Kzam, and her accomplice named Voragine. These individuals will be handed over to us alive and unharmed, or you will be held personally responsible."

Pitogo did not bother denying the accusation. A ship's radiation trail was as unique as a human fingerprint, and he had indeed registered the vessel on Ascham once. Pitogo, his crew, Voragine and Kyra waited for the boarding party.

Kyra never saw Voragine again after they were transferred to the Emperor Otto. He was interrogated and eventually freed. Pitogo and his crew, suspected of smuggling cinerium into the Kzamate, were summarily hanged.

Kyra herself was interviewed at considerable length about the death of the Kzam, his plans, the actions and ambitions of the Kzama, and about Ozim, Ozart and various other sons of the Kzam. She was made to repeat her story several times, in increasing detail. The interviewers were not unkind; indeed one officer, a certain Lieutenant Ruby Aguilar of the Imperial Intelligence Bureau, became quite friendly. Some of what Kyra said confirmed suspicions which Intelligence already held. Some of it was mere gossip or hearsay, but even gossip can be revealing.

Kyra was taken to see Admiral Bazan the next day. He seemed very intelligent, confident of victory and determined, but not without compassion.

As a slave taken from an enemy vessel, Kyra knew she was legally state property. Naval regulations stated that, 'Captured enemy property of no military or strategic use shall be disposed of at market value to defray the costs of war.' But allowances could be made for the fiancée of an Imperial citizen, Lieutenant Aguilar said. She promised to contact Simon Ozwald on Kyra's behalf.

On Ziandakush, Ozim was now called the Great Kzam. But Ozim was not his father.

Worlds which had been independent under their own Kzams before Rurik had unified the Atkoi now declared themselves sovereign once more, and Ozim could not spare the resources to demand fealty by force.

More seriously still, the Kzam's son Khostrounil had also declared himself Great Kzam. He had the support of a substantial section of the Navy, who considered him the natural successor to Rurik. It was rumoured that Rurik had been about to name Khostrounil as his successor when he was killed, or that he had already named Khostrounil as his heir but the Kzama Radmilla had destroyed her husband's will.

Several of the Kzam's other sons, not daring or not choosing to attend the Great Council at which the new Kzam was to be appointed, had effectively sided with Khostrounil, although one of his half-brothers, Ostik, a popular and successful naval commander, had declared himself Kzam of his own fiefdom.

If Khostrounil could remove Ozim and Ozart from the equation, he could become undisputed Kzam of All the Atkoi. He would have to act quickly, before the Imperials could take advantage of this fraternal conflict. A sudden, decisive blow against his rival at Ziandakush could destroy Ozim, Ozart and all who were loyal to them. Then he could turn his attention back to the Empire, and in particular to dealing with the Imperial fleet which was even now wreaking devastation throughout the Atkoi worlds.

Ziandakush was well defended. Khostrounil knew only too well about its defences. That made him all the more certain that Ozim would wait for him there. Khostrounil's warships outnumbered Ozim's. It would make sense for Ozim to fight on his home ground.

Private (Third Class) Artur Thrux of the 4044th Light Armoured Division was still trying to pluck up sufficient courage to desert from his unit, when it surrendered en masse and he was taken prisoner.

The Imperial Fleet had crossed into Atkoi held space near the remote uninhabited system of Bajimond and proceeded to the world of Ctesiphon, now occupied by the Atkoi. They attacked without warning.

Ctesiphon was defended only by the 4044th, which was composed of riffraff recruited on Akkadis and neighbouring worlds. Any man in the 4044th who was not entirely incompetent had already been transferred to other units. The remainder were of little use to the Kzamate except for their nuisance value.

Artur Thrux had now served with the 4044th on several planets. He had soon found that his worst fears about military life had been well founded. His sympathy for the Atkoi cause was greatly diminished after he had met Atkoi officers to whom his relationship to an Akkadisi senator meant absolutely nothing and who expected him to risk his life for their war effort. The one consolation which military life offered was the use of the 'honeypot,' the military brothel attached to each sizeable garrison for the use of its men. One of his favourites was a girl called Emily, from New Wessex, another of the newly conquered planets.

As the Imperial ground troops swept across the main inhabited continent of Ctesiphon, it was clear that the 4044th was losing too many men to hold out for long. These losses were due chiefly not to enemy action, but to desertion.

If only Thrux had been possessed of a little more courage, he would already have fled to the hills as many of his brothers in arms had already done. As it transpired, he was still debating the possible consequences when the 4044th surrendered. It gained the distinction of becoming the first Atkoi division to surrender *en masse*, with hardly a shot being fired. Bazan was delighted with this easy victory. It would help to improve the Imperials' morale.

Thrux was taken prisoner and charged with aggravated rape. Emily had identified him as one of her most spiteful tormentors, and Thrux feared the worst – either hanging, or detention with hard labour on Niflheim. For the first time in his life, he felt alone. Danielz, Stobbins and Ottinger were incarcerated somewhere in the same detention barracks, but were no longer on friendly terms with Thrux. The Senator's nephew now had neither money nor influence.

From Ctesiphon, the Imperial Fleet proceeded on to attack Chirbuliez, and then doubled back on itself and turned its fire on Sibour. These were both Atkoi planets and major industrial centres, and the Admiral had expected them to be defended forcefully. They were not. Bazan had suspected an ambush, a trap, but there was none. He was puzzled by this apparent negligence on the enemy's part, but grateful for it. Chirbuliez and Sibour were both blasted without mercy.

He ordered the fleet to continue to Atkonium, the original Atkoi home world.

Three weeks later, a pall of smoke hung over the burning ruins of all the cities in Atkonium's developed western continent. Half a billion of the planet's inhabitants were dead. The great industrial complexes, whole groups of cities, were gone now. The shipyards, the naval bases and manufacturing centres were now dust blowing in the wind. Even the temple which had stood on the very site where the prophet Tiodor was martyred and where Milos had later preached, had been blasted. To rebuild Atkonium would be the work of centuries.

Bazan watched from orbit as a ball of light streaked through the planet's atmosphere before crashing to the ground. It was a ruined Atkoi warship. He was puzzled, as well as elated. Why had Atkonium not been better defended? They must have known for weeks the Imperial Fleet would come.

Most of his men were simply relieved and happy to celebrate a victory. Many rejoiced at the destruction they had wrought. It was revenge for New Wessex, Canaris, Bonchamp, Nenuphar, and a dozen other outrages. He had heard men say the Atkoi were vermin who deserved everything they got.

But Bazan himself did not relish human suffering. What he did, he did for a purpose. What had been done to Atkonium this day could not be ignored. Whoever aspired to be the Great Kzam would have to come now, and face the Imperial Fleet. A sizeable part of the enemy force would have to leave Imperial space. Bazan's squadrons would scatter now, and ravage Sirmium, Mitylene, Irigoyen, Papegaai and a dozen other worlds. The Atkoi heartlands would be laid waste. Then the Fleet would gather again, in time to face the Atkoi at a place of Bazan's choosing.

That place would be Ziandakush.

On Old Earth, the Chancellor was overseeing arrangements for the wedding and coronation of Admiral Bazan and Lady Demetra Prendergast. The Admiral had insisted on a joint coronation. He had demanded to be an Emperor and not merely a consort, and Arbuthnot-Samar and the cabinet had conceded. Their own positions depended on keeping Bazan's goodwill. The nuptials would be celebrated on Tolon, closer to Bazan's temporary headquarters. The Arch Patriarch himself would travel there from his seat in New Jerusalem to perform the ceremony.

Demetra was both pretty and intelligent, although her intellect did not equal his own, Bazan knew. She was ambitious to be Empress, but she had few plans for what to do when she attained it.

Bazan, though, had many plans. When the Atkoi were defeated, a wave of relief and gratitude would sweep through the Empire. Despite what Arbuthnot-Samar had said, gratitude was a short lived virtue. It would not last long, but it would be enough, and Bazan would seize it with the same resolve he would seize a strategic advantage in battle.

He would allow many more planets to be represented in the Senate. He would extend citizenship to billions more individuals – those who had fought in the war and those who instead paid a sizeable indemnity.

He would pay off the Imperial debt and cut taxes. He would abolish the citizens' allowance and instead offer poorer citizens free passage and land on newly settled worlds. For the first time in two centuries a programme of exploration and settlement of new worlds would be promoted.

Bazan intended his rule of the Empire to last, and not merely for his lifetime alone. He would found a dynasty, and pass the crown on to his descendants. Marriage to Demetra would give it legitimacy. Perhaps he would even retain the name of Prendergast, in conjunction with his own: The Prendergast-Bazan Dynasty. Or better still, Bazan-Prendergast.

The first step would be to appoint new senators, loyal men who deserved reward, to secure his position. He had no intention of becoming a dictator. The Empire had always been a constitutional monarchy, to some extent. He would retain its best traditions and improve upon them. There would be a balance of elected, appointed and hereditary power.

But to be an enduring dynasty, it must never be allowed to grow weak, as the Prendergasts had. Like all Emperors, Bazan would have a seraglio, and concubines. Demetra would understand that, raised as she was in the palace. But Bazan would take it a step further. He would insist on complete freedom to choose which of his sons should inherit the throne. Emperors were mortal, but a dynasty which could always provide a competent heir could rule indefinitely.

Some of Aethelstan's concubines had not been slaves at all, but the daughters of noblemen given to him to cement their families' links with the throne. It was considered a good match for the daughter of a duke or an earl. It was a practice Bazan would encourage. It would enhance his own position too.

The admiral wondered whether any of the girls who belonged to him would be as beautiful and vivacious as the girl Kyra, recently captured from the Atkoi vessel.

On Ziandakush, the Kzama Mother Radmilla waited. She had told Ozim to gather all his forces together there. Khostrounil could not afford a lengthy war. He would want to finish it quickly and turn his attention to the Imperial threat. Ozim could afford to ignore the Empire until Khostrounil was defeated.

It was a pity she had been obliged to use Kyra to get rid of Rurik, but it had been an emergency. Radmilla knew she should have acted sooner, before Khostrounil became so popular. Kyra would have made an excellent diversion for Ozim. She was vivacious and beautiful. She would have diverted Ozim's thoughts from the military situation. Simply waiting on Ziandakush for an enemy to arrive was wearing his nerves to breaking point. He bored easily of his slave girls and turned to cruelty.

Prince Ozim was responsible for the death of one of his concubines in the last few weeks alone. The girl's name was Tamara. Ozim had lost his temper with Tamara over some trivial matter and flogged her senseless. She had not recovered. It was hardly surprising that the girls of his seraglio lived in terror of him and his unpredictable moods.

While Rurik was still alive, Lord Verga, the head of one of the most respected families in the Kzamate, had refused to give his niece in marriage to Prince Ozim. He should have been honoured and delighted at such a proposed union. His excuse had been that the girl was unwell. No one believed that. Their scepticism had been proved well founded a few months later when the girl had been given to a son of the Cabilla family. Ozim had wanted both the Vergas and the Cabillas punished, but Radmilla had urged restraint. If the matter became public, it would be embarrassing at best, and at worst the Kzam would have enquired why his son had been refused.

But Rurik was dead now. There was no longer any risk that he might disinherit Ozim. But Radmilla and her sons' troubles were far from over. Without Rurik's forceful personality holding the Atkoi together, tribal differences were beginning to be felt. When word of what had happened at Atkonium spread, every local kzam and satrap wanted his own home planet or territory protected. That was simply not possible at present. Ziandakush must be defended, at least until Khostrounil arrived. When the Baratkoi threatened to withdraw their support for Ozim, he had agreed to send a force to protect Asphodel. It would deter Bazan from attacking, but it also weakened Ziandakush.

The Baratkoi would be punished later for their disloyalty. But first they would deal with Khostrounil. They would not have to look for him. He would come to them, to Ziandakush. He would have to, to make good his claim to be Kzam of All the Atkoi. And when he came, he would find a surprise waiting for him.

A very unwelcome surprise.

25: DOUBLE JEOPARDY

Study the actions of illustrious men... examine the causes of their victories and defeats... as Alexander imitated Achilles and Caesar imitated Alexander.

Niccolo Machiavelli: The Prince.

The tide of war had turned. With each passing week, the oiku were gaining more ground. The Imperials were recapturing planets which Rurik had conquered, and spreading destruction through the Atkoi home worlds. Khostrounil would have to make a sudden, decisive strike to destroy Ozim. Only then could he give the Empire his undivided attention.

Khostrounil knew what warships Ozim commanded and what defences Ziandakush had, but he was no fool. He did not ignore the possibility of a trap. He divided his force into two waves. The first would weaken the enemy and discover the positions of Ozim's warships and defences. Then at the decisive moment the second wave would appear to deliver the final blow. Khostrounil would himself command the first wave.

Ozim was fighting on his home ground. Khostrounil's fleet would face hostile fire not only from Ozim's ships but from arrays of weapon systems based on the moons and planets of the Ziandakush system. They were automated and programmed to detect and destroy enemy warships. No doubt they were reprogrammed now, to fire on Khostrounil's fleet. There were more weapons systems on unmanned space stations, above and below the plane of the solar system. The most extensive batteries of weapons were concentrated in an asteroid belt near Ziandakush itself, and on a tiny moon of Ziandakush named Nicias, in reality itself a captured asteroid. There were also weapons on the surface of Ziandakush, but their effectiveness was diminished by the planet's atmosphere, which tended to refract and diffuse the beams of neutrino fire.

Khostrounil's fleet shifted out of metaspace on the fringes of the solar system and headed towards Ziandakush itself. They exchanged fire with several weapons arrays, although the intensity of fire was less than Khostrounil had anticipated. Ozim must be holding back something in reserve, he thought.

Three hours later, Ozim's fleet met theirs. The firing intensified. Khostrounil realised that something was terribly wrong. The enemy fire was too intense. A sudden burst of light, followed immediately by a second burst, told him that his own vessel had been hit. A screen indicated that several of his ships were under attack. The Kzam Zimisces had been destroyed. The Avenger of Odenathus was seriously hit.

Khostrounil knew what Ozim had done. He could not have conjured up more warships out of empty space. Most of the enemy fire was coming from the asteroid belt. Every weapon system from every Atkoi world under Ozim's command had been plundered and brought to Ziandakush. No wonder the Imperials had wrought such destruction and suffered so few losses. Ozim had stripped the Atkoi of their defences and left them naked and unarmed to face the oikus' revenge.

A billion of our people died so that Ozim's worthless hide could be kept safe, Khostrounil thought bitterly. *But those innocents will have justice.* It was yet another reason to win this battle. He would expose Ozim and Radmilla for what they had done. They would be impaled as traitors.

Two more of Khostrounil's vessels disappeared from the screen. He could not afford to sustain such losses. Few of Ozim's own warships had even been identified, and none destroyed. He was holding them in reserve. But Khostrounil had come too far to retreat. If he ordered a withdrawal now, the enemy would be picking them off for hours before they could reach the edge of the solar system and shift into metaspace.

What would my father have done? Khostrounil wondered. *He would never have given up, of that I am certain. He would have analysed the information available, planned the best course of action possible, and executed the plan forcefully. And that is what I shall do. I can still win this battle. One by one the enemy batteries are being destroyed.*

Khostrounil gave the signal for his second wave to begin the attack.

There was a flash of light so bright it was visible through the observation window as well as the screens. Another of Khostrounil's ships, the Kzam Sesostris II, had been destroyed. Khostrounil's beloved brother Aradunil had been aboard it.

There would be a time for grieving, later. Khostrounil realised it was an hour since the first weapons had been fired. His losses were worse than he had thought possible, but there were fewer weapons being fired at them now. More than half the enemy targets had been destroyed, and the second wave of Khostrounil's attack force was due to arrive.

There was a blaze of light and Khostrounil knew his flagship had been hit again. A screen gave a status report. The hull had not been compromised, but if they suffered another such blast it could open up the vessel. If that happened, several decks would automatically be sealed off. They were being evacuated now. His men knew what to do. Even before the warning signals finished piping their alert, Khostrounil read another status report. One of his other vessels had not been so fortunate. It was now a lifeless shell of twisted fibresteel.

The second wave of Khostrounil's attack force arrived and almost immediately, another enemy array was destroyed. The balance was beginning to tilt in Khostrounil's favour. Ozim must have realised it too. His fleet, which he had held mostly in reserve, now suddenly appeared, firing with all weapons. It was no ambush, though. They were fighting to survive. Within seconds Khostrounil saw two enemy vessels destroyed. The surface based weapons were also beginning to disappear from the screens. Khostrounil knew it was only a matter of time before all the arrays were destroyed. But in that time he would suffer more losses.

The weapons arrays could not be overruled. Ozim had insisted on that. Once deployed, neither human weakness nor treachery could be allowed to silence his guns. They would continue firing until either every plasma cannon or every one of Khostrounil's ships was destroyed.

But Ozim was losing the battle now. As another of his ships was torn apart, his own vessel, the Rurik Triumphant, began to accelerate away from Khostrounil's fleet. Within seconds, all of Ozim's fleet began heading away from Ziandakush's sun. *Fifteen.* Ozim had fifteen ships remaining. Even as Khostrounil watched the screen one of them flared and disappeared. *Fourteen.* Khostrounil gave the signal to follow the fleeing vessels.

They pursued the enemy, damaging several ships before the remnants of Ozim's fleet shifted into metaspace. Khostrounil could not follow them there, not without knowing their flight coordinates.

It did not matter. Ozim was defeated. He could never be Kzam now. He had nowhere to hide. No Atkoi governor or satrap would dare shelter him. Soon, his remaining men would begin to desert or even mutiny.

Relief overwhelmed Khostrounil. He was the undisputed Great Kzam now. He controlled Ziandakush. The High Priest would realise his error and proclaim Khostrounil the true Kzam. Robotic probes could dismantle the remaining weapons arrays and reprogram them. The fleet had suffered heavy losses, but not catastrophic ones. Some of the weapons arrays might even be repairable. It would not be easy, but they would have a good chance of defeating the Imperials. Khostrounil merely needed a breathing space, a brief respite in which to make repairs and gather reinforcements. The oiku Admiral Bazan was probably still a hundred light years away. When Bazan arrived at Ziandakush, he would find Khostrounil ready and waiting.

But Khostrounil, Great Kzam of All the Atkoi, did not get his breathing space. At that very moment the Imperial fleet was waiting a little beyond sensor range, but close enough to detect the blasts of plasma fire and exploding warships.

Two hours after the last blasts of Ozim's and Khostrounil's exchange of fire had faded, the Imperial Fleet hove into range, firing with all weapons.

26: DEAD MAN WALKING

In time, a successful terrorist becomes a statesman.
Morris West

Khostrounil was defeated and captured. Ozim had fled. The war was not yet over, but the Kzamate was fragmenting. Several planetary and provincial satraps had already declared themselves independent Kzams. Some sought to make peace with the Empire. Others continued to fight.

The Vengeance Is Mine, which had attacked, pillaged and destroyed the Evening Star, also continued to fight. Its crew called themselves the Ziandan Navy. The Ziandan Navy had several vessels and they owed allegiance to a faction called the Ziandan People's Front. Commander Bual, the captain of the Vengeance, was a leading member of the Front.

Bual knew that now was the time for talking. The tide of war had turned, but the Empire was still weak from its losses and the Ziandan Navy could still pose a serious nuisance. Both sides wanted peace. Now would be an excellent time to negotiate a settlement.

Bual himself accepted an invitation to attend a peace conference on Tolon, with the aim of achieving Atkoi rule on Selimpono, or Zianda. There were those in the Empire, especially among the Centralists, who held some sympathy for Bual. He was charming, articulate and charismatic. They considered him a heroic maverick, a likeable rogue. He left the Vengeance to fight on, leaving Toltok in command.

The Vengeance was involved in a brief exchange of fire with an Imperial warship in the uninhabited Artaxerxes solar system in the Anaximander

Province. It sustained several glancing blows in succession, followed by two direct hits which wrecked the propulsion and communication systems and penetrated the hull. Captain Toltok, Krull, Boolg, Smales, Dunlow, Wilson and most of the rest of the crew including two borbods survived the blasts but were obliged to retreat to a small sealed section of the Vengeance.

They did not fear pursuit. The reactor drive had shut itself down automatically, to prevent catastrophic failure. The Vengeance would therefore leave no radiation trail, and the Imperial vessel wasted little time searching for the tiny vessel before leaving the vicinity.

Although their accommodation was uncomfortably crowded, the heating system and water and atmospheric recycling could continue for a year if necessary. The food could last months, although there was very little nourishment suited to the metabolism of the two borbods.

But Toltok knew that the reactor drive and communication systems were beyond repair. At sublight speeds it would take them several centuries to reach the nearest settlement, and they could not signal for help.

He wondered how he was going to tell the crew.

Artur Thrux had been sentenced to incarceration for life on Niflheim.

It was called a life sentence, but it was really a death sentence. That was the only sentence there was, for those condemned to Niflheim.

Deep beneath the surface of the planet, Artur Thrux lay awake in his dormitory. He was wondering, perhaps for the ten thousandth time, how long he would live. He knew it would not be much longer.

Radiation affected people differently. Some prisoners lived longer than others. There were men still alive in the Niflheim Imperial Criminal Correction Facility Number One who had been there for years. One man in Thrux's dormitory, a convicted killer named Peller, had been sent to Niflheim seven years earlier. He was still alive, if 'alive' was the correct term for the walking, skeletal mass of weeping sores that he now was. Thrux wished Peller would hurry up and die. He hated the sight of the festering lesions which covered Peller's face and body, and he hated Peller's incessant screaming when he woke in the night.

Thrux had been found guilty and condemned to hard labour on Niflheim. He had begged and pleaded for mercy. He had said he was really a victim. He had not chosen to go to war. He had been conscripted. He had offered to turn state witness and testify against others. He would have said anything and done anything to get a more lenient sentence.

It was all to no avail. Thrux was sent to Niflheim to operate the machines which cut the precious ore from the ground and pulverised it and loaded it ready to be transported. The supervisors, mining engineers and warders made only brief visits to the surface, wearing cumbersome protective suits. Robots did some of the work, but they were expensive and in short supply and even they did not last long on Niflheim. The radiation scrambled their circuits. It was the convicts who did most of the work.

The ore which Thrux helped to extract was transported to Batteau, a tiny moon where it was partially refined. Then the cinerium and other superheavy metals were ferried to Tolon, where the processing was completed.

Thrux looked up at the ceiling. It was late, and his eyes were accustomed to the dark, so he could see the ghostly pale glow of the solid rock a few feet above him. It was never entirely dark on Niflheim, even in the dead of night. The radiation was always there.

Thrux had been on Niflheim for six months. He had heard that Danielz was already dead, somewhere else in the facility. The news had shocked him, not because he felt any compassion for his erstwhile friend but because Danielz's death made Thrux's own demise seem more immediate. He felt the taste of blood on his lips. He knew his skin was beginning to decay, like Peller's. He had first noticed the signs a month ago.

Thrux wondered if he would outlive Peller.

27: BEST SERVED COLD

Woe to the vanquished.
Livy, History V: 48

Amanda, Honeysuckle and Thomas Alba sat in the front row of the first class enclosure of the Arena in Akkad City. It was an expensive show, but Amanda felt that her family deserved a treat.

There had been many changes on Akkadis. On that terrible, glorious night when the Atkoi War had begun and Gumbo and Mrs Carno had been killed, Amanda had fled from the burning ruins of Akkad City, concealing herself in the streams of tired, frightened refugees.

She had pretended to be searching for her husband, and she drew no attention to herself and aroused no suspicion. She paid an absurdly high price for a very old landcar and some new power cells. Having retrieved the money she and Michael had hidden, and the cinerium Mrs Carno had buried in the woods, she felt she could afford it.

In the hills outside the city are woodlands where she had holidayed with Michael and the children in happier times. There she hid the bulk of the money before continuing on her journey. She rented modest accommodation in a town a hundred miles from Akkad, and it was there that Amanda's baby was born, a healthy girl.

Amanda hoped that the Atkoi invasion, as it had turned out to be, might provide an opportunity to rescue Honeysuckle and Tom. It did not. There was a purge, and those senators and oligarchs considered sympathetic to the Empire were removed and executed, but it did not help Amanda's cause.

Amanda considered the possibility of hiring someone to kidnap Tom and Honey and bring them to safety, but she did not know who to ask. She had trusted Seb Nargal, and he had betrayed them. She could think of no one she could trust and who would be able to help. Honey had become quite friendly with Mrs Grant, who they believed was a lawyer, but Amanda did not know how to contact her. There were no lawyers of that name in Akkad City. It was hardly surprising that the woman had chosen to use a false name.

Then the Great Kzam was killed and the Atkoi began fighting among themselves. The force occupying Akkadis was mostly withdrawn to reinforce Tolon, leaving only a small garrison. The Akkadisi rose up in rebellion and appealed to the Empire for help.

The Empire did not help, but the Atkoi garrison was defeated anyway. They were mostly conscripts from another occupied world. In a frenzy of retribution, the Akkadisi turned on anyone suspected of collaboration or Atkoi sympathies. In a second series of purges, oligarchs, senators, government officials and politicians were killed, proscribed or simply disappeared. Senator Thrux was one of them. Viktor Quindigan was another.

The new oligarchs and senators were as corrupt as the old ones. They reflected the general mood on Akkadis though – a natural hatred for the Kzamate, but also a mistrust and contempt for the Empire, which had failed to protect Akkadis from the Kzam and failed even to help the Akkadisi to liberate themselves from the army of occupation.

Then Amanda saw a picture of Mrs Grant on an infochannel. She found it quite by accident. She studied it carefully. It was definitely the same woman, she decided. Her real name was Mara Plazak, and she was seeking selection as the Reform Party candidate for Attorney General of Akkadis. For that, she would need money, Amanda knew. Michael had sometimes spoken of such things. Amanda was a wealthy woman, now.

She was richer than anyone in the Alba family had ever been. Perhaps they could help each other.

Amanda knew that to approach Miss Plazak would be very risky. She might easily betray Amanda to the authorities and keep the money for herself. But Tom and Honeysuckle could be suffering untold horrors every day, and Amanda had no prospect of freeing them in any other way. Amanda took the chance.

Miss Plazak was initially surprised by Amanda's approach, but she listened to what Amanda had to say and after some consideration she agreed to help. Amanda asked for the writ of proscription against her family to be rescinded, and for the Carnos to be denounced as traitors instead. In return Amanda gave Miss Plazak what she most needed: sufficient funds to persuade several oligarchs to back her campaign to become Attorney General.

It took a significant part of Amanda's new found wealth, but she achieved what she wanted. Amanda, Honeysuckle and Thomas were legally freed. Alicia Carno was proscribed, sold into slavery and her property sold by public tender. Amanda purchased Akkadis Leisure and claimed back her old family home. She rescued Tom's five babies from Seven Fountains and freed Aimee, Ana and Roxana as soon as it was possible to do so. There was, of course, no such place as Happy Valley Farm.

Roxana had taken Mr Bolventor's advice to heart: she could never return to her old life. Instead she began work at the Maidens of Nenuphar, where there was a vacancy for a deputy manager. Amanda needed a replacement for Ronika.

Amanda had not forgotten Ronika's treachery. Ronika had taken Amanda's money, promised to help her escape and then left her to the mercy of the Commission for Public Safety. Ronika was not a freedwoman like Mrs Knott. She was a slave. She belonged to Akkadis Leisure, and Akkadis Leisure belonged to Amanda.

Ronika was sent to die in the Arena. She was to feature in a brief but entertaining performance which Amanda had arranged.

The Albas, mother, son and daughter, all watched the show. It featured a zebra. Amanda knew the stripes were only painted on, but it was superbly done; very realistic, she thought. She personally thanked Mr Smirke afterwards. He seemed genuinely pleased by her compliments. Ronika herself had made a dreadful fuss, Amanda thought. She screamed, squawked and wriggled throughout the show, but she survived for well over fifteen minutes.

28: THE UPSIDE DOWN GIRLS

The Attorney General's office has confirmed that no further investigations will be made into the disappearance of Dr Sebastian Nargal, who was reported missing six weeks ago. Miss Plazak is quoted as saying that she will reopen the case only if new evidence or useful leads emerge....

Akkad City Infochannel News

April Parsons emerged terrified onto the brightly lit platform of the auction room at the Rose Garden. On three sides, the tiered seats were crowded with men and a few women, scrutinising her. April quailed. Like all the girls sold at auction she wore only a very short white skirt which left her thighs bare, and a cropped bolero top which did not close at the front. Each garment bore the badge of the Rose Garden. She was blonde and pretty, tall and slender, with an attractive figure. She should easily reach the reserve price, thought the auctioneer.

"Lot Ten," he announced. "April, aged twenty. Imperial, from New Wessex. Daughter of a public official, and well educated. Trained pleasure slave."

April wished the man had not mentioned that last detail. She wanted to be bought by a nice family who wanted a maid or a cook or a childminder. Why did he have to tell everyone she was trained as a pleasure slave? People would not understand that she was really a good girl, from a good family.

When April was first seized from her home on New Wessex, she had been possibly a little more fortunate than most of her companions.

April and about sixty other girls had been sent to serve in the honeypots attached to the Atkoi units occupying the planet Tura. They were all branded with the bar and circle mark which would proclaim them forever not merely as slaves, but as property of the Kzamate Ministry of War, and as women who had belonged to Atkoi men.

But April was chosen by a senior officer for his own exclusive use. She was blonde, with a very pretty face and good figure, and it was hardly surprising that she had caught his eye. She became, in effect, his personal slave and concubine.

Then after seven months some new recruits arrived for the honeypot, and the officer, who had tired of April, chose a new girl. April was returned to the honeypot to serve as the common plaything of any of the Atkoi soldiers who chose her for their entertainment.

Eventually, the rumours began. Secretly the girls exchanged snippets of information they had overheard or been told. Some said that the Atkoi were now losing the war. Others said the Great Kzam was dead. They had no way of knowing whether the rumours were true or merely the wishful thinking of those who repeated them, but the girls could not help but hope that soon they might be set free.

Then suddenly, the Atkoi divisions occupying Tura were ordered to evacuate the planet immediately, to go to reinforce Chimaera Bis. The girls themselves would not accompany the military. Transport was in very short supply.

But their relief soon turned to dismay. They would not be set free. They would be 'disposed of.' April, together with thirty or so other girls including her cousins Chloe and Zoe, were sold to a private dealer who transported them offworld.

Their journey was a waking nightmare. They were confined naked and pressed together in a freight container no bigger than April's bedroom back home on New Wessex, and allowed out only briefly each day to be fed, watered and exercised and to relieve themselves. Six weeks later they landed on Akkadis, where they were sold to Igor Bleeny, the owner of the Rose Garden slave market.

The Atkoi were gone and Akkadis was independent again, but even when the war ended the girls would be beyond the reach of the Empire. They could not expect to be freed. April despaired of ever returning home.

Igor Bleeny was having a good war. The Rose Garden continued to prosper. When Akkadis regained its independence, Bleeny had reintroduced the ancient practice of branding slave girls upside down. They were strapped, naked and spread eagled on the huge wheel which was fixed upright in the courtyard of his establishment. The wheel was rotated until the girl was upside down, and then the brand was applied.

Frequently, these were Imperial girls. In the aftermath of the war many captive Imperial women turned up in the slave markets of independent worlds. On Akkadis, there was little sympathy for them or for the Empire in general. There were even several new pleasure houses specialising in Imperial girls. One, called The Upside Down Girls, was filled exclusively with girls who had been branded on the Rose Garden wheel. Another, known as Seen But Not Heard, was stocked entirely with mute pleasure slaves, girls whose vocal chords had been surgically removed.

But April Parsons and her companions from New Wessex were not put on the wheel. They already bore the bar and circle mark which identified all of the Great Kzam's property, and it was not the usual practice on Akkadis to brand a slave girl twice. Instead they were simply microchipped, tattooed with a slavemark on their wrists and prepared for auction.

The bidding began at six thousand solidi. April saw several buyers gesture with their hands or paper catalogues as the bids increased to seven thousand. Soon, one of those men would own her, April thought with dismay. In the second row there was even a woman bidding, a smartly dressed lady possibly in her late thirties, accompanied by two younger women. *I hope she buys me,* thought April. *I don't want to belong to a man again. Please God, not that again!* The lady looked beautiful, but rather strict and severe, April thought.

The lady conferred with her companions and made another bid. Seven thousand, five hundred solidi. There was a pause, and then April heard the tap of the gavel. She had been sold.

"Sold!" saw the auctioneer, "for seven thousand five hundred solidi, to Akkadis Leisure." April looked at the lady, but the lady did not seem to see her. She was already looking at her catalogue, at the particulars of lots still to be sold. April was led away. She passed Zoe, who was led onto the platform.

April collapsed shaking on a bench in the holding room. What could Akkadis Leisure be? Some of the buyers had very strange names, like Yelps and Love Bunnies and Entertainment Unlimited and The Upside Down Girls and Seen But Not Heard. But at least she had been bought by a lady. That must be a good sign.

The lady from Akkadis Leisure was in fact none other than its new owner, Amanda Alba. She was accompanied by Honey and Roxana. Amanda had soon realised that the Akkadis Leisure pleasure houses had been mismanaged, or rather hardly managed at all, under Alicia's ownership. She had expected the company to provide an income without any effort on her own part. Amanda decided to attend the Rose Garden herself, to restock her pleasure houses. She wanted Akkadis Leisure to provide its clientele with a little more variety. It had been losing custom to rivals like Top Heavy and Seen But Not Heard. The company needed to adapt, to change with the times.

The girl April was a good purchase. The gentlemen would like her. She was ideal for what Amanda had in mind.

The next girl, named Zoe, looked frightened. *She should be,* Amanda thought. Slave prices were lower than they had been for years and private demand was weak, but the pleasure houses were still buying. She was very pretty though, slender and blonde.

Amanda made a bid of seven thousand. She felt no pity for the girl. Her experiences had hardened her. Amanda was intensely loyal to her family and her friends, but felt only loathing for the Empire whose machinations had brought death and unbearable suffering to her family. Amanda was no longer a Reformer. She was an Akkadisi, and she could never be anything else.

Seven thousand, two hundred and fifty solidi. The auctioneer tapped his gavel. Zoe belonged to Akkadis Leisure now.

At least I've been bought by the same woman as April, Zoe thought. *At least I'll know someone in this terrible, alien place. I hope she buys Chloe too. Maybe she's a kind woman. Maybe she'll buy us both to keep us together. There must be some good people, even in this place.*

Zoe was taken to the holding room. Her twin sister, Chloe, was Lot 12. Chloe was indeed bought by Akkadis Leisure, though not as an act of kindness as Zoe had hoped. The twins, together with April, were destined for the Maidens of Nenuphar where they would be used as pleasure slaves. There were already a number of Imperial girls at the Maidens, including Abi and Trixi, the sisters from Chimaera Bis who were already proving popular with the gentlemen.

Abi and Trixi were now aged twenty-one and twenty respectively. They had arrived at the Maidens not long after the war began. Both sisters had been very shy and utterly dismayed to find themselves sold to a brothel. They had found it difficult to cooperate, but Bowser had dealt with the problem quickly and decisively, with his rattan. Bowser was more than capable of dealing with any such foolishness. Amanda had given him a pay rise.

After that, Abi and Trixi were each punished only for the shortcomings of the other. When Trixi failed to meet her earnings target, Abi was put on the saddle. Trixi merely had to watch. And when Trixi was accused of discourtesy because she had hesitated when Mr Granicus told her to lick his manhood clean, it was Abi who was caned. It had proved a very effective system.

Amanda, Honeysuckle and Roxana stood to leave the slave market.

There was one girl in the holding room who was more lonely and frightened than any of the others, but who was not an Imperial at all. She was a local Akkadisi woman.

Alicia Carno sat silent and alone. She did not know how the Alba woman had suddenly become both free and rich. Nor did Alicia understand why she had been proscribed and condemned to servitude, although she guessed that Mrs Alba must somehow be responsible. She only knew that her worst possible nightmare had become real. Mrs Alba, whose family the Carnos had tormented and almost destroyed, had bought her.

Alicia's world had collapsed since the war ended. She had been spoilt, privileged, very rich and in retrospect, happy. Her mother had been murdered and Alicia had enjoyed owning the family business. She married Jak and they had been married just long enough to become bored with one another when another purge began. Alicia had been arrested, accused of having Atkoi sympathies, and proscribed. Jak had been allowed to go free, after signing documents renouncing his wife.

The Commission for Public Safety and its headquarters at Diskobolus no longer existed. In its place was the Akkadis Bureau of Intelligence, which had proved quite capable of shouldering similar responsibilities. After three weeks in the custody of the Bureau, Alicia had been sent to the Rose Garden and prepared for sale. Unlike April, Zoe and Chloe, she was not already branded. She was put on the wheel at the Rose Garden, rotated half circle and branded. She was an 'upside down girl'. Her brand was still painful.

And now she had been bought by her worst enemy.

29: SEEN BUT NOT HEARD

There is nothing which has yet been contrived by man by which so much happiness is produced as by a good tavern or inn.
Samuel Johnson

Two weeks had passed since the auction at the Rose Garden.

Roxana Keswick was standing in the lounge bar of the Maidens of Nenuphar, near the till where she could see the stage clearly. She was wearing a smart black evening gown, as befitted a deputy manager of such an establishment.

Roxana was watching the stage carefully and critically. A lively Atkoi tune was playing and the new twins, Chloe and Zoe, were dancing. They made a lovely sight, pretty, blonde and slim, and dressed in short flared wraparound skirts and short cropped tops which barely covered their breasts. They were both making good progress, Roxie decided. They were becoming quite popular with the gentlemen.

Roxana gestured to the twins. Relieved, they ran lightly to the bar. Their mortifying stint on the stage was over. They would be serving drinks now.

Roxie nodded to another girl who was already waiting to ascend the stage. The girl's heart sank, but she obediently hurried to the stage and ascended the steps. She too was blonde and attractive, and she wore a short skirt like the twins, but unlike them she was topless. A number of gentlemen in the audience cheered, whistled and laughed. The girl's breasts were full, firm and shapely, and they bounced prettily as she ran. She blushed deeply, but obeyed with alacrity.

The girl's name was Alicia. Once she had been called Alicia Carno. For a while she had been Alicia Zadkine. Now she was simply Alicia, for a slave neither needed a surname, nor was she permitted one.

She's pretty, thought Roxie. *Ironically, she looks less tarty now than she did when she was free. She has to. No pleasure house can allow its slave girls to look like whores. That is the privilege of the free.*

Alicia was indeed very pretty now that the excessive make up which she had formerly worn was no longer permitted her. Her breasts were full and large and firm because Bowser had recently injected biosilicon gel into each of them. He had followed the usual practice at pleasure houses such as Melons, and Top Heavy, and initially injected each of Alicia's breasts with a quarter litre of the gel. A week later, when her flesh had stretched a little, he pumped in a further quarter litre, so that each breast had been filled with half a litre altogether. This was perhaps a little more than the late Mrs Knott would have recommended, but the gentlemen watching did not seem to object. They appeared to be thoroughly enjoying Alicia's performance. Alicia's breasts were still throbbing painfully, but the gel had set firmly and beautifully. Her breasts were full, firm globes jutting proudly forward.

At Table 1, a discreetly screened alcove, sat Honeysuckle Alba, sipping a small glass of white wine. She had come to watch Alicia dancing.

Alicia ignored the discomfort in her aching breasts. She knew her old adversary was watching her perform and she was mortified, but she danced for Honey and for the hundred or so leering men in the lounge bar and tried her best to make her audience enjoy every moment of it.

Alicia dreaded each Wednesday Night Entertainment as it approached. She feared that she would be chosen to perform. She also feared being sent to the breeding farm. Most of all she feared being sent to the Arena, and so she swayed and gyrated her hips and wriggled her breasts with all her heart. Perhaps, just possibly, if she made herself sufficiently useful, Mrs Alba might spare her.

Alicia thought that nothing could be more humiliating than dancing almost naked in front of a roomful of strange men, not to mention Honeysuckle Alba, especially now that she had the largest breasts in the Maidens of Nenuphar.

Then she caught sight of the man sitting at Table 21.

It was Jakob Zadkine: Jak, Alicia's ex-husband, who had divorced her to avoid being proscribed himself. He had not especially minded renouncing his wife, because he had grown to despise her.

Burning with shame, the pretty blonde forced herself to continue. Jak was grinning and watching her.

Roxana had also seen Jak sitting there. She allowed Jak to enjoy Alicia's performance for a few minutes before sauntering over to him.

"Mr Zadkine," she smiled. "Good evening, sir. Would you like Alicia to come and sit with you?"

Jak grinned and said, "All right. Go and get her. And I'll have a beer."

Roxana went to the stage. She sent Alicia to fetch Jak's drink.

A minute later Alicia appeared at Jak's table, still blushing. She curtsied and put the drink on his table.

"Come here," he said. "Closer." He reached out and squeezed Alicia's bare breasts, first one and then the other.

"Oh! Jak! Please, Jak…"

"Keep still," he said. "Take your skirt off."

Blushing deeper still, Alicia removed her skirt which, scanty though it was, was her only garment. She had already learnt that a pleasure slave at the Maidens of Nenuphar could not disobey a direct command from a customer.

Jak scrutinised her carefully. Alicia was standing tall and straight. Her figure was good. Her breasts were firm and full and thrusting. She wore an Akkadis Leisure ear tag. Jak looked at her brand, crisp and clear, a little above her mons and to one side. "Rose Garden," he remarked. "Did they put you on the wheel?"

"Yes," said Alicia quietly.

"Mr Zadkine, would you like to take her upstairs?" offered Roxana.

"No," he grinned. "I had enough of her before, for free. She's not worth paying for. I like her tits though, with the gel." To Alicia he added, "Go and dance."

Alicia curtsied. "Yes, Jak. Jak, can I...please Jak, can I put on my skirt first?"

"No. Go to the stage and dance. Do that one where you shake your tits about."

Dismayed, Alicia hurried back to the stage and began dancing a tsittandi, entirely bare.

"While you're here," said Jak to Roxana, "You can get me the dumb slut."

Roxana understood Jak's demand. He had obviously heard that the Maidens had acquired a mute girl.

The new pleasure house known as Seen But Not Heard was proving quite popular, and Amanda had not wanted Akkadis Leisure to be left behind. She had sent one of her new girls to have the same enhancement. If the mute proved popular, Amanda would send more of her girls for the same treatment. The operation to excise a slave girl's vocal chords was safe and inexpensive. The girl could be back at work in ten days. True, she could no longer speak, but not all gentlemen expected conversation from a pleasure slave. Many preferred quiet obedience.

Roxana went to the reception and returned with the mute.

The girl was beautiful. She had a lovely figure, tall and slender, and a pretty face with dark blonde hair which she wore in kittentails which hung down prettily each side of her head. Like all the Maidens that evening, she wore a short, flared wraparound skirt and skimpy top. She glanced nervously at Jak and blushed prettily, feeling his eyes upon her. She smiled shyly. It was very important to make the gentleman like her, she knew. Now that she could no longer speak it was more important than ever to show by her body language that she would be honoured and delighted to entertain the gentleman.

The girl was April Parsons.

April stood with her back perfectly straight. She had been warned that gentleman did not like girls who slouched. She curtsied and whispered, “Good evening, sir. I’m April, if it pleases you, sir.” She pressed her palms together as if in supplication. This was how she had been taught to introduce herself to a customer.

The removal of her vocal chords does not deprive a slave girl of all ability to communicate aloud. As the breath passes through her mouth, she can still move her lips and tongue to form the words, although she can never again raise her voice above a quiet whisper. Jak could barely hear April’s words above the music, but that did not matter. He was not interested in conversation. He reached out and lifted her chin. He saw the scar, a vertical line on her throat. It was red and raw, but it was healing cleanly.

“She’s charming, isn’t she, Mr Zadkine?” smiled Roxana.

Jak nodded. “All right. I’ll have her,” he said, and stood.

April’s face was lit up once more with a warm smile. “Oh sir, thank you sir,” she whispered gratefully. She held Jak’s hand and led him towards the till.

30: THE LAST GOODBYE

Laws are like cobwebs, which may catch small flies but let wasps and hornets break through.

Swift, Jonathan: A Tritical Essay Upon the Faculties of the Mind

A blushing, slim, pretty brunette named Emma had just taken a tray of drinks to Table 17 at the Maidens of Nenuphar. The ten o'clock bell had just been rung, and Emma had been obliged to remove her top. Roxana caught her eye. "Take your skirt off too," said the deputy manageress. "Then go and dance."

"Yes, miss," said Emma. She was dismayed, but she curtsied and obeyed without hesitation.

Emma had been eighteen when she was sold to Akkadis Leisure and sent to the Maidens. She had been born free on Brizeaux and emigrated to Akkadis as a child with her family. At first her parents had prospered on their new world. They lived in a smart suburb and sent the three children to good schools. But then her father became ill.

It was a very serious and a very lengthy illness. His treatment was extortionately expensive. He died leaving his family deeply, irretrievably in debt.

Emma and her mother, sister and brother fled, unable to pay off more than a fraction of their huge debts. They were not citizens of Akkadis and they were in serious trouble. They had no assets left, except for their own persons. The court had awarded a writ of personal sequestration against them. They evaded the law for a while, but eventually the bailiffs had traced them. They were detained and sent to the Rose Garden.

Emma never learned what happened to her mother and brother. Her sister Jacquie had probably been the most fortunate of the family. She was a virgin and had been purchased by a private buyer.

But Emma was not a virgin. She had hoped and prayed that her boyfriend, Lance, would find the money to buy her and rescue her from her terrible predicament.

He did not. Instead, Emma was sold to a brothel. Now, two years later, she was still a pleasure slave at the Maidens, trained to serve and please any man who chose her.

A young man walked into the reception of the Maidens and paused to look at the dozen or so pretty girls sitting behind the low partition. They were smiling and waving, hoping to be chosen. They all had earnings targets to meet, and none wanted to be chosen to perform in the next Wednesday Night Entertainment.

Without exception, the girls were attractive and well presented. They were dressed in the short skirts and skimpy tops which displayed their figures so well, and they wore their hair in kittentails.

The young man looked carefully at each of them in turn. He would not make a hasty decision. He was not a wealthy man. He was a student in his final year of study at the University of Akkad, and a visit to the Maidens was, for him, a costly treat to be savoured to the full.

Each girl wore a badge displaying her name and number. Carys looked pretty, he thought. So too did Clara: very pretty. Then he saw two brunettes sitting together, so similar in appearance that he guessed they must be sisters. Their names were Abi and Trixi. He looked carefully at Trixi. She smiled sweetly and pressed her palms together, begging to be chosen.

The young man made up his mind. He turned to Bowser, who was acting as concierge that night. “Twenty-four, please. The one called Trixi,” the young man said.

Trixi squeaked delightedly and ran grinning to the gap in the low partition and thanked the young man for choosing her. Together, they entered the lounge and sat at one of the small tables facing the stage.

Emma was still dancing on the little stage. She still daydreamed, sometimes, that Lance would come and rescue her. Realistically she knew that he would not want to marry her now, not after she had danced naked for every man who had paid the price of a drink at the Maidens, and been used by every man in Akkad who wanted her and had fifteen solidi to spare.

Most of the time, Emma tried not to hope. Hope only made her feel worse, because in her heart she knew it was a false hope. She did not think of the future, because she had no future. She would remain at the Maidens, or some other pleasure house, until she was too worn out to be of further use. By her late twenties the gentlemen would begin to tire of her. It would be harder to meet her earnings targets each week, and she would begin to be chosen more often to perform in the Wednesday Night Entertainments. That would get her a few extra customers, for a while at least. Then after another year or so, the company would send her away, either for breeding or to the Arena.

But just occasionally she could not help herself from daydreaming. Suppose Lance was looking for her. He might still be searching every pleasure house in Akkad until he found her. Surely he would understand that it was not her fault that she had become what she was. She would never, never have chosen to be unfaithful to him. She was not that sort of girl at all. It did not matter if he did not want to marry her. She would willingly be his slave. She would be his maid or housekeeper or childminder or concubine or anything he wanted.

Emma was dancing naked to a lively Atkoi tune, thrusting and gyrating to the powerful rhythmic beat, repeating the steps she had been taught. As always when she danced, she tried not to meet the eyes of the men watching. It was too humiliating. That was why she had been dancing for several minutes before she saw the young man sitting at a table with Trixi, halfway across the room.

The man was staring at Emma, transfixed. Emma did not know how long he had been watching her.

The man was Lance.

Emma gasped and for the briefest instant covered her breasts and pudenda, ashamed to be seen by Lance like this, dancing naked in a brothel in front of a hundred men or more. Then she remembered her training. She continued dancing as if nothing had happened. Anxiously she looked around for Roxana, hoping that her mistake had not been noticed. Girls at the Maidens of Nenuphar had been put on the flogging stool or the whipping post for less. It was mortifying, but she must dance as normal. When Lance realised it really was her, he would send for her and put an end to this humiliation.

Emma carried on dancing, sinuously twisting and gyrating to the powerful beat. She continued for two more songs. Lance was still looking at her. Emma saw him speak to Trixi, then look at the stage again. The song ended, and Emma stood still and curtsied. The audience applauded. Lance watched her as she curtsied, naked, to a room full of strange men. The pause between the songs, when Emma had to stand still, was in some respects worse than the dancing itself.

Then the third song began. Why did Lance not send Trixi to fetch her? Had he not recognised her? But if not, why was he looking at her so intently?

Towards the end of the song Emma was relieved to see the deputy manageress approaching the stage. She knelt on the edge of the stage to hear Roxana's words.

"You've been booked," said Roxana. "Go to Table 5."

"Yes, Ma'am," said Emma, descending from the stage. She was confused. Lance was not sitting at Table 5. Lance's table was much further from the stage.

Then with sickening certainty, Emma realised what had happened. Lance had not booked her at all. Another man must have booked her. She hesitated for the briefest moment, but Roxana said, “Hurry up, girl, he’s waiting for you.”

“Yes, miss,” said Emma again. She could not delay any longer. She ran to Table 5. “Good evening, sir,” said Emma to the gentleman.

The gentleman was Mr Granicus.

Mr Granicus grinned and stood. He took Emma’s left nipple firmly between the thumb and forefinger of his right hand. The pretty brunette winced, but followed obediently as Mr Granicus walked her briskly to the till. She stood beside him as he handed over the fee.

Burning with shame, Emma dared not look at Lance now. As Granicus led her towards the door leading to the elevators, Emma stole the briefest of glances towards Lance. Lance was still looking at her.

It was the last time that Emma ever saw him.

31: MAY YOU LIVE IN INTERESTING TIMES

The institutions of slavery, concubinage and the seraglio have benefited the Empire immeasurably. Our ruling class tends to marry within itself, to consolidate its power; but through concubinage, new talent can enter the ruling class and strengthen its gene pool. Everyone benefits: the Imperial family and the ruling class, the young women themselves, their families, and society as a whole. No other polity, and scarcely any other institution in human history, has survived for as long as the Empire with so few changes to its ruling elite. True, we have had civil wars; but for humanity as a whole, the Empire had brought peace on an unprecedented scale, and much of the credit for this peace and continuity must be given to the institution of the seraglio.

Itchenor, E.: The Causes and Consequences of the Atkoi War, Vol. 1. (Cornubium University Press: Nenuphar, 3020)

Ruby Aguilar, the intelligence officer aboard the Emperor Otto, had brought Kyra the shocking news: Simon Ozwald was already married to someone else. He had no wish to claim Kyra. Simon's wife in particular did not want him to have any communication with Kyra. Most emphatically she did not want Kyra given to Simon as a concubine.

Kyra asked how Simon was, but she resisted the temptation to ask about his wife and where she was from.

As soon as she was alone, Kyra wept. She was proud, despite her servitude. She had known, really, ever since she was taken to the Rose Garden, that she could never be Simon's wife, but it had been a shock to have it confirmed in a message from her former fiancé himself.

Feeling for Kyra's pain, Ruby decided to have the matter investigated further, if only to satisfy her own curiosity. She asked her colleagues on Nenuphar to find out a little more about Simon Ozwald.

The consequences, for Simon, were disastrous.

It turned out that the young eunuch Gaspar had indeed managed to rescue several girls, including Jemima, from the beleaguered Imperial Seraglio on that dreadful night when the berserkers arrived. Gaspar had hidden the girls in a house in the city until the owner of the house was able to transport them to an isolated rural property he owned. They hid there until Nenuphar was liberated, but during that time Jemima and the owner of the house fell in love. The owner smuggled Jemima off planet and they were secretly married and lived together on Petwen.

The man's name was Simon Ozwald. As a result of Ruby's investigation, he was arrested charged with theft and rape. Jemima was, after all, still legally the property of the Emperor.

Admiral Bazan had decreed that for the time being the Emperor Otto would continue to serve as his headquarters. Kyra also remained on board, waiting to learn what would become of her. Bazan would decide her fate.

The Admiral had spoken kindly to Kyra several times. He was self-assured, intelligent and yet considerate. He was not arrogant, but he always seemed sure of victory and certain that he was making the correct decisions. He made other people feel confident, too. Kyra imagined that if she were a marine or a soldier she would have liked Bazan to be her commander.

Once, Ruby Aguilar remarked to Kyra, "The Admiral likes you. He told me to make sure you have everything you need. He often asks how you are." Ruby smiled. Kyra blushed, and Ruby grinned more broadly, as if sensing the younger woman's thoughts. Kyra blushed deeper still.

Bazan invited Kyra to his quarters. To Kyra's relief, Ruby accompanied her. It would have been frightening to go alone, and embarrassing to be seen going or returning alone. After a while, Ruby left, leaving Bazan alone with Kyra.

"Kyra. I have been busy with naval duties, but I have been looking forward to seeing you again," he said.

"So have I, master. I mean, looking forward to seeing you." Kyra blushed, flustered.

"I would have liked to see you sooner."

"Yes, master."

Kyra could think of nothing else to say. *Will he think I am foolish?* she wondered. But he smiled and invited her to sit down, and as they continued to talk, Kyra relaxed. They had dinner together, and continued talking. They talked altogether for five hours and discussed many things. He seemed genuinely interested in Kyra's story and background. Whatever Kyra began to explain, Bazan seemed to understand immediately, and he drew conclusions from it before Kyra had even finished speaking.

Finally they stood and Bazan said, "It is late now. Ruby will be here in a moment, to escort you back to your cabin." He lifted Kyra's chin gently and kissed her. Wide eyed, Kyra said nothing. Bazan put his arms around her and squeezed her, and then kissed her again. "I will see you again, soon."

Kyra did not sleep that night. She hardly dared hope that her feelings were reciprocated. *Is this what it feels like, to fall in love?* she wondered.

Kyra knew that Bazan was the most important man in the Empire. To all intents and purposes he *was* the Empire. Yet as the weeks passed he regularly made a point of seeing Kyra or sending her a message. Sometimes if she heard nothing from Bazan for several days, Kyra felt disappointed. She knew it was illogical. Bazan's responsibilities were immense, and the war was by no means over; but she could not help it.

Then Ruby broke the news to Kyra: Bazan would be leaving the Emperor Otto to travel to Tolon for his wedding to Lady Demetra.

They were to be crowned jointly as Emperor and Empress, but it would be Bazan who truly ruled the Empire. He would rule under the name of Baldwin V. The first Emperor had been named Baldwin, and the name was a powerful one which would add to his status and legitimacy.

Kyra realised that she felt jealous of Lady Demetra. She was sunk in depression until she was told that the Emperor would return to his flagship immediately after the ceremony and the Empress Demetra would return to the Imperial Palace on Nenuphar.

32: SAINTS AND SINNERS

Saint Athanasia, Virgin and Martyr, 2977-3000. Daughter of the Emperor Aethelstan IV, married to the Great Kzam Rurik III, Athanasia was martyred for refusing to convert to Arianism and instead attempting to convert the Atkoi to the true faith. The Holy Orthodox Temple of Saint Athanasia, with its beautiful domes and spires set amidst lovely gardens, is now a peaceful idyll amidst the bustle of the city, popular with locals, tourists and pilgrims, but it stands on the site where the Kzam's palace and seraglio once stood, in the days when the planet St Athanasia was known as Ziandakush. The altar marks the very spot where Athanasia died.

His Holiness Arch Patriarch Boniface VI: Lives of the Saints (Ecclesia Press: New Jerusalem, 3026)

Kyra had been invited to the Emperor's quarters again. She curtsied deferentially. Had his feelings changed towards her? Had he merely been playing with her? But he kissed her, and smiled. Later, he explained some of the difficulties he had been facing.

At an appropriate moment Kyra said, "Master, what are your plans for me?" Finally she had dared to ask.

"I want you for myself. Forever," Bazan replied. "It's all being done properly. I've had the legal department draw up the Deed of Transfer. It's signed and endorsed. I'm sending you to Nenuphar as soon as it's safe. You will wait for me there." He paused for a moment as if he had realised that Kyra was really asking him a different question altogether. Then he said, "Kyra, I love you."

"I love you too, master," she said, feeling as if her heart would burst with happiness. "When did you realise?"

"When we had dinner, that first time. I didn't tell you then. I wanted to wait, to be certain."

"Master, will I truly belong to you forever? Always and forever?"

"Yes. I promise. Kyra, this is for you." Bazan reached for a small box and removed a ring, and put it on her finger. It was too large, so he tried it on her middle finger where it fitted better. It was simple in design, and of gold. "It belonged to my mother," he said.

Kyra was overwhelmed. Such a gift, for a concubine, was rare indeed. She could never be Bazan's wife, but she would be more than a common slave.

Perhaps he sensed her confusion. "There are many things I want to talk to you about," he said. Then he kissed her again and said, "But first, I want to look at you properly." He loosened the strap behind Kyra's neck, so that her dress slid to the floor. Beneath it Kyra wore a white camisole. The dress and the camisole had both been gifts from Bazan. When Kyra had opened them, alone in her tiny cabin, she had blushed.

Now Bazan slid his hands slowly over the silky white fabric to where her slim waist began to curve out to her hips. He loosened the thin straps of the camisole so that it too would have slid down had she not clutched it instinctively to her breasts. Beneath it, she was entirely bare. "It's all right, Kyra," said Bazan. "Let it fall." Wide eyed, Kyra obeyed, grateful that Bazan had dimmed the lights. The flimsy garment slipped to the floor.

Bazan's gaze shifted first to her face, her sweet face framed by fair, almost blonde hair, and then down to the firm hemispheres of her breasts. He saw her injured nipple, bruised but recovering. He saw her flat, smooth stomach and slender waist. His eyes returned to her breasts.

"It's almost healed now," he said. "You haven't painted anything on them, have you?"

"Oh no, master! I would never…" she began, before realising that he was smiling. It was a joke. She giggled with relief and embarrassment. He stroked her hair.

It was arranged elaborately into a single plait, the usual fashion for virgin slave girls in the Empire. "Untie it," he said, quietly. Kyra did, and shook it loose. Bazan ran his fingers through her hair, and kissed her again. Kyra simply looked at him, wide eyed. He slid his hands down to her slim waist. He traced the impression of the brand with his fingers. Kyra blushed in shame and looked at his face, trying to discern his thoughts. It was Kyra's last great fear: what Bazan would think when he saw her brand, the Kzam's mark, the indelible reminder that she had belonged to another man, she had been the slave of an Atkoi.

"The Kzam was saving you, to celebrate a victory," said Bazan. "But *I* have won the victory, and so *I* will celebrate."

He understood. He understood completely. Kyra's shame evaporated and she sank gracefully to her knees. How was an Imperial slave girl supposed to make obeisance? She had no idea. She had been told very little since she had been aboard the Emperor Otto and she had been too embarrassed to ask Ruby, so she did it in the Atkoi fashion, touching her forehead to the floor at his feet.

Bazan did not order her to rise. Instead, he bent forward and took her gently by the shoulders. She rose lightly to her feet.

"Kyra, you know what I'm going to do to you now, don't you?" he said quietly.

Kyra hesitated. "I think so. Yes master." She blushed.

"Are you afraid?"

"Yes master. But I am happy, too. I want nothing more than to belong to you."

"You do. And I am happy too." He picked her up lightly, and carried her into the bedroom. He put her gently on the bed and kissed her.

He carried me like a bride, Kyra thought joyfully. *I was carried like a bride, instead of kneeling at the foot of his bed and crawling on my knees.* She closed her eyes as she felt his hand slide down over her intimate parts. *This is what it feels like,* she thought. *This is what it feels like to be touched by a man who I love.*

Later, as Bazan was drifting off to sleep, Kyra composed herself to perform one final duty, as she had been taught in the Kzam's seraglio. Bazan felt her slide down the bed. He felt the tickle of her tongue as she began to lick him clean.

"No," he said. "Lie here, beside me."

"Did I do something wrong, master?" she asked anxiously.

"No. No, you did nothing wrong, Kyra. I liked everything. But tonight I want to talk to you. Those things can wait, until you are ready."

"Yes, master. Thank you. Master, may I speak?"

"Yes. I want us to talk. When we are alone, Kyra, you can call me Giorge."

"Yes Mast—Giorge," she corrected herself. "Thank you. Giorge, you said you were sending me to Nenuphar to wait for you. Is it – would it be possible -- for you to keep me here, with you?"

"Yes, Kyra, It would. I will," he grinned. In the dim light, Kyra also grinned.

Eventually, Bazan drifted off to sleep.

But Kyra could not sleep. For the first time since that terrible night on the Evening Star, she realised that she was no longer afraid. She stroked his hair gently until he woke. "Giorge. I love you, Giorge," she said, and kissed him again.

EPILOGUE

St. Peter Scamander, Martyr. 2949-3000. Peter Scamander was canonised in 3004 and is the patron saint of the Imperial League for the Rescue of Distressed Ladies. Famous for his compassion towards the oppressed and underprivileged, his good works took him to many parts of the Empire and beyond. His belief that God's love extends to all intelligent creatures led him to work among the borbods of Borobudur. On another mission, to rescue fallen women on Akkadis, he was martyred, probably on the orders of the owner of one of the planet's notorious 'pleasure houses.'

Even in his dying moments, his thoughts were for his flock; the splendid statue of Peter sculpted by Odinzo which stands in the portico of the Patriarchal Temple on Nenuphar, bears a plaque inscribed with his last words: "Feed My Lambs."

His Holiness Arch Patriarch Boniface VI: Lives of the Saints (Ecclesia Press: New Jerusalem, 3026)

In the rolling Segonzac Hills of northern Coromandel there stands a fine stone residence, set in spacious grounds amidst ornate gardens and surrounded by crumbling stone walls covered in moss, lichen and clinging ivy. An arched gateway set between two castellated towers provides landcar access. Above the arch is a shield carved in stone, depicting a griffin holding a single star in its talon. A visiting stranger might imagine that he has somehow been transported to an ancient manor house on Old Earth.

In fact the house is no more than a few years old and the appearance of antiquity was achieved at some considerable trouble and expense. The moss and lichen were genetically engineered to establish themselves quickly, and the walls were purposely designed to crumble in places.

The residence affords fine views over the gardens and fields of oilroot plants where the harvesting machines can often be seen working, silently and busily. Further afield are hills and forests and a small river which winds its way through the valley.

A flag flutters from a pole in the light breeze, depicting the same device as the stone shield: a golden griffin with a silver star, on an azure field. It is the griffin of the Welbecks, and the house was built by Sir Hektor Welbeck, first Earl of Segonzac and Knight of the Most Illustrious Order of The Thousand Suns. Sir Hektor's daughter Kyra held the exalted position of Preferred Concubine of the Imperial Seraglio. His sons were Imperial senators and his two other daughters were married to an admiral and a cabinet minister respectively.

Demetra was the Empress, but it was Kyra whom the Emperor loved and who became the mother of four of his children. The first was Otto, named either after the great Emperor of that name, or the ship on which he was conceived, and who eventually succeeded his father to the throne as Otto II. Under him and his successors of the Bazan dynasty, the Empire continued to recover and grow.

Kyra herself became known for her charitable work. She had been disappointed by the lack of progress made by the Imperial and Akkadisi authorities in finding the victims of the attack on the Evening Star. She founded The Imperial League for the Rescue of Distressed Ladies to rescue all victims of the slave traffic, and help them to begin new lives. The League rescued Nysha, Clara, Carys, Janina, Juliet, Daisy, Millie and several others who had been seized from the Evening Star.

Officially the Akkadisi authorities agreed to cooperate fully with the League and allow its agents to inspect the pleasure houses to search for abducted Imperial women. In practice the pleasure houses learned to evade and adapt to these arrangements. Amanda Alba, for instance, had contacts in positions of authority and was invariably warned of such visits before they took place. She would arrange for any Imperial girls to be moved away temporarily whenever a pleasure house was due to be inspected. Occasionally a few older Imperials, who were due to be disposed of anyway, would be left for the authorities to 'discover.' As the League paid compensation for the women they rescued, Amanda was always able to purchase replacement girls. Often the replacements were themselves Imperial.

Leah and Rebekka Hart were never found. Mr Ipoletz, who had purchased Bekka from Akkadis Leisure, was so fond of her that he allowed himself to be persuaded to buy Leah too, and he had taken the sisters with him when he emigrated to one of the independent worlds. No one at the Maidens knew precisely to which planet they had gone. It might have been Anckarstrom or Brizeaux, or possibly even Oriflamme.

But the two sisters were grateful to Ipoletz and served him loyally. He treated them well. They each bore him several children, and when he died the sisters were freed under the terms of his will and given generous legacies. They remained with their children on their new home world.

Nor was Mintika, who had formerly been called Philippa Warburton, ever found. Her Atkoi master, Noruo, took her to the Great Plateau of Akkadis, to the region where his tribe, the Irtukoi, lived and where the writ of the planetary government hardly ran.

Mintika bore her master a son named Arnulf and eventually presented him with four more children, but for years her life was made a misery by Zinnia, her master's eldest daughter by his legal wife. Zinnia was beautiful, but spoiled and arrogant.

When Noruo died fifteen years later, Arnulf became head of the family. He gave Zinnia in marriage to the ugliest man in the village, an elderly tanner who could never quite rid himself of the odour of the goats' urine he used in his work. The tanner could scarcely believe his good luck. The couple were blessed with sixteen children.

In total, fourteen survivors from the Evening Star were found: fourteen out of a total of two thousand, six hundred and fifty passengers and crew. Several of those fourteen had borne children in slavery and chose to remain with their children rather than return home.

It was a pity that the Arch Patriarch Boniface insisted on canonising Scamander and declaring him patron saint of the League. Kyra protested to the Emperor about this, but Baldwin was adamant that the League could not afford to antagonise the church. Politics, he said, was the art of the possible.

Bazan's first task was to restore order in the weakened Empire. The Levellers had already been defeated. Borobudur was to be abandoned. Its human inhabitants were already leaving in a steady trickle. The Empire would continue to employ borbods as mercenaries.

Selimpono, now called Zianda, was to become independent with Commander Bual as its first prime minister. He called himself Admiral Bual now. No criminal action would be taken against him or any of his party. Some Imperials genuinely admired Bual. Others merely pretended to.

The Kzamate broke up into a number of successor states: four large ones and a dozen or so smaller entities, some at war with their neighbours. Only Ziandakush, the old capital of the Kzamate, was to be annexed to the Empire. It was renamed Saint Athanasia in honour of the Princess, who was canonised.

The former Kzama Radmilla was to be detained for life in the Reliquary, the only part of the Kzam's seraglio which would be left standing. Adriaan Voragine was appointed Chief Prefect of Police of Saint Athanasia. He had saved Kyra's life, and the Emperor was grateful. Kyra also persuaded the Emperor to drop charges against Simon Ozwald. The eunuch Gaspar became the Chief Eunuch of Baldwin's seraglio.

Jakob Satkisant and his team retained their positions. Indeed, they were busier than ever, despatching Atkoi war criminals. When Jakob retired, his nephew Mikal did indeed become the new High Executioner. Mikal had a long and distinguished career, but he never forgot Athi and he never executed a prettier convict.

On Akkadis, Doctor Nargal's remains were never found, nor did Amanda's part in his disappearance ever emerge.

Prince Ozim was murdered by one of his own men.

His fleet shifted out of metaspace near Psellus Ter, the last inhabited world of the Kzamate on the side furthest away from Imperial space. There they hoped to take on board supplies and continue on. It was rumoured that there were human colonies on various worlds in unclaimed space beyond the Kzamate. Ozim had lost the Kzamate, but with a fleet of modern warships he might still become lord of his own domain.

But the remnants of Ozim's navy began fighting among themselves. Not all of his men wished to go into exile, and not all of the officers accepted the Prince's leadership.

Ozim himself was killed, not by a rival for power but as an act of revenge. He perished at the hand of the brother of Tamara, the concubine who had died beneath his whip.

Probably the last casualties of the Atkoi War were the surviving crew of the Vengeance Is Mine, drifting helplessly in space. Krull was the first to die. The borbod Ugeos, driven mad by hunger, tore off his arm. Toltok blasted both borbods and vacuumed the three bodies. Only later did the remaining survivors regret disposing of Krull. That was after they had turned to cannibalism to survive.

Boolg was the last to die. Three months after he killed Wilson, he turned the pistol to his own head and pulled the trigger. The Vengeance was discovered over a century later, when a tramp freighter travelling off the usual trade routes happened to detect the emergency signal it was still transmitting.

Made in the USA
Columbia, SC
20 April 2025

56874813R00120